······ ★ ······

Liberty Lanes

WEST WORD FICTION

Liberty Lanes

ROBIN TROY

UNIVERSITY OF NEVADA PRESS ▲▲ RENO & LAS VEGAS

WEST WORD FICTION

University of Nevada Press, Reno, Nevada 89557 USA
Copyright © 2011 by Robin Troy
All rights reserved
Manufactured in the United States of America
Design by Kathleen Szawiola

Library of Congress Cataloging-in-Publication Data

Troy, Robin.
Liberty lanes / Robin Troy.
p. cm. — (West word fiction)
ISBN 978-0-87417-857-9 (pbk. : alk. paper)
I. Title.
PS3570.R696L53 2011
813'.54—dc22   2011010452

FIRST PRINTING
20 19 18 17 16 15 14 13 12 11
5   4   3   2   1

····· ⭐ ·····

Life begins with L.
Life itself is a beautiful thing.
It was given to us to enjoy,
So use it to the fullest.
L is for living.
L is for laughter,
L is for loving.
The 3 L's will carry you through
Life on a cloud of Happiness.

—EVAUN CROUCH, Montana

······ ★ ······

Liberty Lanes

CHAPTER 1

Nelson

Nelson sat at a two-person table in the dining area of the bowling alley at 7:00 a.m. He wore his blue jeans and a plaid button-down shirt with short sleeves, though it was December. None of the other tables were set up with napkins and jellies and round mini-tubs of margarine like his. At his table, he had all of that, and ketchup and syrup and a cup of coffee in a narrow white mug that would need to be refilled again and again. He had a comb in his front jeans pocket, just in case.

"You going to keep on waiting, Nelson, or you want your breakfast now?" The waitress, Charla, spoke to him from behind the service window, which was trimmed with plastic holly.

"I'm waiting," said Nelson. "And I'm just going to want the one hotcake this time."

"You're all wound up today," Charla said as she helped herself to a plank-shaped frosted donut.

"What's that?" Nelson's hearing wasn't as good as it used to be, and he found himself irritated when he missed something. Charla was about his age, her hair was silver like his, and she was from the eastern part of the state like he was, out where it was ranchland and the climate was harsher than it was here in the city. He didn't like to think he was aging worse than someone else his same age and circumstance.

"These are deadly," she said, looking at the donut. "Someone needs to put these clear across the room." She took a big bite and then held her hands up to her neck and made loud choking sounds.

"That's not funny, Charla," Nelson said. "Quit it."

"You're not going to save me?"

"It was a one-time thing."

"You don't love me?"

"Hey," he snapped.

She pushed the donut aside. "You're no fun this morning. You're normally fun. Anyone seen the fun Nelson?" she called into the empty bowling alley.

Nelson shushed her and looked around. "I might be a little nervous," he said.

"You want more coffee?"

Nelson nodded. The lights were off everywhere in the bowling alley except above the dining tables. Were they always this way in the morning? He looked over his shoulder at the door. This girl, this reporter from the newspaper, was late. She'd talked very fast on the phone, and Nelson had had a hard time keeping up with her.

Charla came out and filled his mug. "So you're going to be famous," she said.

"What?" Nelson touched the comb in his pocket. "No," he said.

"Are you going on the front page?"

Nelson blushed and put a spoon in his coffee and stirred. "Stop it, Charla," he said. "You're going to make me nervous. I didn't do anything anyone else wouldn't of."

"The other paper should've put you on the front page of Our Town at least."

"I don't even know why these ones want to talk to me. I already told everything I have to say."

"There she is, coming," said Charla, looking to the door. She touched her hair. "She's got a big bag."

Nelson turned to look and leaned toward the darkness. The girl walked across the navy carpet in the dark lobby and paused by the front desk with all the bowling shoes. She had long hair that was wet—from the shower, Nelson figured—and she peered at him and Charla there under the few lights.

"She's taller than I pictured," he said quietly.

"Mr. Moore," the girl said, breezing into the lit-up dining area. "It smells like an ice-skating rink in here." She sniffed, not so much to smell, Nelson thought, as to stop a drippy nose. It wasn't double digits outside, and her nose was shiny. "I've never been in this place before," she said. "I drive by all the time." She dumped her bag and held her hand out to Nelson. "Thanks for meeting with me, Mr. Moore. I'm Hailey James. Thanks for having me here."

"This is where I have breakfast," said Nelson.

"I've never been in here." The girl looked at Charla but didn't shake her hand. "It happened in here?"

"In there." Charla pointed behind them, to a glass door that led to the bowling alley's bar, across from the rental shoes.

Nelson followed Charla's finger. He pictured Fran Murray's scared face when she'd gotten that happy-hour chicken-wing bone stuck in her throat. He remembered how her rib cage had felt like a stack of potato chips beneath his fists, and how odd it had been to touch her again, to touch a woman who wasn't Bethany. Bethany was much rounder and softer than Fran, and Nelson had thought afterward that if Bethany ever choked on a bone, he wasn't sure he'd be able to find the right place to put his hands. He'd picked out Fran's ribs one by one. Bethany had watched the whole thing. She had reached down and plucked the chicken-wing bone off the floor and saved it in a cocktail napkin in her purse.

Nelson took a breath.

"I do league bowling Mondays, Wednesdays, Fridays," he said to the girl.

Charla asked if she could bring coffee, and the girl said yes loud enough to make Nelson wary.

"What did you say your name was again?" he asked.

"Hailey James," she repeated.

"Hailey James," he said.

"Yes." She was still looking toward the door to the bar. "I'd like to go in there later. I'd like you to walk me through what happened." Then she sat and took a laminated menu from its wire holder. "What do you eat? I don't normally eat breakfast."

Nelson watched Hailey read the menu. Her cheekbones were broad, with pink brushstrokes beneath her eyes. Nelson sometimes painted outdoor scenes on an easel in his spare bedroom. The alley owners hung a few of his paintings around the bar—wild flowers, the Clark Fork at sunset, a barn up in the Missions—because they'd known Nelson twenty years and his spare bedroom had canvases stacked wall to-wall. But he'd never been any good at painting faces. Now he watched Hailey's face, her lips moving as she weighed her options, and also tried to remember if the menus had always stood up in the wire holders like that. He looked around to the other tables. They all had a single laminated menu standing in a wire ring. "I have a hotcake and coffee," he said.

"I never eat before noon," she said. "I can't handle it."

"You can't handle it?" Nelson was puzzled. He reminded himself he didn't have to talk to any reporter if he didn't want. He could explain there'd been a mix-up, this wasn't what he'd pictured, and the last interview hadn't been so great anyway—it had been over the phone, and that had felt strange, and he wasn't a hero by any measure—and then he could eat his hotcake and go about his day like it was the same as any other. This girl talked very fast. He could smell the cold air coming off her red coat.

"Fried eggs," she said. "That's light." She shoved the laminated menu back in its holder and dug into her bag. She pulled out a tape recorder and a pen and a skinny pad of paper.

Nelson straightened up.

"I'm going to let this run," she said, punching down a button on the recorder.

Nelson eyed the recorder like it might spit at him. "I don't know about this," he said.

"It's just so I don't have to write the whole time," she said. "So I can talk to you like a normal person."

She made a scribble on the pad to check that her pen worked. In the winter, Nelson's pens didn't always work right away either. Sitting at the table by the window in his kitchen, before the bowling alley opened, he had to scribble on an old bill envelope before he could do the crossword.

Nelson picked up the recorder, held it close to him, and shut it off.

"Are you a normal person?" he asked her.

"God, I hope not." She winked, but Nelson wasn't sure if she meant to. He wished young people would stick to "gosh," but he'd given up with his own grandchildren.

"Well, I am," he said. "So you can talk to me like a normal person like this, like we're meeting up for breakfast. I'd feel funny," he said.

He could see Hailey trying to decide what to do. She rubbed her eyes, and Nelson thought he might have upset her, but she didn't seem to him like a girl who upset easily. She dug around in her bag and then squirted two drops from a small bottle into each eye.

"Allergies," she said. "The neighbor's cat got into my apartment."

Charla filled up their coffees and took Hailey's order. Neither Nelson nor Hailey said anything more until she'd gone. Hailey peeled open three vanilla creamers, poured them in her narrow mug, and stirred. Then she licked the spoon clean and aimed it at Nelson.

"I can't do this without the recorder," she said. "I wouldn't be able to get everything. I might make a mistake, Mr. Moore, and I wouldn't want to make a mistake about your story because I'm serious—"

Nelson turned on the recorder himself. "Did anyone ever tell you being the boss is not an attractive quality in a girl?" He leaned into the recorder as he spoke. Hailey raised her eyebrows, and he could see he'd gotten her attention. "Now," he said, readjusting himself. Hailey stirred her coffee even though it didn't need stirring. She clanked the spoon down on the table, and Nelson watched a dribble of coffee work its way toward him. Then she started in. She asked Nelson the questions listed on her skinny pad. They were the same questions he'd answered for the daily paper last week, for the article they buried in the back of Friday's Our Town section: What was your first thought when Fran Murray started choking? Did you think twice about helping, or did you know what to do? Where did you learn the Heimlich? Do you feel like a hero? Is the bowling alley's bar really going to give you a free beer every day for the rest of your life? You are seventy-four, correct? Have you talked to Fran Murray since?

"For heaven's sake," Nelson said. "I've known Fran Murray forty-five years. We've bowled the same league twenty-eight."

These questions, he thought. Who, what, when, where. Chop, chop, chop, chop. Nelson pictured a vending machine. Better to stick a quarter in a person's ear and select the answer to fall out his mouth than this, he thought. Neither reporter had asked him to tell about how he'd gone into the army, Fort Drum, New York, all the way from Havre, when he was sixteen. How after that he'd gone to Las Vegas, worked on the railroad, and shared a room with a tattoo artist named Zil who'd done an eagle on Nelson's left arm. Then he'd gotten married and divorced, saved up money for a used Chevy Coupe and driven it back to Montana. By that time he was nineteen. He was twenty when he got the route for Dawsen's Trucking and married a second time. He was twenty-two when his first son was born, fifty-six when his second wife got sick and died, seventy-one the first time he kissed Bethany and they both agreed they didn't want to be married again, seventy-four when Fran Murray choked on a chicken-wing bone at happy hour. The last bit was all anyone cared about. How was it, he wondered, that the world made stories out of such small things?

"I don't see how you're going to write something different than what the other paper got," he said to Hailey.

"We're a weekly," she said. "That's different already."

"What?"

"What would you like to tell me that you didn't tell the other paper?"

She sounded rude, and at this rate Nelson didn't want to tell her much of anything. Their food had come and he spread some jelly on a part of his hot-cake. Before Fran choked, he'd been in a newspaper only two times—once in elementary school when a horse had gotten loose in downtown Havre, and a truck swerving to miss it had whacked a fire hydrant, and Nelson had run out from the grocery where his mom was paying, and the newspaper had showed up right then; and a second time when his sister, fifteen years his senior, had gotten married in Great Falls and they'd run a picture of the wedding party. Nelson had been a gangly usher next to the full-grown men.

Now this.

"Fran Murray and I are lovers," he said.

A flicker of excitement crossed Hailey's face and vanished. "Mr. Moore," she said.

"You don't think we are?"

"I—" she caught herself, and Nelson could see her paralyzed with curiosity. Young people would always want to know about this. He knew because he could remember wanting to know himself. He could remember being surprised, happily, that his plumbing still worked at sixty-five, then seventy, and then he had stopped being surprised.

"You can't print that in the newspaper, though," he said. "It wouldn't be decent."

"Of course it would," said Hailey. "It would be a love story. Everyone loves a love story."

Nelson caught her checking to make sure the tape was still rolling.

"How long have you two been—together?" She inched forward in her seat.

"Six months," he said. He wasn't sure why he didn't stop himself. "Bethany told me I call her too much—"

"Who's Bethany?"

"My girlfriend," he said, which was true, as was the fact that Bethany had told him not to call so much, not every time she arrived home or he arrived home, or she was two minutes late. "We've been together three years in February."

"Does Bethany know Fran?"

"We all bowl in the same league," said Nelson.

Hailey hooted and tapped Nelson's arm like they were friends, like they were speaking the same language now.

"Does she know *about* Fran?" she asked.

"I would hope not," said Nelson. "I imagine that wouldn't be good for me."

Hailey laughed again, and Nelson wanted to tell her she should smile more often.

"Was Bethany there when you saved Fran?" she asked.

Nelson nodded. "She saved the chicken bone in her purse."

"No way."

"Yes," said Nelson. "In a napkin."

"Are Bethany and Fran friends?"

"We're all friends," Nelson said. "There's a group of us gets together for drinks in the bar after bowling."

"Really," Hailey said, which Nelson took to be—in his brief experience now with reporters—a stumble. A stalling for time. This wasn't the story she'd come for, he thought. This didn't fit the list of questions on her skinny pad. Ha, he wanted to say out loud. This is bigger than a chicken bone. But he looked into his coffee instead. His mug was still full from the last go-round, and he and Fran Murray hadn't touched each other in years.

"Do you think—"

"You can't print any of this," Nelson said. He felt nervous about what he'd started—about what inside of him had made up this lie at all. "This is just so you know there's more to the story."

Hailey chewed her lip. She'd popped the yolks of both eggs but taken only one bite. Charla came over with more coffee, and Nelson hoped Hailey wouldn't ask any more questions right then. He held his hand over the mug, but he thanked Charla anyway as she walked away.

"Mr. Moore," Hailey said slowly.

"You can call her an old flame," he said. "Fran. That gets at the truth enough. You can keep it to that."

In fact that *was* the truth, and as he spoke Nelson wondered why he hadn't simply told the plain truth to begin with. He'd gone with Fran for several years long before he met Bethany, and then Fran had gone on to date Jim Bowers and then Marshall Hicks and Dale Johnson and Stu Larsen and had been back with Jim off and on for a few months now. In fact, Fran had dated about half of the men in their group that met for drinks in the bar after bowling. She packed little bottles of wine in her purse and bought one drink from the bar and then refilled her glass from her purse. She had three daughters and two sons spread out from Montana to Arizona, and two dead husbands. She was a good deal of fun, and sometimes Nelson missed being in the middle of that. Especially when Bethany got too busy these days, he missed how he'd felt with Fran.

He watched Hailey write "old flame" on her skinny pad and underline it. He didn't like the look of it. It was the truth, but it didn't look like much. A part of his life plunked down like that. He watched Charla in her window counting out forks and knives to roll up into paper napkins. She did it every day, one hundred rolls on the nose, and stacked them in a blue plastic tub labeled "Prep." When she finished, she always asked Nelson if he had room for another cake, and sometimes he said yes and sometimes he said no. The truth was Nelson was so bored he thought he might die. The truth was that a million years ago he had been in love with Fran Murray.

"Mr. Moore?"

"Oh, sure," he said. "You can print what you want." Then he felt Hailey remove her hand from his wrist, and he wondered how long it had been there. He wondered how he could have missed it.

"I want to print the truth." She laid her hand flat on the table.

"Well, there you have it," he said. "There's your story. Nelson and Franny, sitting in a tree."

"You call her Franny?"

"I used to," said Nelson.

Hailey hesitated. She looked as if she didn't trust him.

"She doesn't like it," he said. "She says it sounds too close to you-know-what."

Hailey went blank.

"Your behind," Nelson said. "Your can."

She checked her watch and consulted her pad. "Will you show me the bar?" She pushed back from the table. "Where it happened?"

"Oh," Nelson said. "Right." His legs were unsteady as he stood up. What had made him think this girl would be interested in his story in the first place? He was an old man, an old man who still had sex and compared his greatest love—well, no, not his greatest, but his last big one still alive—to a fanny. He and Fran both had big old fannies. It sounded disgusting even to him.

"Mind if I turn the lights on in there?" he called to Charla, matter-of-factly.

"She wants to see where it happened. I'll come back and finish this." He gestured to his hotcake.

"I don't mean to rush you," Hailey said.

"Be careful of the vacuum," said Charla. "The cord is wound all over everywhere in there."

"That's fine," he said to Hailey. He walked ahead of her to the bar, found the lights, and unplugged the vacuum and wound up the cord. He took his time, wondering how he'd gotten himself into this. He felt like a fool. He turned around and found Hailey standing by a high table with four high chairs beneath a big-screen television. She'd put her pad and her recorder on the table and looked distracted. He thought again about telling her she should smile more often. He thought of a joke to tell her, but then she said, "I think maybe it's not a smell after all."

"What?" Nelson asked.

"I was thinking out loud," she said.

"I missed it," he said, and waited. Hailey looked smaller to him now that they were both standing. Her chin was raised, and Nelson thought of the deer out his window when they picked up a scent down the river. He'd done a few paintings of them that he liked.

"I was thinking," she said, "maybe it's not a smell in here at all that reminds me of an ice rink. Maybe it's the temperature."

"They don't turn the heat up all the way until nine o'clock," Nelson said. "Bill and Sandy do that when whichever one of them comes in."

Hailey didn't say anything.

"They're the owners," Nelson said. "You might want to ask them some questions."

"I think it's the smell and the temperature," she said. "I took skating lessons when I was a kid, and I always knew when my mom had arrived to pick me up because I'd catch her perfume in the cold air. That waitress must wear some."

"I believe she does," said Nelson. Hailey seemed calmer right then. She didn't seem to be focusing on him, which made him more comfortable. The joke he'd wanted to tell her had slipped his mind, and so he asked her, "Did you skate down there at Wilson's Community?"

"Oh," she said. "No. I'm from Pennsylvania. That's where I skated."

"Oh," he said. His parents and his grandparents had lived their whole lives in Montana. His siblings had lived their whole lives there, too. And so had his children, though they lived so far east they might as well be in North Dakota, and he was lucky to see them on Christmas if the roads were clear. Pennsylvania. "That's not around here," he said.

"My parents got divorced," Hailey said, as if that explained it.

Nelson didn't know if he should say he was sorry. His parents had never divorced. He thought of something else he could tell her, if she were someone he knew better, but then she said,

"My dad stayed in Pennsylvania, and my mom brought me and my brother here."

"Oh," Nelson said again. He wanted to ask her if she missed Pennsylvania, but he'd never heard of talking to a reporter like this, asking his own questions. He didn't imagine a reporter like Hailey went around talking this way to everyone she interviewed, and for a moment he thought that maybe she really was interested in his story.

Hailey folded her arms across her chest. Her hair hung straight down the sides of her face, and Nelson tried to think what he should do. "I've got a daughter all the way in Miles City," he said. "I've got a niece in Hawaii."

Hailey nodded. Nelson considered whether he had said this a few minutes earlier and forgotten. "I have a sister and two brothers, but they're dead," he added.

"My brother's in New York," she said, like this was comparable. "My mother met her second husband here and moved to LA, and my dad married a woman from our hometown who has four other kids." Hailey raised her eyes to Nelson's.

He was confused. "Families move around more these days," he said, though the truth was he had no idea what to say to a girl Hailey's age, telling him about her life out of the blue.

"They wouldn't understand your story," she said.

"Excuse me?" Nelson felt for a high table behind him.

"Real love," she said. "Selfless action."

Nelson felt his hands go clammy.

Hailey shook her head. "Anyway, I stayed out here," she said. "I went away for college, but I came back. I don't have any desire to leave."

Well then, Nelson thought. He wasn't sure what direction any of this was going, but he did know from his own experience that people who stated what they wanted usually wanted something entirely different. He wondered if

Hailey had friends, or if she was all alone, or if she was married. She wore no ring. She was old to be single, probably in her late twenties. He wanted to ask. Instead he said, "Who's interviewing who?"

Hailey looked away from him.

"I'm just joking with you," he said, but he could tell he'd lost her. She picked up her pad, added something.

"I've never been to Pennsylvania," he said.

She didn't write that down.

"I'd like to see the Liberty Bell," he said, but she didn't respond. He was afraid she might leave, and so he asked, "Have you ever been to the Maize Dayz over there in Helena?"

She squinted at him then. Nelson imagined she was picking out which screw had untwisted in his old brain. "No," she said. "Not yet."

He watched her flip the pad shut, and he wasn't sure if she still wanted to see the spot where he'd saved Fran. He felt his stomach tighten, that nervous feeling that made his hands hot and had been sneaking up on him ever since he was a boy. In Havre, where he grew up without his older sister who was already out of the house by then, his parents slept in separate twin beds, and he slept in a twin bed down the hall. If he heard any creaking at night, it was only his mother or his father going to the bathroom, or a deer who'd come right up on the front porch. He had memories of cold, wide floorboards and tiptoeing through the house, even in daylight.

He didn't want Hailey to leave yet. He wasn't sure about her, either, but he didn't want her to leave. "I'm from Havre," he said to her. "I lived there with my parents until I was sixteen, and then I went into the army at Fort Drum. That's in New York."

"That's young to leave home," she said.

Nelson shrugged. "My sister was already out of the house. I was the youngest." He pushed the vacuum cleaner back and forth over the carpet. He paused for one more second, then decided it was okay to tell her even though he hardly knew her. "My parents didn't love each other."

Hailey stood still. She didn't say anything, and Nelson wondered if she was thinking it was odd that a man his age still talked about such things. A man his age who was still having sex. A man his age who was an accident.

But then she got a look on her face. Nelson couldn't call it a smile. It was something in her cheekbones, in the looser brushstrokes, by her eyes. He couldn't say what it was except he knew it was between them, and it put him strangely at ease. He knew he didn't need to tell her she couldn't print all that. It was the truth.

"It happened over here," he said, and he led her to the big table where they'd all been sitting when Fran Murray choked on the chicken-wing bone. He pointed to the carpet where the bone had fallen. Hailey leaned down with her hands on her knees, but there was no spot on the carpet or anything like that. She straightened up and stared at the big, square table.

"Were you sitting next to her?" She ran one hand along the back of a chair.

"No," Nelson said. "I was sitting next to Bethany, over there." He pointed across the table. "Jim was next to Fran."

"What did he do?" Hailey asked.

"Well, we all kind of froze up at first. We all weren't sure what to do."

"You were," she said.

"Well."

From inside the walls came the sound of air churning to life. Nelson felt a puff of warmth. "Bill and Sandy must of come in early today."

"Did Fran do anything special to thank you?" Hailey asked. "Anything romantic?"

"Oh, no," Nelson said too quickly, and he saw Hailey's interest falter. He and Fran were no lovers. Disappointment filled him up and then waned. A lie was nothing but a lie anyway, no matter how close it got at the truth. "We're all friends," he said.

"You loved her," Hailey said.

"A whole lot."

There was the churning in the walls, the puffs of warmth spreading.

"Not everyone would have done what you did," Hailey said.

Nelson shrugged, but he let himself smile.

"It's good to meet you," she said.

Nelson blushed, and thought it was interesting she had waited so long to say so. That was the kind of thing he said first when he met somebody, out of habit.

"I tried to call Fran," Hailey said. "But I got no answer."

"No," Nelson said. "She doesn't have an answering machine."

"No."

Nelson rocked Fran's empty chair forward and back in his hands. When Fran had loved Nelson, too, they used to sit on lawn chairs at her family's old place up Rock Creek and eat Winston's peanuts from the can. "You could talk to her here," he said. "You could meet all of them."

Hailey looked like she was considering it. "Not in time for my story," she said. "But another time."

Nelson wasn't sure if that meant she was coming. He wanted her to.

"Do you always sit at this table?" she asked.

"It's the only one where we fit," he said. "It's four tables put together."

"How many of you?"

"Oh," Nelson said, "fifteen, sixteen. It depends."

Hailey was quiet a moment. Nelson thought she might be wondering if there'd be room for her, and he wanted to tell her yes. But then he saw her look at her watch.

"Are you going to be late?" he asked.

"I should go." She reached into her pocket and pulled out some folded-up bills.

"Oh, no," Nelson said.

"I can expense it," she said.

"What?"

"What time to do you all meet in here?"

Nelson pulled out his own wallet and looked through it. "Like I say, we have drinks after bowling. We finish up around three o'clock."

"You finish bowling?"

"Around three," he said. He wasn't sure if he should be inviting her. How would that be? A girl in her twenties, who wasn't married, who wasn't any of their granddaughters. He couldn't think about it fast enough. "You could meet some of the others," he said.

"I could rent some of those shoes," she said.

Nelson didn't know if he should explain league bowling was seventy and up, or if she was trying to be funny. Before he could decide, Hailey thanked him, and so he thanked her back. He turned off the lights in the bar, and by the time he returned to the dining area, Hailey had already paid. She was leaving three dollars on the table for a tip. Nelson thought that was steep, but he didn't say anything. He put his hands in his blue jean pockets, felt the comb in there, and then took his hands out. Normally he wouldn't let any woman pay for his breakfast, but this time he did. This time, it was just the one hotcake, and there was no saying when he might save a life again.

CHAPTER 2

★

Bethany

Bethany never drank more than two beers after bowling, and now this was three. On her cocktail napkin, where Nelson had written her name with a ball-point pen like always, the ink had run so that only the *B* was clear anymore. Across the table, Fran Murray sat next to Jim Bowers, emptying a second mini-wine bottle from her purse into her glass. Bethany was surprised Fran could fit all that free wine in her purse, what with the three copies of the *Free Press* she'd stuffed in there, and she told her so. Right across the table for everyone to hear.

"Honey," Nelson said.

Bethany ignored him.

Fran bobbed her head toward the bar—like a woodpecker into a telephone pole, Bethany thought—and put a rose-polished fingertip over her lips. "You know who."

"If you think Doreen doesn't know you bring your drinks in your purse," said Bethany.

"Doreen's like family," said Fran.

"What does that have to do with anything?"

"Honey, please." Nelson fiddled with the corner of his cocktail napkin, on which he'd written his own name with a ballpoint pen. He'd had half a light beer so far. "Doreen is Charla's daughter."

"I know that, Nelson," Bethany said, though she was interested to hear Nelson remember it. Doreen had been bartending at Liberty Lanes eight years, and her dad, Charla's ex-husband, had run the bar twenty-some before that—but there was no telling what Nelson was going to remember and what he wasn't going to remember these days. He might remember all four of his children's birthdays but go blank on his son's name. He might remember the shortcut to Grubber's for two-fer Tuesdays but not know what he and Bethany were doing in his car once he'd parked.

Bethany was sure the others noticed. No one had said anything, but they couldn't have missed the glaze in Nelson's eyes when they all sat around after bowling, the way he laughed too late when someone said something funny. Bethany was half-mad at them for keeping quiet, half-glad she didn't have to go down that road yet. But most of all, she was worried. The week before Fran choked, Bethany had gone ahead and told Alastair Wells as much. He was mostly blind, which had made her justify in retrospect that he was the safest one in their group to tell. They had been changing out of their shoes after bowling when Alastair had asked her if she was all right. How he could have known she was upset she didn't know—he couldn't tell a shoe from a bowling ball in front of him—but he had been a good listener. He had told her that sometimes when you lost one of your senses the others were heightened, and that maybe this would happen for Nelson. Bethany was encouraged by the idea, even if she didn't see how having a strong sense of anything would matter if your mind was shot, but she was open to any possibilities that might stop her from worrying about Nelson.

She worried about him all of the time now, living in that Burr Street house alone. And because she and Nelson had been together three years, she didn't feel she could talk to the others behind his back. She had thought about calling one of his children, all of whom lived a two-days' drive away, but she didn't see how they were better suited to help than any of his friends. All she'd seen of them in three years were Nelson's birthday cards and one holiday visit when they'd made it clear they didn't need a new mother in their father's life, not that the role remotely interested her either. In any case, she hadn't called. Instead she'd started snipping at Nelson, at him and all of their friends for not doing something about the change, for not saying the things she couldn't bring herself to say, like, *Hey, how come Nelson doesn't tell his jokes anymore?*

"Do you think Doreen's pregnant?" Fran said, altogether too loud.

Bethany hushed her. She was sick of Fran calling attention to herself.

"Do you?" Fran raised her own finger to her lips.

To Bethany, Fran was one of those people whose head always seemed to be moving. It was no wonder she had choked on the chicken-wing bone; she was a careless, twittery little bird. How she was the only one in the group never single, Bethany couldn't figure. She knew some of the other women were jealous of Fran, but she was more inclined to feel sorry for her. Bethany had a tendency to feel sorry for everyone. When Fran had sat with her makeup running and spit on her chin after she'd choked, she'd felt sorry for her then. Every time Fran showed up at Liberty in another one of those sequined tops, ticking off the holidays like a blithering human calendar, Bethany felt sorry for her then, too. Fran seemed to be lit up from the outside in instead of the other way around.

Even now, mad as she was, Bethany felt sorry for her.

"What?" Fran's mouth hung open like she was waiting for a worm.

"Doreen's fifty-one." Bethany checked to see if Doreen had looked over from the TV behind the bar. Court TV was on. "She's fat," she said. "And she's getting fatter."

In fact, Bethany estimated Doreen's hips had doubled in the past year. Doreen's dad had had a heart attack at sixty, and Bethany couldn't help noticing that Doreen was well on her way to becoming her father's size. She was unmarried. Her knees bothered her. Bethany worried about her, too.

"She should go on Atkins," Fran said. "That's what I do."

Everyone knew Fran had been doing Atkins for three months and eleven pounds.

"You mean that diet?" Clarette Luther said from across the table. She was thin as a pencil, and everyone said it was because she drank bourbon, not beer.

"It's where you don't eat anything that crunches," said Jim.

"I thought you could have all the bacon you wanted." Stu Larsen stopped watching TV.

"Cheese no crackers, burgers no bun," said Jim.

Next to Stu, Marshall Hicks sat with his fists on either side of his beer. He was still wearing the Mountain Lines shirt he wore when he filled in shifts selling tickets at the bus depot. "Didn't I read somewhere the Atkins man died?"

"And no ice cream." Jim shook his head.

"If it has nuts, you can have it," Fran corrected him. "They're protein."

"My daughter told me his heart gave out," said Stu.

"I thought it was a fall," said Marshall.

"But nuts crunch," said Clarette.

That stumped them.

"And buns don't," she said. She looked around the table. "I believe it was ice he went down on."

"Buns crunch if you toast them," said Jim, but it wasn't good enough. Bacon crunched, too.

"Maybe he went down on ice *because* his heart gave out," Clarette said.

They got quiet.

Nelson had been quiet the whole time. His eyes were glassy, and he looked as if he was trying to figure out a way to leave. These days, he wanted to get everywhere early and leave everywhere early, and Bethany just wanted one normal evening out. She wanted one evening where she didn't have to worry about anything. He already had his hand on her thigh, and she knew he'd squeeze it soon and wink toward the door—only he wouldn't want to sneak off and have any fun. That's what he used to want. They used to stop to play the slots at The Lucky Button long enough for one free glass of wine, and then go home.

For a second, Bethany wondered if Nelson was tired of her. But, no, she knew that was wishful thinking. The truth of it was she was tired of him. She was mad about the article, too, sure—she hadn't lived through three husbands, eight children, and twenty-two grandchildren to be made the fool—but the truth was that if Nelson wanted to get back with Fran, that was a load off her mind. Every day, he was more and more a shell—the wink without the kick. Bethany imagined him hollow right beneath his bones.

He squeezed her thigh. "Honey, is it about time—"

She was mad at him, of course, for failing.

"Fran's diet is where you eat free chicken wings and drink free wine," she snipped. "It's not for everyone."

Everyone looked at her.

Nelson crunched up his brow so tight it looked like he might wring tears out of his eyes.

Even Bethany had to admit it was mean. She felt her face flush because mean wasn't in her nature—ask anyone. Ask any of her eight children and twenty-two grandchildren and three dead husbands. You can't go to all those christenings and graduations and have a mean bone inside of you. Not when you're so busy logging miles to Great Falls or Butte or Helena or Havre you forget to even have your lunch. Not with one child in rehab and another with diabetes and two with children in the war and another zoned out on Xanax and two others divorced, and all the babysitting around the clock so that maybe they can smooth over their bumps, hit some groove, get rolling with their own lives. Isn't that what a mother wants?

Bethany wanted one day to herself.

Now Nelson never wanted to be alone. He wanted to come over and sit in her armchair and watch her TV.

Bethany knew she was supposed to say she was sorry.

Clarette tinkled the ice in her drink. "I hear Doreen's not going to make any more of those chicken wings," she said seriously. "So you know."

"We should think more about what we eat anyway," said Marshall Hicks.

Stu Larsen was watching the court case on TV. A woman their age was on the stand, crying. Stu's own wife was in a nursing home and didn't know who he was. "We're all blessed for what we have," he said, and no one said anything to that. The whole table went quiet, and then Jim went ahead and said what they all weren't saying.

"I thought it was a good article," he said.

Everyone caught that.

Nelson pressed his forehead against Bethany's ear. "I'm sorry, honey," he said. "I didn't—please don't be mad at me."

"I'm not mad at you."

"You pulled off a good one, Nelson." Jim raised his beer.

There was half a beat before Stu raised his glass, too, and then Fran and Marshall and Clarette and the rest of the table did the same. Jim smiled, and the rest of the table followed suit. He was a decent man, Bethany thought. He was generous when he didn't have to be, and she figured if anyone might speak up and do something about Nelson, it might be Jim.

"Nelson always has the best jokes." Clarette clinked her glass against Marshall's.

"My hero," Fran said.

Nelson started to smile and caught himself. He squeezed Bethany's knee again. His face was red. Next to him, Alastair smiled politely, looking in slightly the wrong direction. Because he was blind, Alastair put a piece of tape on the lane when he bowled so he could feel where to stand. Some of the other bowlers felt this was unfair, but they only said so to each other. Bethany didn't know Alastair as well as she knew most of the others—another fact she attributed to his blindness—but after talking with him the other week, she wondered if he knew that some of the bowlers felt this way. If he could sense it.

"If someone would read it to me," Alastair said, "I'd like to hear the article." He reached out and found Nelson's arm. "I hear it was a good article."

"I don't think so." Nelson clenched his teeth.

Bethany saw Fran reach for her bag and hesitate. "Go on and get it over with," she said.

Fran looked to Jim.

"Hand one over," said Bethany. "You've got enough."

"I brought copies in case anyone wanted to see," Fran said.

"Right." Bethany waved a hand. "Give me one. Alastair wants to see."

So Fran handed a rolled copy of the *Free Press* to Jim, who handed it to Stu, who handed it to Marshall, who handed it to Alastair, who patted it like a dog before handing it to Nelson, who grimaced as he handed it to Bethany. She snapped it open. Nelson had made the front page.

"A Wing and a Prayer." Bethany didn't care for the headline. "On any old Monday, Nelson Moore brings super-heroism to life."

"Who writes this fluff?" Stu Larsen made a face.

"This is the *Free Press*," Fran reminded him.

"Hailey James wrote it," Nelson said. "She's from Pennsylvania. Her parents got a divorce."

Bethany looked at him.

Then she cleared her throat and began to read. She read about how Nelson had saved Fran when she'd choked on the chicken-wing bone. She read about how Nelson had learned the Heimlich in a first-aid class he'd taken when he'd retired from driving a truck for Dawsen's. She read the part about how, as thanks for the rescue, Nelson would get a free beer at the bowling alley every Monday—not every *day*, as the *Daily Chronicle* had printed incorrectly—which was the day he had saved Fran Murray. And she read all the details the girl had gone into: what Nelson had to eat the morning they'd met for the interview—a hotcake with jelly, and black coffee—and what he was wearing—blue jeans and a plaid button-down short-sleeve, even though it was freezing outside—and how his silver hair did a little swoop across his forehead not unlike Superman. Bethany had to admit it was a good article. Reading it was less like reading the news than a story, she'd thought the first time she'd read it at home. The girl had even got Charla in there, the way she came around with more coffee every time you took one sip. It was only the part near the end that Bethany wished the girl had left out. Bethany blamed herself for not being there with Nelson. She was so mad at herself she could have screamed.

"'Lest anyone fear that chivalry is dead, take heart,'" read Bethany. "'Moore and Murray may be teammates who meet three times a week to bowl with a group of longtime friends, but Moore says there's more to the story than that. "You can call her an old flame," he says of Murray. Then he lifts his mug and blushes. The truth is, he says, that he and Murray remain more than friends. He gets a twinkle in his eye and calls Murray his lover. And after an hour of eating fried eggs and talking to the seventy-four-year-old Moore, you don't doubt him for a second. After all, Liberty Lanes is, as Moore has proven, a place where life goes on.'"

Around the table, there was a dusting of applause. Alastair thanked Bethany. He couldn't see Nelson's pained expression, or he might not have said, "Nelson, you dog."

Nelson clung to his beer bottle. "No," he said. His eyes were half shut.

"Plenty of men are dogs," Clarette said.

Bethany thought about ordering a round of whiskeys.

"Remember the one about the mutt, the astronaut, and the showgirl?" Clarette elbowed Marshall.

"Now listen," Nelson said.

Bethany added up that sixteen whiskeys would be forty-eight dollars, because only beer and wine were part of happy-hour specials, and that was too much. She tried to think of how else she could save him, but she couldn't remember the mutt joke.

"Jim," Nelson said then.

Bethany heard the word fall like an old apple from the junked-up backyard of Nelson's brain.

"Jim, I respect you. I respect you as a person, and as a man, and I meant no disrespect," he said.

Jim chuckled. "Lighten up, Nelson. I've known you long enough—"

"No," Nelson said, right where the old Nelson would have said: *Did you hear Monica Lewinsky is moving to Rock Creek?* "I want to air this thing out," he said.

She wanted to be closer to Clinton, Bethany finished. It was one of her favorites. When she'd first moved from Spokane with her second husband, they'd rented a place in Clinton so he could go over and fish Rock Creek. Thirty minutes down the interstate, and she hadn't been to either for years.

"I want to be clear, and I want to get on with it," Nelson said. "I like you, Jim, and I mean no harm. I give you my word."

"Okay, Nelson." Bethany patted his arm.

"Sometimes a man's brain doesn't work as quick as his Johnson."

Then everyone roared.

Good old Nelson hasn't lost his touch—Bethany could see that's what they were telling themselves. They clapped their hands and tossed back their heads and covered up the cracks. They drank their beer like Fran Murray hadn't almost died before their eyes, like Nelson still had all his tools in the drawer. It was their best option, and Bethany knew that, but she couldn't swing it herself today. She excused herself to the bathroom.

Fran was waiting by the door when she came out.

"Beth." Fran grabbed her forearm. "I don't want things to be tense between us. You seem angry about this, and we've been such good friends."

Bethany resisted rolling her eyes. *Good friends.* The only time she and Fran had done something together outside of the group was a Christmas shopping trip to the mall last year. Bethany had found Fran's taste so mismatched with her own that they'd separated and met up just long enough to say good-bye in the food court.

"Nelson saved your life," Bethany said. "I'm not angry."

"Nelson and I haven't been intimate since 1998," Fran said.

At that, Bethany laughed. She wondered if Fran had been preparing these words for some time.

"I wanted you to know." Fran was serious. When Bethany said nothing, she went on. "I know you and Nelson are committed. Everyone knows that. I wouldn't do anything to get in the way. Nelson and I were a long time ago, and it's true, we will always share—"

"Fran." Bethany stopped her. "I'm seventy-four years old."

Fran looked puzzled. "I know, Beth. Remember we all signed that card—"

"How old are you?"

Fran puckered her lips like this might be a trick question. "Seventy-two?"

"Do *you* want to be married again?"

Fran went silent. She looked to her side, to one of Nelson's paintings. Bethany followed her eyes and saw their reflections, ghostly, amid a stretch of nodding onions blooming up Pattee Canyon in August. Bethany knew the flower's name because last year Nelson had brought her a sprig of the purple blossoms, and the way they bent forward on their stem, they hooked just right behind her ear.

"Well, I don't," said Bethany, freeing her arm from Fran. "I want to come down to bowling and have a good time."

"That's what I want, too." Fran brightened.

"I've killed three already," Bethany said. "That's enough."

Fran's eyes went wide. She pulled a Kleenex from her pocket and held it over her mouth. She let out a low moan like she was in over her head.

"I've got a beer out there," Bethany said.

Fran sniffed and nodded. She looked around and then squared her shoulders to demonstrate that she was pulling herself together. "Okay, Beth," she said. "You're a good sport. That's what Jim says."

"We always have a choice," Bethany said.

"You're right," Fran said, though Bethany doubted she understood her. "It's just that—"

Bethany waited.

Fran twisted her Kleenex. "I've been thinking that—" She shook her head, and around her collar snowflake sequins shimmered. "I don't know how to say this."

"I'm not looking for you to say anything else."

Fran shifted her glance sideways, to the floor. "Jim and I do talk about getting married." She let go of the Kleenex without seeming to notice, and Bethany watched it drift to Fran's toes. "But that's not what I was going to say."

Bethany thought of picking up the Kleenex like she had picked up the chicken-wing bone without hesitation. It had taken her a week to throw it away. She didn't know why she had kept it, except maybe to respect what had happened—or, to acknowledge what *could* have happened.

"Do you think Nelson is okay?" Fran said then. Her voice was like a feather, and Bethany wasn't sure she had heard her right. She looked at Fran and saw that she appeared frightened.

"Do—?"

"No," Bethany answered. She was quick, and she was direct, but that was all she could bring herself to say. She had to admit, she was stunned. Here was Fran, out of all of them, speaking up first, and Bethany was disappointed in herself for not saying what she believed.

Fran was shaking her head. "I don't want to think it, Beth. I don't."

"No," Bethany said again, and that was all. There was so much more she wanted to say: about what was happening to Nelson, what it meant for the rest of them, what they should or shouldn't do. But now she saw that once you entered that conversation, you were in it, and there was only one way out. She saw how she was stuck—how all of them were stuck—with no good place to go. "I don't either," she said. "I don't want to talk about it." And she wasn't surprised, in that instant, to have something in common with Fran.

Fran reached down and picked up the Kleenex herself. She sniffed but pushed the Kleenex into her pocket without using it. "Well," she said nervously, patting the pockets on both of her hips. Bethany saw there were pink flowers embroidered across the top of each pocket. Fran's nail polish just about matched. "Anyway." Fran looked around. She gave an odd, high-pitched laugh as if someone had snuck up on her. "You know what I think?"

Bethany wished she could find the courage to keep talking. She thought it was possible she had underestimated Fran.

Fran was looking at Nelson's painting, not at Bethany. "Sometimes I think he misses me," she said.

Bethany waited to hear that she was kidding.

"I do." Fran started to smile. "Whatever you say, I do think we all want to be married. I think Nelson does. I think it's the natural thing. And sometimes these days I think Nelson is jealous of Jim."

Bethany had felt anger before. She had felt it when each of her husbands died, when the state trooper told her that her daughter had been in a wreck, when her youngest son dropped out of school. She knew how that sort of anger set you on fire at first and then filled your blood with lead and held you down in your bed for days. But this anger was different. This anger was working itself from the outside in. It was pushing deeper and deeper inside her, and it wasn't going to change course, because she could never say she was angry at Nelson; because these were her friends and she couldn't call them all daft for wanting to go ahead and live the rest of their lives; because apparently, given the chance, she couldn't do any better than the rest of them anyway.

Fran must have noticed Bethany's face darken, because she said, "All three of them had cancer, Beth. Right?"

Bethany stared at Fran. For the first time, she noticed what appeared to be a small rug burn on Fran's chin. She remembered Fran lying, curled up, on the bar's carpet when the paramedics arrived.

"Right," she heard herself say. "All three of them died of cancer."

"That's just the shuffle of the deck, Beth."

"Yes," said Bethany.

"That's not you."

"Yes, thank you, Fran."

If Nelson hadn't remembered the Heimlich, Bethany thought, Fran Murray would be dead.

Fran patted Bethany's arm, appearing to feel better about things. "Well," she said. "I think it would be great if you and Nelson got married." She smoothed Bethany's blouse for her. "Jim and I have already said that if we get married, we're doing it in Vegas." Then she did a little shimmy with her shoulders that started a whole blizzard on her sweater, and she headed back out to the table.

Bethany followed.

In the bar, Charla was turning up the TV so they could hear the Power Picks.

"Hurry up." Jim waved her in. "The balls are whirling."

"Damn it." Bethany stopped by the end of the bar with her hands on her hips. She said it loud enough for them to hear. "Damn it to hell," she said. And then she gave the nearest stool two kicks, first because she had forgotten to buy the Power Pick tickets, and second because none of the group talked like that in front of each other. They might slap each other's behinds now and then, but most of them went to church on Sunday, and none of them swore in front of the others that she could remember—except for once when Nelson had been over at her place and knocked a bowl of potato chips off the counter and then dropped the Dust Vac on his toe. It had been just the two of them on Nelson's birthday, and Nelson had been mad his daughter hadn't made the trip from Eureka after all.

"I forgot to buy the tickets." Bethany had her hands in her hair. But how could she have forgotten? They'd each been putting in a dollar to buy Power Pick tickets every Monday for umpteen years. They rotated whose turn it was to go to the Kwik Stop to fill out their numbers for the next week's drawing, and this week was her turn. She'd known it was her turn and then somehow she'd forgotten. The pot was up to $600,000.

"I flat out forgot," she said.

The table grew quiet, and Bethany could see them all trying to remember if anyone had ever forgotten to buy the Power Pick tickets before.

"Don't worry," Alastair said then. He could always be counted on for something nice to say. Maybe that was why Bethany had confided in him after all. "They probably won't have our numbers anyway," he said. "You don't have to worry, Bethany."

Clarette, too, could be counted on to say something cheery. If Clarette was mad, then you knew you were in trouble. Bethany looked around but didn't see her at the table. She wondered where she might have gone.

"We won enough to have the party at The Silver Bow last year," said Fran.

"We'll hitch to Hawaii if it comes to that," Jim said. That was their goal: to win the Power Pick pot and take a cruise in Hawaii all together. They were going to dance in grass skirts, and Stu Larsen's joke was that he was going to wear his skirt with nothing on underneath.

"I got the tickets," Nelson said.

Bethany turned to him. He drew the tickets out of his shirt pocket.

"I saw you hadn't done it," he said to her. "The baggie was there by your phone."

He was right. The baggie had been there by her phone, a corner of it wedged under her pen cup, and now she could see it. They always pooled their money in a Ziploc bag. Whoever went to the Kwik Stop picked the numbers.

Bethany stared at the tickets fanned out in Nelson's hand.

"Here." He put them down on the table and pushed them toward her seat.

"Thank you, Nelson."

He nodded seriously.

Doreen had the TV turned up, and Bethany took her seat in front of the tickets, and they all listened to the Power Pick girl do the numbers. The balls spun around inside a metal cage and popped out one at a time.

Bethany watched as two of their six numbers came up—eleven, twenty-six—one number short of winning fifty dollars, which they'd only done a few times. Four matches got you into the thousands, which they'd never done. All six got you enough for tickets to Hawaii.

"We almost won," Fran Murray cheered. It was what Clarette always said when more than one of their numbers turned up. "Where'd Clarette go, anyway?"

They looked around the bar. Clarette wasn't there.

"I don't know," said Nelson. Suddenly, he was scowling.

"Well, we almost won," Fran repeated.

"No, we didn't," said Nelson.

"Who's wound up today?" she said.

"Not me," he said.

"Fooled me," she said.

"Suit yourself, then." Nelson's face reddened. "But I don't like it when Clarette says that every time. And I'm not saying so because she isn't around to hear. I'm saying so because it's nonsense. There's no such thing as almost winning, and that's just the way it is."

Even Doreen, who had come over to take more orders, stopped to see if there was going to be a punch line. But there didn't seem to be.

"You either win or you don't," said Nelson. "And you might as well get used to it."

Bethany took his hand. "Okay, Nelson."

"Lighten up, old man," Jim said. "Anyone seen where Nelson went anyway?" He was trying to make a joke, but Nelson's face was angry. Bethany thought it might even be an anger that she understood. She wished all the others weren't there right then. She wanted to be alone with Nelson. But she wanted someone else to recognize what was happening, too. Here was something wrong. Right here in front of them all, and she wanted someone to say so. Or did she? Hadn't Fran said something? Bethany did not know what she wanted except she didn't want to feel sorry for Nelson. When Doreen came around to her, she said no to another drink because she'd already had more than she'd intended. She squeezed Nelson's hand and asked him if he'd had enough, and when he said, yes, he'd had enough, they stood up to go. Except for Fran, who still had half a glass of wine, the rest of them ordered one more drink and sat there talking while Bethany and Nelson stood up to leave.

Bethany drove Nelson home along Memorial, past the ball field, out by where the new office park was going up. The way they were angling the buildings, you could still see the mountains from the parking lot. That was good, she thought, though she didn't share as much with Nelson. She drove over the Third Street Bridge and alongside the park where she and Nelson had sat at a picnic table last fall when she'd first said how she didn't need him to call every few hours, or come over before breakfast with the part of the crossword he couldn't do. In the mornings, she liked to have time to herself, for a walk. At night, she thought it was important to call around to her sons and daughters to see how everyone was keeping it together. On league days, she liked to go down to bowling and have a good time. As she drove, she wondered if the rest of the table was talking about her and Nelson right then. If they were, she couldn't blame them. When you left the table first, people were always going to talk, no matter if you were a saint, no matter if you were one sandwich short of a picnic. Bethany was just curious to know what they were saying. She was curious to know if they were starting with *Poor Nelson* or *Poor Bethany*.

CHAPTER 3

····· ★ ·····

Clarette

Clarette pulled up a stool at the Fivemile and wondered how she could still be getting away with this scot-free. Three Mondays in a row, not one of them had asked her where she'd been going, leaving Liberty early. In the back of her mind, their not-asking bothered her because it suggested they might be collectively slowing down. But for the moment, all that mattered was that they hadn't. Because if any one of them had asked where she'd been going, she could hardly say to go meet Louis Black. She didn't even know what she'd say, except it wouldn't be to tell how she'd met Louis four weeks back when she went to the Fivemile for a bourbon by herself. Which was what she did plenty of the time when Dean was still alive. Clarette had gotten in the habit of getting her drinks where she wanted, when she wanted, because Dean was always too cheap to go out with her, and if he wanted to sit on the recliner with a Bud after fifty-nine years married, then he could sit on his recliner and Clarette could go on down to the Fivemile and pay for her own bourbon. No sense getting twisted up about what you can't change, Clarette swore up and down. You might as well get on with it. Dean's heart stopped while he was eating his dinner in the recliner. Five months later, Clarette still hadn't called a handyman to fix the door frame where the recliner jammed when she pushed it out to the front lawn for anyone to take for free. She was proud of moving the recliner by herself, at seventy-nine. Shane, the bartender down at the Fivemile, was twenty-four and he didn't believe she'd done it, but she had. She had good legs. She was strong. Louis Black was no dummy. And someone had come and taken that recliner off her lawn that very night.

One thing about Louis—besides the fact he was sixty-three—was he was always late. Clarette sat at the Fivemile's bar and wondered if she should be mad about this, but honestly she wasn't. As much as she liked dating Louis, she liked the parts of their dates that didn't involve him as much as the parts that did. She liked to lay her blouses out on her bed to see which ones went with what. She liked to get home after dinner, leave her clothes in a heap, and, still in her stockings, have one last nip of bourbon in front of the TV. She liked to sit at the Fivemile's bar before Louis got there and eat peanuts and wonder about things, and not feel alone. Sometimes she wondered about who was sitting in Dean's recliner now. Other times she wondered what the group would do if she invited Louis to come bowling. He wasn't old enough, but if he came with her, she wondered what they would say.

Tonight she wondered about Nelson. He had always been the ringleader of their group, ordering whole rounds of beer at a time, but recently it was as if he had shut down a part of himself, as if he was shifting to a lower gear so he might get the best mileage for this last stretch. The thought made Clarette feel quiet, too, and she considered that the rest of the group hadn't slowed down so much as grown preoccupied, each in their own way, with what might be going on inside of him. Clarette herself had to admit that she was probably attracted to Louis because he was still of an age where his mind and his big body weren't quitting any time soon. She could sit at the bar, split an order of meatloaf and onion rings with him, and talk about the day. Louis would want to finish her half of the onion rings, but she wasn't about to let him. She would fold them up in her napkin and save them for lunch. She would heat them up in the oven and mull over what the group would think if they knew Louis Black was sixty-three.

She saw him walk in behind two men in baseball caps. Louis wore a base-ball cap, too, but it sat taller and squarer than the other men's, and Clarette knew it said *Miller Genuine Draft*. He didn't look happy, but then again, Louis usually didn't look happy. His wife had left him eight months back, and he had a natural scowl and one big bank of thick black eyebrows besides. Even when he was happy, he didn't seem to get too excited about anything, and Clarette filed this away as a difference between them that might cause trouble if they kept on together.

"A ten-inch drill press came in right when I was leaving," Louis said as soon as he got close enough for Clarette to hear. The bar was filling up with the afternoon crowd. "Then two oak headboards after that, and it was only me and Kay, and she can't haul her own ass."

Louis worked part-time at Jack Cash Pawn on the edge of town, not because he needed to but because he had rented a trailer in the Boundary Bluff Court across the street after his wife left. She'd abandoned a lot of her things along with Louis—her figurines and knickknacks and whatnot—and his new trailer was only half the size of the previous one. So out of convenience, he'd hauled her things to the pawnshop and then ended up—not that he was proud to admit as much, he'd told Clarette, but you do what you do in this life— checking on her things there most days until he figured, why not get paid for his time. At least that was how he told it to Clarette the first night they met.

"I hardly got here myself." Clarette pushed a stool out of the way so Louis could join her. That was the other thing about Louis Black: He had a tummy. Not just a little tummy, but one round enough that he didn't like to sit on a stool. He liked to lean with his forearms on the bar so it looked to Clarette like his behind was guarding him from the whole world except for the bartender. And her. Louis wasn't afraid to put his hand on her thigh right there at the Fivemile, and even as thin as she was and as important as she felt it was to keep a trim figure, she didn't mind the feeling of his fat, damp palm covering her leg. Dean had only ever wanted her to rub his shoulders or scratch his head.

And the group at Liberty kept saying how she was doing so *well*. How she was so *up*.

Damn straight. If they wanted mourning, they'd have to knock on a different door.

"What size headboards?" she asked Louis.

His beer appeared without him asking, because Shane knew Louis only drank MGD. "Full," he said.

"Shoot," said Clarette, "I've got those two twins, and I was going to say if those headboards were twins and not too dinged up, I might take a look."

Louis took two long sips of beer. "These were fulls," he said. "I haven't seen a pair of twins come in there I don't think ever. But I have an idea where I could find you some. I could get you a good price."

"I don't have a need," Clarette said, "so much as it's fun to stumble across just the right thing."

Louis took off his cap and put it on the bar. He smoothed his hair. "Well, like I say, I could get you a good price."

Louis was serious like Dean, only nicer, Clarette had decided. Louis was serious because he was sad, and that was a lot different than being serious because he needed to make her do every little thing for him just so. Louis didn't have one joke in his whole body. He had forty extra pounds since his wife left, and Clarette imagined whittling them off of him, like a craftsman, one chip at a time.

If the group wanted mourning, she thought, they should go knock on Louis's door.

She ordered a bourbon then, and Shane put menus in front of them.

"We don't need these." Louis stacked the menus and handed them right back. "We'll have the meatloaf and the onion rings, and a second plate."

"You might change your mind." Shane knocked the menus against the bar, and Louis squinted at their noise.

"Not today," he said.

"Not today," Clarette said. "I'm hungry as a bull."

Louis smiled at that, and Clarette wriggled on her stool.

"You're like one of them hummingbirds," he said. He put his hand on her back. "I read somewhere they weigh less than a penny." He ran his hand up and down her spine, and Clarette felt safe—which was odd, because she'd never consciously felt the opposite, even since Dean's death. She hadn't locked the front door of her house in so long she wasn't sure where the key was anymore, and she'd had a black bear in her kitchen more than once. She wasn't the type to spook easily. But this latest bit with Fran and Nelson might have gotten to her. The idea you could have seven decades under your belt and go out on a chicken wing—Clarette preferred not to think about it.

Still.

"Did you read in the paper about Nelson?" she asked Louis. Clarette had told him the whole story about Fran choking the first week they met at the Fivemile. "It was in the *Free Press* there last week," she said.

"I read the *Chronicle*," Louis said, which Clarette knew was a nice way of saying the *Free Press* would only be of interest to him if he had a puppy to house-train or a fire to get started, and he had neither.

"It was the story about how he saved Fran Murray," she said. "She and Nelson went together a long time ago."

Louis nodded, frowning like a big fish.

"The article stirred things up," she said.

Louis waited, his big bar of eyebrows raised.

"There was almost a blowup at Liberty this afternoon." Clarette rubbed her palms together. "I thought Bethany was going to explode when Fran waltzed in with a half-dozen copies of the paper."

"Bethany's the one goes with Nelson?" Louis had lowered his hand so the tips of his fingers tucked into Clarette's back pocket.

Clarette mapped out the history for him with five peanuts from the bowl: Nelson and Fran, then Fran and others, then Nelson and Bethany, and Fran and Jim, and now this:

"The newspaper came right out and called Fran and Nelson lovers," she said.

Louis looked at her.

"As in, *today,*" she said.

Louis smoothed his dark hair again even though it was already smooth.

"Fran used to go with Nelson and now she's with Jim." Clarette repeated it for him. "Nelson and Bethany have been together three years—"

"They used that word?" Louis stopped her.

Clarette stopped.

"Lovers," Louis said, leaning in like he was dropping a coin in her bourbon, like her bourbon was a fountain.

Clarette felt a little whoosh go through her. *Lovers.* She saw Louis's face twitch like he was trying to hold in a grin, and right then she wouldn't have cared if anyone in the group had asked her where she'd been going. When she was with Louis, she was having fun, and she would recommend the experience to any of them. She bet Nelson would have understood where she was coming from. Whatever the truth about him and Fran, he had had that word *lovers* at the front of his mind. For all Clarette knew, his mind wasn't in any trouble at all, just fuzzy about where they all were in their lives by now, trying to keep up their fun even when the reality of things was nipping at their brains, their bones, their splotchy skin. Why not be lovers? What else were they going to do?

"Yes." Clarette gave Louis's belly a poke. "That's what I said. I thought that was quite a word."

"I don't think I've ever read that word in the newspaper," said Louis. "Not in the *Chronicle* anyway."

"There you go," said Clarette.

"Can a newspaper use that word?"

Clarette thought about that. "I suppose if it's true," she said. She held her bourbon in both hands just below her chin, like a buttercup. "They were playing it off as a joke at the alley, but I don't think newspapers are in the habit of printing jokes. I don't know, but if it's true, there's going to be a whole lot of hairs flying down at Liberty."

"You mean fists," Louis said.

"I mean hairs," Clarette said. "We're not young as you."

Louis breathed through his nose like he was steamed. "If it was me, it'd be fists," he said. "And I'd mean it. I don't care if I'm a hundred. It'd still be fists."

Shane brought their meatloaf and their onion rings, along with ketchup and Tabasco and two sets of utensils wrapped in paper napkins.

"We need the second plate," said Louis.

"I don't have three hands," Shane said as he reached under the bar for their plate.

"Watch it." Clarette winked. "Louis here is ready to pop someone."

"I'm hungry and I'm tired," Louis said. "And I'm ready for another beer." He crunched into an onion ring and shook his head. Clarette slipped the knife from her napkin roll, cut a small piece of meatloaf for herself, and lifted it onto the second plate.

"I swear to God," said Louis. "That Kay can't even haul her own ass."

Clarette watched Louis load up the rest of the meatloaf with salt and Tabasco and pour a pool of ketchup for the onion rings. He shoveled his food. If he wasn't sixteen years her junior, she felt certain then, she wouldn't date him. But there was his relative youth, like a fairy tale, that she wanted. And then there was companionship, and touch, and now this article. Clarette hadn't considered that Nelson's article might have made her mind fuzzy, too—she'd met Louis two weeks before it ran—but now she wondered if she'd still be sitting here with Louis if it hadn't. She'd been thinking about the article an awful lot—the double edge of it. Maybe Nelson and Fran *were* lovers. Or maybe Nelson was just losing it. Either way, the word wouldn't have appeared in black and white, about their own lives, if Fran hadn't almost died, and right there was the bittersweetness. The honest truth was there was a jag between what any of them wanted now and what this life could give them. It was a full-time job to keep seeing the good, to read a word like *lovers* and say, *you bet, why not, count me in.*

Beads of sweat had appeared along Louis's hairline. His meatloaf was nearly gone.

"Did your mother ever tell you to chew your food before you swallow?" Clarette teased.

"Did your father ever tell you not to mess with a man and his dinner?" Louis swayed his butt toward her just enough for Clarette to know he wasn't completely serious.

"No, he did not," said Clarette. "I never laid eyes on him."

Louis looked at her. Clarette could see him trying to figure out if she was serious.

"Where was he?" Louis asked. "Was he dead?"

"No, he was not." Clarette pursed her lips to show him just how serious she was. "He was having the time of his life. But that's all I need to say about that." She emptied her bourbon and signaled Shane for another.

Louis waited until Clarette's drink arrived, then polished off the meatloaf and washed it down with the last of his second beer. He ordered a whiskey with his next one. He crumpled his napkin into a tight ball and dropped it on his plate. Then he said, "We could go out to Flat Springs sometime if you want."

It might have been the bourbon, but Clarette didn't know what to make of that.

"We—I have a cabin," Louis said. "There's a wood stove and a porch, and the springs are right out back. We'd have to consider how much snow is in them this time of year."

Clarette gave Louis a punch in the arm. Louis squinted. "You're talking about Flat Springs *hot* springs," she said. "I thought you were back on the twins and fulls and whatnot. I was going to tell you to give it a rest."

"No," Louis said. He scowled, and Clarette realized she hadn't given an answer. She realized Louis Black had asked her to go away with him, and she'd punched him in the arm.

Louis's drinks arrived and he swallowed the whiskey at once.

Clarette wondered if she should say yes, or say no, or say sorry. She sipped her bourbon.

Then there was a girl beside them. Clarette could have kissed her.

"Excuse me," the girl said. "I don't mean to interrupt."

She was young—somewhere in her twenties—with long hair that gave Clarette a flash of her own daughters, Annabel and Cynthia, at that age, before they both moved to California and had their children and cut their hair short like hers. This girl sounded more with it than Annabel and Cynthia, who were down to "Bel" and "Cyn" by now and always seemed to be in the middle of an exercise video or a TV program when she called. But Clarette felt flush with relief that neither of them was in the same state right then while she was being invited to go away with a man who was in spitting distance of their age.

"I'm with the *Free Press*," the girl said, "and I'm—"

"We're eating here," said Louis over his shoulder.

"We were talking about the *Free Press* two seconds ago." Clarette swung around on her stool. She tried to remember the name of the girl who'd written about Nelson.

"I'm working on a story about the Fivemile," the girl said to her.

Louis clunked his beer down. "I don't talk to the newspapers."

"About the plans to tear it down," the girl said.

"They're going to tear down the Fivemile?" Clarette sat up straight.

"They've been talking about that twenty years." Louis gripped his beer. He gave the reporter a once-over. "Since before you were born."

Clarette couldn't believe what she was hearing. Tearing down the Fivemile. "Why on earth?" she said.

"For a travel plaza," the girl answered. "Now that they've finished the exit ramp off 90." Clarette watched the girl inch toward her, so she clammed up. Not that she had any trouble speaking her mind; it was just that Nelson's piece had got more of them reading the *Free Press* these days, and it occurred to Clarette that if her name ended up in the paper, she'd have to explain what she was so busy doing down at the Fivemile while the rest of them were still sitting with their beers, waiting on Doreen's mini-pizzas.

The girl flipped backwards through a pad in her hand. "The plans include a mini-mart, a Laundromat, a video store, and a pizza parlor," she said to Clarette.

"And they'll charge two dollars a slice for pizza." Louis grimaced.

Clarette looked around the bar.

"And another two dollars for a quart of milk," he said.

Clarette knew at least a dozen faces here. She'd been coming to the Fivemile since her daughters were in diapers. When Dean was on day shifts for Bell West, she'd brought them down in the afternoons and nobody gave a hoot. "They can't tear down the Fivemile," she said.

"Who's they?" Louis shifted sideways so his butt wasn't smack in the girl's face.

"W. W. Gooden and Sons," said the girl. Clarette thought her voice was like one of those radio voices—crisp like the sound of wine glasses clinking in the movies. Clarette imagined a voice like that could sing beautifully, and she wondered if this girl had ever been in a choir. Or led a protest. You could get a lot of attention with a voice like that, and they might need a protest if this thing with the Fivemile gathered any steam. She almost asked the girl what she knew about protests, but then the girl turned over the pad in her hand and revealed a small recording device. She raised it between them. "Would you mind if I—"

"I said I don't talk to the newspapers," Louis said.

The reporter looked to Clarette. Clarette looked at the recording device in the reporter's hand. She considered making a comment without giving her name, but then she remembered Nelson saying how he had grabbed the recorder away and turned it off. Clarette was struck by how this girl's hand didn't have even one brown splotch on it. No rings either. Just the whitest, smoothest skin that Clarette thought didn't even belong in the Fivemile, with all its smoke caked onto the walls and black grime built up on the arms of the ceiling fan. She wondered how this girl had ended up working for the *Free Press* in the first place. They had their office above another smoky bar downtown, and Clarette couldn't imagine many girls wanting to go to work above the bar behind windows with the *Free Press* signs propped up in them so you probably couldn't even see the sky. And then it struck her.

"You're the one wrote the story about Nelson," she said.

"Yes." The girl's voice rounded out like a big gust of wind. "I'm Hailey," she said.

"Well, that's right." Clarette smacked her own knee. "You're Hailey from Pennsylvania. And I know Nelson. We bowl the same league down at Liberty. I've known him since forever." She felt her own voice rising, like she herself had some celebrity here. "And I was there when it happened. I saw the whole thing."

"He was a hero." Hailey lowered the recorder.

"You wrote a good article," said Clarette. "We all said so."

"Thank you." Hailey nodded,

"We all kept our copies, and they're talking about paying to take a few of them to a print shop and get them—" Clarette made window-washing circles with her palms—"done up," she said.

"Laminated," said Louis.

"That's it." Clarette pointed at him.

"How is he?" Hailey said, and simple as it was, that got Clarette's attention.

"Nelson?" She cleared her throat like she was preparing for something. "He's fine. Why wouldn't he be?"

"Because of the way newspapers turn everything around," Louis said. His beer was gone.

"Did he like the article?" Hailey asked.

Clarette wasn't sure how to answer that. She didn't want to seem like she was stalling, but she couldn't say as Nelson had enjoyed the attention so far. "Well," she said, "I think so." And just like that, she saw how you could end up saying something to a newspaper that you didn't mean. She wondered if this was how Nelson felt when he'd said the bit about Fran, and she found herself wanting to protect him. "That man is basically all heart when you get down to it," she said. "When you get down to it, there isn't anything he wouldn't do for another person. But when you're all sitting around like we do after bowling, he can get under your skin. He's got his jokes, and he'll go ahead and give you a squeeze once he's had his beer."

Louis scowled, and Clarette would have pinched herself for saying too much except she already knew that all men were jealous, and there was nothing you could do about that. She might have gotten married at nineteen, but she'd still been around the block.

"I'm getting another beer," Louis said. "Do you want one?"

To Clarette's surprise, he was talking to Hailey.

"It sounds like you two have enough to talk about," he said.

"I'm working," Hailey said.

"Not in the Fivemile, you're not," said Clarette. She hopped off her stool and pulled over another from a table against the wall.

Hailey checked her watch.

"It's going to be MGD," said Louis. "That's what I drink."

And in Clarette's mind, Louis went up a notch right there. He offered to buy Hailey a drink only because he thought it was something Clarette wanted, and that was as much as any man had ever done for her.

"I can't," Hailey said.

"Says who?" Clarette shrilled. The bourbon was making her a little lippier than normal.

"I'd like to," Hailey said. "But I shouldn't."

"It's either a 'yes' or a 'no,'" said Louis.

Hailey lowered her bag from her shoulder. She looked at the stool for a second before taking it. "One beer," she said. She pulled the stool in closer to Clarette and Louis and lowered her voice. "I told Nelson I wanted to meet the rest of your group. He said we could meet in the bar after bowling."

"That's Nelson," said Clarette.

Hailey didn't say anything right away. Louis handed her a beer, and she thanked him. "I don't normally keep in touch with people I interview," she said.

"That must be hard to do after a while in a town this size," said Clarette.

"You're just starting out then," said Louis.

"No." Hailey sipped. "This is my second year."

"That's just starting out," said Louis.

"That's not how it feels," Hailey said, and Clarette caught a bite in her voice. She watched Hailey take a few more big sips of her beer and wondered if Louis would pay for a second one, too.

"What does it feel like, then?" Clarette asked. "I've never been inside a newspaper office before. Can you see out those windows?"

Hailey nodded but didn't answer the first part, which was the part Clarette was curious about. Hailey seemed serious for such a young girl, and Clarette wanted to know why. But all Hailey said was, "Nelson was different."

Clarette waited for her to say different from what.

"He wasn't pushy," Hailey said. "He was quiet. Other people call me all day long, *demanding* that their stories be written."

"He never used to be quiet," Clarette said, though she was interested that this girl had seen something good in Nelson's demeanor. "He used to ride with a motorcycle group."

"It was almost like he didn't want his story written."

"Which you can't blame him for," said Louis.

"Which made me like him." Hailey finished her beer. "Which made me feel a little bit bad for writing it." She didn't stop Louis when he signaled Shane for another. She watched Shane pour the new beer, carry it over, and put down a fresh napkin beneath the glass. "Sorry," she said as if she had caught herself going on too long. She picked up her glass. "So, he is okay?"

Clarette wanted to ask her outright what she meant. "He's not getting any younger, if that's what you mean."

But Hailey just smiled. "No," she said. "That's not what I was saying."

Clarette felt a wave of relief come over her. She felt her shoulders relax, loosen up. "Well, okay now," she said. "He's a boy compared to me and a geezer compared to him." She rubbed Louis's back.

"I'm not that young," said Louis. "I ran my own plumbing operation twenty-six years before I retired."

Hailey raised a hand in apology. "I meant—"

"Me and Louis are sixteen years apart in age in case you're wondering," said Clarette. "None of this is for the paper, though."

"No," said Hailey. "We're just talking."

"Banging gums," said Clarette.

"I wasn't sure what he wanted me to say," Hailey said. "In the article. Normally people let you know exactly what they want you to write. They *tell* you what words to use."

"And you say whatever you want anyway," Louis said.

"Sometimes." Hailey gave him that much. "But Nelson didn't seem like he knew. And so I wasn't so sure—" She stopped. "He surprised me." She tucked some stray hairs behind her ear, and Clarette was impressed again by how white her fingers were. Her thin wrists. Clear skin wasn't something Clarette saw much anymore. When she used to slip her wedding ring into her change purse and go over to Manny's Excuse Room, sure, but that was a million years ago. Dean was on nights by then, and Annabel and Cynthia could drive, and she herself still looked young enough to be in school. Not to be turning roasts and packing lunches and dusting curtains just so. But none of that was anything to lose sleep over this far down the road. You do what you do in this life.

"I wouldn't have thought I would relate to him," Hailey was saying.

"To Nelson?" Louis was squinting.

"You have a lover, too?" Clarette said flat out, and beer sprayed from Hailey's nose. "Because we were sitting here talking before you came," Clarette kept going, "saying we've never seen that word in the paper before. We weren't sure you could use that word in the paper, but we figured, well, if it's true, maybe that's why you can put it in."

Louis handed Hailey a cocktail napkin, and she wiped beer from her upper lip.

"So," Clarette said to Hailey. "Is it true?"

Hailey sat dumb.

"Are Fran and Nelson lovers?" Clarette leaned toward her, watching her eyes. "You wrote the article. You must know."

Hailey shifted on her stool. Clarette didn't normally set out to make a person uncomfortable, but on this particular question she was prepared to bend her own rules. She'd spent too much time on this question herself not to take advantage of having the actual reporter from Nelson's article right here.

"I wrote what Nelson said," Hailey said.

"So it's true," Clarette said.

"It's what Nelson said." Hailey's voice sharpened. "You know him better than I do." She stared right at Clarette, like she was trying to see what it looked like to be a person so close to someone who had saved a life. "Are you always sure of every word you say?"

Clarette only had to think a second. "Well, yes," she said, and the bourbon made it that much easier to say. "Pretty much I am."

"So I could tell you I'm the duke of somesuch and you'd print that up?" Louis said to Hailey. "Just because I said so?"

"Nelson and Fran are lovers," Hailey said right back. She put down her beer, almost untouched, and slid off her stool.

"Well, now I'm not sure what to think." Clarette wrung her hands together as Hailey pulled her wallet out of her bag.

"Put that away," Louis said to Hailey.

"Do you think he would make it up?" Hailey said to Clarette.

"I don't know," Clarette said, and then heard how that contradicted what she'd just said about being sure of things. She felt how, in her gut, she wanted to believe that it was true, how she hadn't realized, until that moment, that she might have *needed* it to be true. She moved her hands flat against her thighs and said, "No. No, I don't. And you can tell from the way everybody's acting down at Liberty that it's true. Everybody's half in the clouds these days. They're acting like fools." She felt much better for having said so. "You caused a stir down there, you know."

Hailey stiffened. She pushed bills back into her wallet. "I hope I didn't cause trouble," she said.

"A *stir*," Clarette repeated. "That's not trouble. At our age that's a tune-up— except maybe for those ones who'll always be looking for trouble, but not me." She smacked the bar. "Do you drink bourbon?"

"Not right now." Hailey shouldered her bag.

"What are you going to say about the Fivemile?" Louis asked.

"I tried to figure out what Nelson wanted me to say," she said.

Clarette reached out and clasped Hailey's arm with a firm grip. "You did a good article. Nelson's at a point in his life, but he's his same self at the end of the day. That's what you have to remember."

Hailey looked puzzled, and Clarette figured it was just as well they weren't having more bourbon.

"You aren't going to put us in your article," Louis said.

Hailey buttoned her coat. She looked first to Clarette and then to Louis like she wasn't quite sure what she was going to do next. She stepped away from them but tripped on the stool's leg, stumbled, caught herself, and apologized. "I'm going to say the duke of somesuch bought me a beer," she said, dead serious. She let Louis take a breath through his nose before she winked at him, and Clarette thought that was all right. She thought how Annabel and Cynthia had never seemed much good at poking fun. They'd always been bored around grown-ups.

"Tell Nelson I didn't mean to cause any trouble," Hailey said.

"It's good for him," Clarette said.

Hailey paused like she wanted to say something more. Instead she thanked Louis for the beer, checked her bag to make sure she had everything, and then wove her way through the crowd. Clarette watched her red coat disappear into the evening. She was going to ask Louis if he thought Hailey had been pushy or skittish—or if a reporter worth her salt could be both—but when she swiveled back to the bar, there was a glass of something gold waiting for her.

"What's this?" she said.

"Laphroaig," said Louis. "Fifteen year. It's eight dollars a glass."

Clarette didn't think she should take one more sip of anything. "Is it going to make me young?" She picked it up. "At that price?"

"It's a single malt," Louis said seriously.

"When did you get so flush?" she asked, and as she said it she remembered about Flat Springs—his invitation dangling out there—and she grew quiet.

"Today," he said. He sounded glum as ever.

Clarette sniffed her drink. "From those headboards?"

"What?" Louis was hunkered down over his glass.

"Those fulls," she said. "Those fulls and that other thing you came in here going on about—"

"No," Louis said.

Clarette tilted her drink and felt it warm her up before it ever touched her lips. She remembered the first time she'd had a top-shelf drink. Dean had been promoted to supervisor, and they were celebrating at the vfw. "Okay," she said. "So, what?"

Louis's head hung so low he barely had to lift the glass to get his sip.

"Are you mad we talked to that reporter?" she asked.

"She was all right," he said.

"I thought so," she said. "She told us what we were after."

Louis's mind seemed to be somewhere else. He wasn't concerned anymore with what was getting printed in the paper.

"Did you play some of those Power Picks?" Clarette asked. "We play every week, except for this week—"

"No," Louis said. He sighed, and Clarette watched his big shoulders balloon and sag. She wondered if it had made him sad to see a young girl like Hailey; sometimes those moments made her sad. Sometimes they made her realize how far away the world was from her by now, and sometimes they made her tickled she was still right smack in it. Bourbon could do that to her, too, and she wasn't sure which was bouncing her heart around tonight.

"There weren't any headboards," Louis said.

Clarette put down her glass and made sure she'd heard him right. She felt herself grow sober and stern in equal measure. "What do you mean there weren't any headboards?"

"I just said that," Louis said. "I made that part up."

"You made that part *up*?"

Shane glanced over at Clarette from down the bar.

She could forgive a lot of shortcomings—she'd forgiven acres of shortcomings over the years—but lying wasn't one of them. People are mostly good. People are mostly flawed. But good, flawed people don't lie. That was the way she saw it.

"You had me going on about twins and fulls and you made that part—"

"Nan came in," Louis said.

Nan being Louis's ex-wife. Clarette didn't say anything to that.

"She heard I had her things up for sale," he said.

Clarette remembered Louis telling her about porcelain dolphins and giraffes and dolls in costumes from exotic countries. She made a fist on the bar. She didn't want to be mad at him. "Well, what did she expect?" she said. "Did she expect you to drag your duff around dusting every little—"

"She bought it all back," he said.

"Oh." Clarette didn't want to picture how sad that scene was.

"She paid cash."

Clarette didn't want to picture Louis packing those boxes. Carrying those boxes, since Kay can't haul her own ass. No matter how you sliced it, that was a sad scene, and it was a scene where Louis and Nan's lives were still tangled up in some mess that didn't exclude love, and Clarette felt hot thinking Louis had waited all this time to tell her. All this time they'd been talking about head-boards and lovers, and he'd just been up to here in it with Nan.

People are mostly good, and they are mostly flawed, and Clarette didn't consider herself different from anybody else.

"I'd go up to those Flat Springs if you want," she said. It might have been the right thing to say, and it might have been wrong, but it was what she had. She'd never considered herself a jealous person until that moment, and she couldn't say she was proud of it.

Louis was just about in his glass. It was a small glass, especially for a drink that ran eight dollars, but the way Louis hung onto it, his whole body pressed toward it, it seemed to be holding him up. Clarette fixed on the shiny gold liquid and imagined it turning solid, turning into a gold pole that went straight through the bar and into the ground so you could hang on to it, or swing yourself around it, or hold a protest where you don't let go until they say they'll never tear the Fivemile down. Until they'll just leave things the way you remember them. Clarette reached her hand out over Louis's and held on. His skin was rough, and she imagined her hand felt bony to him. She expected he might tell her he didn't want to go to Flat Springs anymore. The way his frown twitched up, though, she was pretty sure no matter what Louis said next, she had done her part. She figured whether they went to Flat Springs a hundred times or never, she had managed to whittle away at least one night's worth of the loneliness that was weighing down his heart.

*   *   *   *   *   *   ★   *   *   *   *   *   *

CHAPTER 4

Hailey

Hailey went in to the office on Saturday to finish the city council piece. It was a short article—the council had decided to install benches, not lampposts, along Main Street—but after Nelson's story had come out last week, she hadn't been able to get much done. Her editor, Craig, wasn't happy with Nelson's story; he said it was too soft for the cover, all feel-good and no edge. Forget that he'd okayed it in the first place. Hailey had had a nervous rumbling in her stomach ever since the article ran. She wasn't bothered that Craig would find out she'd used "lovers" even though Nelson had told her not to; she was concerned that she had done it in the first place. And though she'd told herself over and over all weekend that it didn't really matter—not to her job, not to her life—if a seventy-four-year-old man was miffed over a little misstep in a human interest story that would be forgotten before the next issue hit the stands, she couldn't stop worrying that Nelson Moore would think badly of her.

That she had done him wrong.

That she had done something that she had sworn she would never do.

On her desk, an old slice of pizza lay on top of notes for two other stories that had to be written by Tuesday. Hailey sighed. She looked at the paragraph on her screen and thought about calling Nate, her fellow staff reporter, to see if he might make her feel better. Nate had a big, open heart inside a broad, solid body, and those were most likely the reasons, Hailey knew, that she had gone ahead and started dating him.

She was reaching for the phone when it rang.

Seriously? she thought. *On a Saturday?* Sometimes she came to work on weekends to write without the interruption of the calls. There were so many of them—so many people wanting to tell her about themselves, about their causes, about why their voices more than any others should be heard.

She let the call go. She was sick of all of them but Nelson Moore. She rubbed her hands over her face and heard a door open downstairs. Then she heard keys fall to the ground, a paper bag crinkle, Nate's heavy boots running up the stairs.

He might have been the only person she wanted to see.

"Sunshine," he said, walking in.

"What are you doing here?" She picked up the phone. "I was about to call you."

He put a paper bag on her desk. Her message light was blinking.

"I thought you'd be here." He kissed the top of her head. "But no one else is, right?"

Two weeks earlier, she wouldn't have been so happy to see him. She would have still been irritated at herself for getting so close to a coworker, but she'd felt different since the article ran. Or, really, she had felt different since her interview with Nelson.

She shook her head. "What's in there?"

Nate opened the paper bag and withdrew two cartons of orange juice and two bran muffins. He'd never brought her breakfast before. He had started bringing her lunch on occasion if he was taking a lunch break before she did, but no one in the office was the wiser. No one knew that they had first kissed in Nate's car while covering the VFW's annual Thanksgiving Day auction, and no one knew that Nate had said, pretty much right away, way before Hailey would have dared, *I love you.*

"You're saying I should eat breakfast?" she said.

She hadn't said, *I love you, too.*

"Who are you calling?" Nate said, and only then did Hailey realize she was still holding the receiver.

"Oh." She punched in to voice mail. "I just missed a call."

"Yes," said Nate. "You should eat breakfast. Breakfast is the foundation of—"

"Shhh." She held out a hand to silence him, because on the other end was Nelson Moore. He was saying he was going to be in the neighborhood. He was saying he was going to stop in if she had a minute. She played the message again. She listened for anger or friendliness, but his tone betrayed neither.

"What is it?" Nate pulled up a chair next to Hailey's desk. "Something wrong?"

Every other time he had asked her that question in the past few weeks, she had wanted to tell him that, yes, something was wrong: His declaration was hanging out there, and she didn't think she was ever going to return it. She wasn't sure she had the ability, and so what were they doing anyway?

"Hailey?" Nate touched her arm.

"Why would Nelson Moore stop by at 10:00 a.m. on a Saturday?" she said. She hadn't told Nate what she had done.

"He's the chicken-wing guy?"

"He wants to know if I have a minute."

Nate shrugged. He tore a piece off his bran muffin and appeared to swallow it without chewing. "You wrote a good article."

"No one gets in touch because they're happy," she said. It was true, and it was something she and Nate had talked about plenty. People only followed up if you hadn't said exactly what they wanted.

"Sometimes they do."

"On a Saturday morning?"

"Is he senile?" Nate said.

That brought Hailey up short. Nate had a way of keeping things simple whereas she was always overanalyzing, and in this case it unsettled her. To her, Nelson had seemed pensive, maybe shy, but what did she know? No matter how much she had been thinking about it recently, she had no idea what it was like to be old.

"He is, what, seventy-something?" Nate said.

Hailey had thought Nelson's friends at the Fivemile had had the same concern. But what preoccupied her about Nelson—what drew her to him—was his matter-of-factness, the way he just stated things about his life with no cushioning. He loved Fran Murray. He saved her life. His parents didn't love each other. He spoke as if it were easy to say who you were and what you wanted and what got under your skin. Hailey considered that maybe that was what it was like to be old: to have yourself figured out. It sounded lovely—except Nelson didn't seem like he had things figured out, not entirely. He seemed to her like a much younger person rattling around in an old man's skin, his mind busy with the concerns of someone closer to her age than his own.

If he were her age, Hailey thought, they might be friends.

"He told me that his parents didn't love each other," she said.

Nate had pulled off another hunk of muffin but stopped short of eating it. He looked at Hailey funny.

She surprised herself, too, by saying it.

"He's seventy-four," she said. "Do you think that's strange? To still be talking about his parents?"

"You mean, because he's old?" Nate said.

"I mean, do you think we'll be talking about whether or not our parents loved each other when we're seventy-four?"

Nate looked like he was going to ask her again if something was wrong. He popped the hunk of muffin in his mouth. "I don't know," he said. "But if we are, it'll be a short conversation. Mine do."

"Mine don't," Hailey said. Had she ever said it out loud?

"Well, they're divorced." Nate shrugged.

She had never considered that she might share something so fundamental with someone Nelson's age, and ever since the interview the idea of it had made her want to see him again.

"So," Nate said, like that settled the issue.

"So?" Hailey squinted at him. As much as she liked Nate, she wasn't sure how much she really shared with him.

"Nothing," he said. "But if they're not together, then it sort of goes without saying . . . Never mind." He faked a yawn. He did that when he was trying to fill a silence. "What were you asking him? That he would tell you that?"

"I don't remember," Hailey said. "We'd gone into the bar to see where it had all happened, and he was telling me about his life. Things I hadn't asked him about."

"I hate when people don't answer the questions."

"No," Hailey said. "I'd already asked my questions."

"People go on and on like you're there to write their life story."

"It was okay," said Hailey. "I didn't mind."

And maybe it was because her magnanimity was out of character, or because her voice had grown distant, that Nate asked, again, "Hailey, is something wrong?"

She looked at him. Yes, she wanted to say. Something was wrong. Her parents were divorced. She wasn't good at sharing much with Nate, or anyone. Nelson Moore was at a point in his life, but he was his same self at the end of the day. That's what his friends had said.

"I know that Nelson and the woman he saved aren't lovers," Hailey said. "But I wrote it anyway."

Nate smoothed his hands over his chair's arms, watching her.

"I ran a lie," she said, and doubted, suddenly, that Nate would be able to make her feel any better about it. "And now I don't know why I did."

Nate clasped his hands over his head and up into a stretch—another move he used to pass awkward moments—and gave a nervous laugh. But then he looked at Hailey's face and sobered. He leaned forward and picked at the remainder of his muffin.

"How do you know?" He creased his brow the way he did in story meetings when Craig listed mistakes in the previous week's issue. "That they aren't?"

It was a fair question. Nate was a clear thinker. Hailey didn't *know* Nelson. All she knew was what he'd said. All she knew was that she'd liked him, that compared to the usual ego-swelling, earth-saving showboating she weathered in her interviews, Nelson hadn't seemed proud of himself at all.

"At first, he said that they were lovers," she said.

"He used that word?" Nate sounded hopeful.

"He didn't say I could say it," Hailey said. "He told me I could use 'old flame.'"

"But he did say they were lovers? He did use that word?"

Hailey nodded. Sure, he'd said it. But the whole point of reporting was to find the truth, and she'd known from the get-go—the smallest shift, a tiny stumble—that it wasn't true. And yet there was this dull certainty inside of her, a kind of childish insistence, that made her believe, in brief moments, that it *was* the truth she'd printed. Not that Craig would agree. Or that Nelson would give her a gold star for doing it. But . . .

"I think it was what he wanted me to say," she said.

Nate looked puzzled. "So if he told you he was running for president—"

"I know," she said. "I'm not dumb." She thought of Nelson's friends the duke of somesuch and his older woman—and felt embarrassed for herself.

"Well, obviously it was what *you* wanted to say," Nate said.

Hailey looked to the floor, to the gritty bare wood splintering. In her parents' old kitchen in Pottstown, the floorboards buckled by the sink from a leak. She thought of her parents, arguing at the kitchen table, Budweisers between them. Hailey stood eye level with the cans.

Yes, it was true, wasn't it? It was what she wanted to say, and she almost resented Nate for making her own poor decision so clear. "It does make a good story," she said. She tried to look out the windows, but *Free Press* signs were blocking all but a few inches of gray sky. "Old people," she said. "Forever young. I did think about that." She was ashamed to admit it was true. "Everyone saves a life." She cleared her throat and wondered if her parents had spoken in years. "Not everyone falls in love," she said.

"Hailey," Nate started.

She looked at his calm, wind-blown face. He had never brought her breakfast before. A few weeks ago, he had told her that he loved her, and the way he looked at her sadly now, Hailey felt she was in trouble. Not in trouble with Nate, or in trouble with Craig, or in trouble with Nelson—though likely with all of them, too—but just in trouble. Just missing some piece she was supposed to have that everyone else had to hold themselves together. Some bit of glue that she hadn't been aware, until recently, wasn't there.

She couldn't bring herself to say, *You, too.*

She was supposed to have said, *old flame.*

Nelson Moore had saved a life.

And his parents hadn't even loved each other.

"But he is seventy-four," Nate was saying. He tilted his chair back on two legs. "I wouldn't worry about it."

She looked at him. She'd been counting on him to make her feel better.

"He probably doesn't remember exactly what he said, or you said, and even if he did—"

"You mean, if he were younger—"

"He's a hero," Nate said. "And he's old. And he said the word. I'd drop it." He rocked his chair back down and pulled close to her again. He placed his hands on her thighs and rubbed them. "You wrote a good article." He leaned in and kissed her neck. "I'm sure he wanted you to say it. Don't you dare bring this up with Craig."

Nate's knees were touching hers, and his hands felt good on her legs.

"Everyone loves a hero," he said.

She leaned toward him. It was Saturday after all, and her articles didn't have to be long, and she did *want* to want this—and so she kissed his cheek, back by his ear, and his temple. She was going to kiss his lips next, but there was a noise downstairs—the door opening again. She pulled back and whisked her chair away from his. They listened. The steps were soft, not sharp like Craig's. Not quick like Michael the photo editor's. Not really tense enough for any of the *Free Press* staff.

"Did you leave the door unlocked?" Hailey picked up her phone again to look busy.

"I think so." Nate stood and brushed crumbs off his lap. He sighed, and Hailey saw him shake his head. And then there was Nelson Moore.

"They can stick a newspaper up above a bar?" Nelson said loud, looking around. His face was red with cold. He looked large in the narrow door frame.

"Mr. Moore." Hailey stood up. She glanced at Nate, who was watching her. "I got your message," she said. "You look cold." In fact, Nelson's eyes were tearing, and his eyelashes were either laced with frost or white to begin with.

"I walked all the way from over there on Glen," he said. "The bus dropped me there."

Hailey realized she had no idea where Nelson lived. An apartment. A house. But she knew he drove a car. She couldn't tell if he was angry.

"I didn't want to mess around with the parking downtown," he said. "You got my call?"

"I did," she said slowly. She was working to assimilate the pieces: Nelson and Nate in the office on a Saturday.

"Am I interrupting something?" Nelson looked from Hailey to Nate. Nate appeared stern. Nelson stepped farther into the office, and Hailey saw he was carrying a paper bag in his bare hand.

"No," she said.

"Not a thing," Nate said to Hailey.

"This is Nate Whitfield," Hailey said. "He's our other staff reporter."

"He's not your husband?" Nelson said.

"Whoa." Nate raised his hands like a cop had showed up.

"No," Hailey said, uneasy about Nelson's question. It didn't make much sense. Nelson Moore was in the office on a Saturday. He'd said he was in the neighborhood, then taken a bus downtown instead of his own car far none of it made much sense. "No," she said again.

"Well, I thought maybe that was why you hadn't come down to the bowling alley," Nelson said. "I thought maybe you had a husband who thought it was a bad idea."

"That's not it," Hailey said, and stopped short of telling him about her run-in with his friends. They'd made her nervous, and now she felt guilty for thinking Nelson hadn't really wanted her to join them. "I thought you might not want me hanging around," she said.

"I only asked three times," said Nelson.

"Before the article," Hailey said.

"Before I knew if you had a husband." Nelson winked at Nate. Nelson's red face was puffy with cold, but he didn't seem angry to her. He just seemed out of place.

"Hailey won't even tell anyone that we're dating," Nate said then.

Hailey banged her hands on her desk. "We *work* together," she said to Nelson.

"So I don't think marriage is on the table," Nate said.

"Who are you?" Nelson squinted at Nate.

Hailey couldn't tell if he was being funny.

Nate furrowed his brow like there was a mistake.

"You're not the husband," Nelson said. "We've got that straight, but I—"

"Nate Whitfield," Hailey repeated.

"I'm the *Free Press*'s other staff writer," Nate said. He held out his hand to Nelson, but Nelson was holding the paper bag in his right hand.

"That's okay," he said to Nate. "I figured I'd come down and see how you're doing," he said to Hailey.

She didn't say anything right away. She was thinking that parking was only a problem on weekdays, and Nelson had taken the bus on Saturday morning. "I'm fine," she said, though the truth was she felt sad. "I'm writing a story about the benches the city council voted to put in along Main."

"On your dime," Nelson said. His eyes were watery.

"How are you?" Hailey asked.

Nelson bobbed his head side to side. He made show of looking at all ten of his fingers, then shifted his weight to his heels and pretended to inventory ten toes through his thick-soled boots. "I still put my briefs on before my trousers," he said. "I still run at about sixty-five beats a minute. But I wanted to get a few extra copies of the article to send my kids if that's okay with everyone around here. And I brought you breakfast because you said you don't eat breakfast, but it looks right there like maybe you do." He pointed to the bran muffin and orange juice on Hailey's desk.

"Oh, no." Hailey dismissed Nate's offering. "That's nothing. Nate brought that."

Nelson paused. He looked at the second carton of orange juice and the crumpled-up wax paper on the floor next to the chair where Nate had been sitting. There were crumbs all over the floor. He scanned the empty newsroom and flushed. "My apologies, sir," he said to Nate. "I meant nothing by it. I just came for those extra copies." He rolled his own bag tighter shut. Hailey wondered what was in there. Nelson ran his free hand along the wall, along three light switches that were still off. "So, what, it's the two of you run this place?" he said.

Hailey didn't want to embarrass him. She didn't want Nate to be right, for Nelson to be bats.

"In the movies, newspaper rooms are always full of racket," Nelson said.

She didn't want him to realize it was Saturday. Not in front of her.

But Nate said, "We try not to work on weekends."

There was a second before Nelson caught it. For one more he stood there with a glint in his eyes—here, he'd walked in on a little something—before Hailey saw him get it. Lights off. Newsroom silent. Boy and girl sharing breakfast, one token computer humming. She watched his eyes shrink back in his head.

"There were parking spots up and down," he said, incredulous. He clapped his free hand over his forehead. "Oh my gosh." He blinked his eyes shut hard. "I'm so sorry," he said to Hailey. He looked like he was lost. "I feel foolish," he said.

"I drove to school on a Sunday once," she said, which wasn't true. She'd gotten as far as the shower before realizing it was her stepfather's alarm going off the first weekend of hunting season. "We've all done it."

"I can't believe this," Nelson said.

"This is perfect." Hailey wanted to save him. "Our publisher doesn't like to give away extra copies, but he's not here. Today I can give them to you."

Nelson didn't respond. He seemed to have lost interest in the task at hand. "I don't know how I did this," he said. He was bent forward slightly, like he was ducking from something that might hurt him. "Both of you, this is not like me. I am so sorry."

"We were here anyway," Nate said.

"How many do you want?" Hailey didn't know what to do.

Nelson's head hung forward. "I have the two daughters and the two sons," he said.

Hailey didn't remember him mentioning any sons. "Have a seat," she said.

"That's okay." Nelson scrunched his paper bag tighter.

"The copies are in back." Hailey pointed toward the far end of the office. She wanted Nelson to stay the hero, to get the girl. Not this.

"You're right about the parking," Nate said, and Hailey turned to him. He'd widened his stance and crossed his arms. "This town is overgrown."

"Not today, it isn't," said Nelson.

"There's been no planning." Nate didn't skip a beat. "I've been here six years and watched it get worse and worse."

Nelson lifted his head. "I've lived here fifty-one years."

"Damn," said Nate.

"I was on the city council sixteen of those," Nelson said. He looked toward the *Free Press* signs in the windows. "I wouldn't do it again. You get a group like that together, you're going to figure out the coffee machine and not much else."

Nate laughed, and Hailey followed. She watched Nelson loosen up and envied Nate his ability to keep things level.

"I ride my bike downtown," Nate was saying to Nelson. "Do you ever ride a bike? You look fit."

Hailey could have hugged him. Sturdy shoulders, sure hands, big heart. He knew what to do. That, and he was right. Nelson did look fit. Hailey hadn't noticed before, but he looked trim in his blue jeans.

Nelson blushed. "I'm trying that Atkins deal," he said. "Only bike I've been on was four cylinders."

"For real?" Nate said, and then they were going. They were talking torque and compression, and if they noticed Hailey walk away, they didn't acknowledge it. Hailey slipped inside the back storage room and closed the door. Stacked newspapers insulated the tight space. Dust hung like breath. Hailey fumbled for the light switch and wondered if Nelson had been close to his sister and two brothers. Hailey hadn't talked to her own brother in months—he lived with his girlfriend in New York—and she wondered how often he thought about their family. She wondered if her parents would ever talk to each other again. She wondered if they would live to be Nelson's age, and if a person recognized when he was losing his mind. Would it be a loosening or a tightening? A buzzing or a silence? Would it be so natural that you just felt free, that people called you crackpot at the exact same moment you got to the bottom of yourself? Was *that* what growing old was all about?

Hailey found the light switch and saw ten years of stories filed all around her, yellowed edges curling. She located the stack with Nelson's story and took a dozen copies. On the cover was a photo of Nelson standing in the bowling alley's bar with ten pins lined up artificially behind him. It was the photo editor's dumb idea. Hailey had complained to Craig, but Nelson hadn't commented on it either way. Nelson had said that he and Fran were lovers. He had said he loved her a whole lot. Whether his mind was coming clear or bottoming out didn't seem critical to Hailey. She wanted to believe such love was out there. And if it wasn't? Well, Nelson was still the most genuine interview she'd ever done.

"You tell me," Nate was saying to Nelson as Hailey walked back. They were standing by the windows.

"I'm not sure I'd listen to me," Nelson said. He looked over at Hailey coming across the room with the stack of papers. "You could have your own paper route with all of those," he said to her. "You could deliver them to my house."

A house, Hailey noted. You couldn't run your own house and lose your mind at the same time, could you? "I'm going to put them in a shopping bag," she said. The papers were heavy, and she worried they might be too much for Nelson to take back on the bus.

"I don't need all those," Nelson said.

"Is it too many?" Hailey pulled an old shopping bag from under her desk.

"Nelson once carried a whole bed into breakfast." Nate grinned.

"You what?" She worked all the papers into the bag.

"It's part of a joke," Nelson said. He glanced at Nate. "But it's not one I'm going to repeat right now."

Hailey looked at the two men standing close to each other by the windows. Had they been whispering? She didn't want to know what they'd been joking about. She wanted to love Nate just like Nelson wanted to love Fran; they had that in common. "I'll walk you out," she said.

"Did you hear that?" Nelson raised his eyebrows at Nate.

"Watch yourself." Nate clapped Nelson's shoulder and started chewing on a straw.

Hailey pulled on her coat. She carried the papers down the stairs and Nelson followed. Outside, the sun was burning through the clouds, making streaky patterns on the brick buildings and the empty streets. On the sidewalk, blue chalk outlined a rectangular space where a bench would go in a few more months. Smaller orange chalk squares on either side of the blue marked proposed planters.

"Those are going to be benches," Hailey said to Nelson, pointing. "The council had them outlined all along here before the vote. I have to write an article about why they chose benches, not lampposts."

Nelson stared at the blue rectangle and the orange squares. "Why'd the benches win?" he asked.

Hailey didn't care. She wanted to tell Nelson she was selfish for printing his lie, but instead she said, "I don't know. They say a bench isn't going to come loose in a storm and fall on someone's head."

"If it were my deal, I'd want a lamppost next to my bench," Nelson said. "And a trash can. People like to eat their lunch on a bench. They like to feed the squirrels." He looked up and down the street. "There aren't any trash cans."

"So it would be okay if I came down to the alley on Monday?" she said.

"Honey, I've already told you—"

"Sorry." She put the bag on the sidewalk. There was salt ground into the cracks. She didn't want to make him angry. Nor did she want to hide anything from him—she wanted to be clear—and so she said, "I saw a couple of your friends at the Fivemile on Monday. They bought me a beer."

"Who bought you a beer?" Nelson turned his whole body toward her.

"I didn't get their names," she said, which seemed odd to her now. "I was working on an article about the Fivemile."

"There was a group of them?" He sounded put off.

"Two," Hailey corrected. "A woman and a man. She was skinny, well dressed. He had a baseball—"

"Clarette Luther lives over there by the Fivemile," Nelson said. "She wears blouses."

"She had on a blouse," Hailey said.

"She was with a young guy?" Nelson raised one hand to suggest a person who would come up to his nose.

"She said he was sixteen years younger." Hailey nodded at Nelson's raised hand, though she'd only seen the man bent over.

"Not her grandson?"

"What?"

"She's got a grandson who teaches at the elementary school out there." Nelson pointed west of town. "The sciences. He's got hair the color of a tomato."

Hailey followed his finger. Her blank face must have been enough for Nelson, because before she could decide whether it would be a good idea or a bad idea to tell him Clarette Luther had not been drinking with her grandson, he said, "You said this was Monday?"

"Yes," said Hailey. She considered that Nelson might be ticked that Clarette was the first to buy her a beer. "This past Monday," she said carefully. "Around four. I told them to say hi to you."

"They didn't."

"I was working on a story—"

"Son of a gun," said Nelson. He wasn't smiling, but he looked like he'd discovered something good. His eyes were more alert than they had been earlier. "You said sixteen years?"

"I—"

"Son of a gun." Nelson smacked his thigh.

"Mr. Moore—"

"Call me Nelson," he said, and that was all.

Hailey was hoping he would continue. She had felt more confident talking to him when she'd had her list of questions. Interviewing gave her license to come out and say what she wanted in a way she couldn't when she was just talking like Nelson was her friend.

Was it odd that she might like to be his friend?

"You could bring your boyfriend if you want," Nelson said then. "Monday."

"He's not—" Hailey caught herself. "He shouldn't have told you that."

"It's nice he brought you breakfast," Nelson said.

"It's unprofessional. If anyone found out—"

"That's a sign he cares about you," Nelson said.

Hailey didn't say anything. She watched her breath puff in the air and was surprised not to feel cold yet.

"That's what matters once everything else has come and gone," said Nelson. Then he unrolled his bag. "I get the donuts from over there on Glen. The cake donuts."

Hailey looked at the bag. In their old kitchen, her mother always kept a bread box with pastries on the counter. Her father liked the apple turnovers. "I've never brought Nate anything," she said. "Now I wish I had, but I've never thought of it."

Nelson nodded. "I always like having someone to share a meal." He peered into his bag. "But now I think I shouldn't of brought you breakfast. He probably doesn't like the idea. Your boyfriend."

Hailey didn't correct him. "He won't mind," she said. "I love cake donuts." Fall weekends, before they left Pottstown, her mom bought apple cider and cake donuts at the farmers' market. The donuts came in a cardboard box, and Hailey and her brother dipped them into the cider as it heated on the stove.

"I don't want to make anybody mad," Nelson said.

"That's funny," Hailey said.

"What's that?"

"Nothing," she said.

"If I'd known—"

"He's not my boyfriend." Her voice grew firm. "Not really. We work together."

Then Nelson narrowed his eyes. He studied her like he was disappointed—not disappointed she didn't really have a boyfriend, but disappointed she'd think he was this dim. Hailey felt a little rush go through her chest.

"I've never been in love before," she said in explanation, and then wondered if Nate might be right: If Nelson were younger, if she thought his knowing this about her would be of any consequence, would she have told him? "So I'm not sure—"

But, no, she thought, age had nothing to do with it. She wouldn't be talking like this if Nelson hadn't told her his story. But he had told it. They were two people similarly on their own. "Anyway," she said. "It's a secret."

Nelson pouted his lower lip like he was considering something. "Okay," he said. He looked past her, up the street. "Then I won't print that up in an article if I ever write one."

"I'm so sorry," she said instantly. "Mr. Moore—Nelson—I am so, so sorry." Her throat tightened. She felt her face get hot.

But Nelson didn't flinch. He was looking up at a cardinal on a phone wire across the street. "I said it," he said. "I'm not sorry."

Hailey wasn't sure what she was supposed to feel. She wasn't sure she'd be able to recognize if her own mind started to go. She was wondering what it would be like, if it would be a flooding or a drying out, when Nelson said, "I called her up the other day. Fran."

"You did?" Hailey looked at his red skin and pale eyes. She wondered if it would be a winnowing or an explosion.

"I remembered her number off the top of my head."

A wilting or a bloom.

"I asked her if she'd want to go out to Rock Creek," he said.

A train wreck or a celebration.

"She said she'd have to think on it." He sounded calm and clear. "She's been off and on with Jim, you know."

"Yes," said Hailey.

"I'm not sorry," Nelson said. "It's what I wanted to do."

Hailey didn't feel the relief she would have anticipated. Instead, she was thinking that her parents had always done what they wanted to do, too. They'd fallen in and out of love, moved back and forth, said things they'd meant and didn't mean. Hailey knew Nelson and Fran weren't lovers, but she would write the same lie again this second. She would buy Nelson's friends a round and swear it on her own life. Nate was right; she gave him that much. She wanted it to be true.

"I'm starving," she said.

"This is going to be a bench," Nelson said. He walked the few steps across the sidewalk and into the center of the blue chalk rectangle. He glanced back at her as he pretended to wipe clean a seat that wasn't there. "How do I look?" he asked, his breath white in the air.

"Cold," Hailey said.

"There's room for two," he said.

She joined him. Nelson unrolled his paper bag and handed her a donut and took out another for himself. Then he crumpled up the bag and made a show of looking around. "I need a trash can," he said.

"I'm happy you came by," she said. Her hands were cold now, and her feet were getting there, too. She took a bite of the donut and thought of hot cider. She wiped crumbs from her lips and thought of Nate waiting upstairs. She wondered if he might be watching them through the window above the *Free Press* signs. If so, he probably saw the cardinal, too, as it flew down from the phone line and landed in the middle of the street. It hopped around, puffing up its red feathers like it owned the place.

Nelson ate his donut in big bites. He watched the cardinal, too. When he finished eating, he wiped the back of his hand across his mouth. "It's a hell of a thing," he said, maybe about the cardinal, maybe not. He didn't elaborate, and it didn't matter to Hailey either way. The streets were empty, and the sun was out, and you could see your breath like clouds.

"This is delicious," Hailey said.

"This is Saturday," Nelson said.

And though she could feel goose bumps prickling her legs, Hailey stayed still next to Nelson, weighing the cold against the sun. A punch of wind came up, and she imagined a single car moving along Main Street, the driver slowing down to look at them. Would he see a hero and a stranger? A daughter and a dreamer? A lover and a liar? Or maybe a cardinal, flying to safety, landing where a bench would be come spring.

CHAPTER 5

Fran

"You know I was Wagon Days Queen in 1948," Fran said, to test out how it felt. She used to feel proud, telling people. "And runner-up 1949 to 1952." Now she was fixing Jim a hamburger for lunch. "I've told you that," she said. She wore the chili-pepper apron that he'd given her for Mother's Day. At the time, she considered it a thoughtful gesture, as he wasn't her husband or the father of her children, but Eileen, her oldest daughter, had nudged her at the dining room table—Fran herself had cooked the ham—and said he needed some work in the gift department.

Jim sat at her kitchen counter, shuffling through Fran's coupons. "It rings a bell," he said.

"Everyone said I would of had a longer streak if Charity Summers hadn't moved to town," Fran said, but her heart wasn't in it.

"That was her real name?"

"I couldn't care less about it anymore."

"Excuse my French, but Charity Summers—"

"Get your head out of the toilet, Jim. I'm fixing lunch here." Fran flipped Jim's hamburger and forgot about being Wagon Days Queen. She'd been cooking Jim burgers just the way he liked them—rare but not bucking—off and on for years, and she wondered what he had done for her lately. It was a line from a song her instructor Marie played in the Stretch 'n' Go class at the Y that Eileen had signed them both up for. Right after that line they swung their hips side to side. Fran did a little hip swing to herself. She could go through with this, she told herself. Today she could speak her mind to Jim. They'd broken up several times before, but this time things were different.

"What's that all about?" Jim said. She turned around, and he was pointing at her hips. He had a gleam in his eyes that she used to find romantic, but this time it made her think of a greedy dog.

"I have a tune in my head," she said. Where she might once have told him the name of the song and sung it for him, now she just stayed quiet. She didn't tell him he looked foolish, or that ever since the chicken-wing bone, the whole world looked like her backyard last August when a bolt of lightning hit down by the strawberries: razor sharp and done up in lights—and terrifying.

She ripped apart one English muffin for Jim's bun and a second English muffin for herself. She brought down the low-fat peanut butter from the cabinet and took cottage cheese from the refrigerator. She'd told Jim she was rejiggering her diet after hearing that that Atkins man's heart gave out, but the truth was she didn't have a taste for meat anymore.

"Is this why you look like you've been at the beach?" Jim held up a coupon for a bronzing lotion called Sure As Sun. Fran kept her coupons in a white wicker basket, organized into categories: Household, Travel, and Body.

"Put those down," Fran said. "They're in an order." Which was true—the coupons were ordered by expiration date—but besides, Fran didn't want Jim to see what she was buying. A woman has her secrets, and Jim had lost his chance to be on that inside track. He had sat there like a fencepost while Nelson saved her life. And week after week, he was continuing to sit there—like Bethany, like Clarette, like Alastair, like *herself*—doing nothing about their friend.

Nelson might never again remember she was Wagon Days Queen.

Nelson might remember he and Fran had been lovers, but his years were all scrambled up.

Fran shook her head. She had liked those years with Nelson. All things considered, she thought she would enjoy going back to them very much.

"Do you think a massage parlor has this many lotions?" Jim was thumbing through her coupons like a flip book.

Nelson had given her paintings, perfumes.

"What?" Jim was staring at her like she was being difficult.

The Heimlich was what you *did* when someone was choking, she wanted to tell him. That, or you called 911. You just *did* it. You took action, and then things were okay again.

"I wouldn't know," Fran said. "You've never bought me a massage."

Jim looked at Fran.

She didn't know what you did when someone was fading out of his own body.

Jim jutted his lower jaw forward the way he did when he was thinking hard, and Fran knew he was trying to see if she was serious about the massage. She hadn't talked to him like this before. When they'd broken up in the past, it hadn't been for any reason; they just came together and drifted apart like those cold, dark tides Fran had fallen in love with on Long Island a couple years back while visiting her middle son, Chuck, and his wife, Annie, for Thanksgiving. She'd thought about using the comparison on Jim today, but she didn't feel so poetic anymore.

Now she felt like something had to be *done*. Not that she hadn't been worried about Nelson before she had choked—she had—but having her own glimpse of death had scared her so profoundly that now she saw his situation with new urgency. What if he left the stove on at night? What if he drove his car through a stop sign? Was he scared like she was? He must know what was going on inside him, and Fran wondered if he felt like she did, both more alive and more afraid of everything than she'd ever been before. Big pills. Yellow traffic lights. The possibility of frozen pipes. She saw her mortality at every turn, and she imagined she and Nelson had this in common. Jim seemed frivolous to her now, waiting for his lunch. It was Nelson who needed her—who might have still loved her—and it was he, too, who had saved her life.

She wanted to tell Jim he would be lucky to have half the bond with her that she had with Nelson.

Instead she got the A.1. out of the fridge.

"My point is you don't listen," she said.

"What are you talking about?" Jim said. "You're talking about being Wagon Queen. We're having lunch."

"I'm making *you* lunch, and you're getting into *my* business." She moved the white basket to the opposite counter.

"I don't know what's going on here." Jim slapped the coupons down.

Fran felt herself start to shake. She stood up for herself so rarely she didn't really know how to do it. And the thing was, despite his shortcomings, Jim wasn't a bad man. He was kind and tall. Truth be told, none of this was his fault. Mad as she was at him, her anger wasn't about him, but about the fact there *was* no maneuver, no 911 call, to return Nelson to his old self. It was easier to take it out on Jim. Where the old Fran would have been happy to wear his apron and please him with another good burger, this new Fran was so scared and charged up about life that she was dizzy with the need to break out of her routines and take action. Any action. And if Jim was going to sit around and do nothing, he'd be doing that without her.

"I'm not like I used to be," she said then. It wasn't how she'd practiced, but it was a beginning. She had hoped to have the guts to talk to Jim about what she saw happening to Nelson, but she didn't know how to work it into a breakup conversation. Also, after Bethany had all but dismissed the topic when Fran had brought it up at Liberty, she didn't hold out much hope for Jim to be any different. He could be territorial, and he had done nothing to help her, and for both those reasons, she plain wasn't attracted to him anymore.

"We need to talk," she said to him.

"I'll say," he said.

But Fran felt a little dizzy. She got nervous now more than ever before. And so she said, "I signed up with Free the Fivemile," which was absolutely not the direction she'd intended to take this. "Clarette got me turned on to it."

Jim stood up like he sensed her legs were about to give. "Do you want to sit down?"

Fran hung her arms at her sides and closed her eyes. She took two deep breaths. This was the trick with these new nervous bits.

"Why don't you turn off that stove," Jim said.

Fran did a neck roll the way they did at Stretch 'n' Go. She took one more deep breath and opened her eyes. "I'm fine," she said. "I'm going to be a team leader." She'd never spoken those words aloud, and only as she did so did it hit her as obvious why on earth she cared about the Fivemile in the first place. "I'm in charge of recruiting ten volunteers to go door-to-door for signatures to save it." She felt the blood move back into her head. "I'm getting involved."

"Don't they already have the demolition set?" Jim sat back down.

"That's not the spirit, Jim," Fran said. "The spirit is to fight for things. The spirit is you can *do* something."

Jim shrugged. He was looking beyond Fran to the stove, and she knew he was worrying about his lunch.

"It's a filthy old bar," he said.

"It's a landmark," she said.

"It is?"

She didn't have to know a thing about the Fivemile to know that if Nelson's mind were sound she wouldn't be giving the place a second thought. She had no idea what it took to be a landmark, but she didn't see how the Fivemile couldn't be. All she knew was it was old as dirt. "To some of us it is."

"When have you ever gone there?"

It was a fair point. Though she hadn't said as much to Clarette, Fran had never once gone inside the Fivemile. She had waited in the parking lot one afternoon while her second husband, Clive, had gone in to fish out their oldest son, Jesse, who'd cut school and made the sorry mistake of parking Fran's own Chrysler in the front. A beefy patron on his way in had looked her over and told her church was the other direction, and she'd asked him how he'd know. But still, she'd felt good about saying yes to Clarette when she'd asked for help. For twenty-six days since she had choked, Fran had been spinning around with this nervous energy she thought might make her short-circuit. But the idea of fighting for a cause, of channeling all that energy as if it had showed up inside her purposefully—that made her feel strong. It made her feel like there were answers out there after all.

"That's not the point, Jim," she said.

"What's the point?" Jim got up and turned off the stove himself.

Fran undid her apron. The point was it was human nature to want to save a thing. To do something important. Sure, she had spent a lot of years thinking it was all about keeping yourself up—smooth skin, firm legs—but now she saw that if you were going to keep going, you needed to get involved and not just sit around like the world was so lucky to have you here, when really it was the other way around, a fact that too many people didn't figure out in time.

"What are we talking about?" Jim was saying. He'd put his burger on a plate. "I thought I knew, and now I'm not so sure."

Fran spread peanut butter over her English muffin and scooped cottage cheese onto her plate. She swiped the extra peanut butter off the knife with her finger and licked it. The peanut butter stuck to the roof of her mouth and made it even harder to say what she was going to say. She liked Jim. She'd half thought they would go down to Vegas in the spring and pick out one of those frilly chapels. He wasn't a bad man. He was good with people, and he was good at conversation. But when things got sticky, when it wasn't all fresh lipstick and free lunches, he didn't have what it took. That's what she'd found out.

"You didn't do anything," she said.

Jim's burger was up in his face, and Fran saw his eyes narrow, his eyebrows come together. He chewed a big bite and put the burger down.

Fran took two more deep breaths to ward off dizziness.

"What?" said Jim.

"At Liberty," she said. "With the chicken wing."

Jim went silent. His jaw was forward, lips pressed together, and Fran could see his tongue moving over his teeth like he was picking out burger. He was looking sideways, to the window, and Fran might have started apologizing if he hadn't had a look on his face like he had had about enough of this.

"Why didn't you do anything?" she asked as plainly as she could. She was nervous, but also impressed with the way she was coming across calm. "Were you scared?"

Jim flinched. He didn't speak, but when he opened his mouth Fran could see his tongue reaching up in his back teeth like he was really working on something.

"Why did you just sit there?" Fran's pulse was up. "What was going through your head?" She paused, but then figured it was either now or wait until the next time she invited him over and cooked his burger and worked up her nerve, which suddenly sounded like more work than she was interested in. "Where were you when I was dying?" she said.

"Oh, come on now." Jim stopped her. "Don't get ridiculous."

Fran felt her heart buckle, but she tried not to show it.

"For heaven's sake." Jim had his hands on his hips. "Everyone gets some food down the wrong—"

"I was choking," Fran said firmly.

"You weren't dying," Jim said.

"I couldn't breathe," she said. "What do you call that?"

Jim shook his head.

"You sat there," she said, burning. How dare he try to tell her what she'd been doing.

Jim pushed his burger away and scowled at Fran. She hadn't gotten to the part she'd wanted to say about how she wasn't just anybody—she was Wagon Days Queen, with the legs and the get-up of someone half her age, and *you don't have what it takes, Jim Bowers*—but still she'd made her main point. Jim had sat there while she was dying, and she wanted to hear what he had to say about that.

He cleared his throat and tucked his paper napkin under his plate.

Fran knew that meant he wasn't done eating, or he would have balled up the napkin on top of his plate. The thought that he was going to have it out with her and then go back to eating the burger she'd cooked for him got under her skin. It occurred to her that in all the years she'd known Jim, she'd never once seen him cook his own burger. What kind of a man didn't ever want to step up and do his own grill?

"This is about Nelson," he said.

Fran hadn't seen that coming.

"This is about Nelson being your hero," Jim said.

Fran knew her face was red. She was hot and she could feel her heartbeat in her palms. She considered taking the burger away from Jim but had enough of her wits about her to realize that doing so wouldn't really have anything to do with anything.

"This is about you and Nelson still having something," Jim said, and Fran felt her last wits flutter from her fingertips. He wasn't wrong. Nelson's mind might be all scrambled up, but what rose out of that tangle when he saw she was in trouble? What came clear when a reporter asked him about his life? It was a love for her. That's what he had said. And even if it was an old love for her, it still existed inside him, and it had been set free precisely because his mind was losing its grip.

"Are you going to tell me that you don't?" Jim said.

"What?" Fran's mind was at her parents' old place up Rock Creek, at the bend in the road where you could see the creek frothing from the front porch.

"Are you telling me it's true what's in the paper?"

"I'm not telling you anything," Fran said. And then it struck her: of course she would go with Nelson. "You wouldn't understand."

"I can't believe this," Jim said.

"It's about history," she said, as much to herself as to Jim. "It's about history, and it's about *doing* something. Like being a team leader. So we can at least try—"

"And I tried to make a joke of it." Jim cut her off.

"We have to at least try," Fran said.

"I tried to let Nelson off the hook easy because he seemed upset, and all along, you two—"

"Oh, come off it, Jim. You're not listening to me," Fran said. "We are decent people. Nelson and I. We aren't running around, and you know it. We sit with the group and have a drink after bowling. We are old friends, like all of us. We are friends who remember how things used to be, and we help each other out when we are dying."

"I've had enough of this." Jim stood up.

"*I've* had enough of this. That's what I'm saying."

"Well, we have that in common." He was looking around, and Fran knew he was trying to figure out where she'd put his parka.

"Why didn't you do something, Jim?" she said.

"What would you have liked me to do?" He stretched his neck forward like he was trying to read fine print. "Should I have knocked Nelson out of the way?"

He had a point there—she might have died if Jim had fought for her. Except Jim had been sitting right next to her, while Nelson had had to rush from clear across the table.

"I know why," she said. "It's the same reason you didn't put up a fight when Bethany read Nelson's bit in the newspaper. It's the same reason you haven't said one word about Nelson until now. It's the same reason you have half a mind to finish that burger after we're done with this." She swallowed the last hint of peanut butter in her mouth. "It's because you don't have what it takes," she said.

Instantly, she regretted it. They were the words she'd been hoping to say, but in the actual moment they came out, they sounded too nasty. They *were* nasty, and she was not. She was a person who liked to please people; only now she was more alive and more scared of everything than she'd ever been before, and this new sensation was mixing everything up. It was making her wonder who she even was.

Jim was circling the coffee table, his hands in fists. "Where the hell is my coat?" he said.

"In the bedroom." Fran looked at the floor.

Jim marched past the kitchen to the bedroom and returned with his parka in his hand. He didn't bother to put it on. He didn't look at her, either, and she was wrong about the burger. He went straight for the door. He threw it open, and Fran was surprised to see so much bright light. The sun was glaring, and then right behind it came a blast of crisp air. It was so cold it made her feel intensely lonely and frightened and alert.

"Wait." She rushed after Jim, one hand to her forehead against the sun. She clutched at the parka in his hand, though she hadn't planned anything to say. Suddenly, she was crying. She was sorry for what she'd said; only that wasn't what she told Jim. She wanted to tell him how everything felt so frightening and thrilling since the chicken-wing bone, how she felt like she could try anything now—and also how she could be done in by a patch of ice on her front steps—only she didn't know how to say that either. It was hard to put into words. It seemed impossible to explain what it was like to have someone save your life, to have one other person touch you like that, under those circumstances.

"Do you ever worry about how you're going to die?" she said to Jim. It was exactly what she'd wanted to say for weeks.

"No," he said.

"Well, I do," she said. Her cheeks were wet with tears. "I worry about all of us. All the time now. I get nervous on the couch and at the grocery and in the rain and—" She felt herself out of breath. She wiped the tears from her face. "If I'd died," she said slowly, "Nelson would of been the last one to touch me. Not you."

Jim didn't look angry, but he looked very far away. "Well then, I guess I'm making the right decision," he said.

"I made this decision," she said.

"Well, we're done touching each other either way."

That made Fran so sad. There was a finality in Jim's words that was exactly what she'd been after, but stating them like that seemed unnecessary. She and Jim had been together off and on ever since she'd bought this house and he'd brought the river rocks to line the first garden she'd planted, which had since quadrupled in size. They'd gotten in the habit of walking along the banks of the Bitterroot on summer evenings and picking out four rocks—one for each hand—every time. An hour ago, Jim had hugged her and kissed her when he'd arrived, and now he wouldn't hug her or kiss her again. That was the last time. She already hardly remembered it—it hadn't been anything extraordinary sixty minutes earlier—but now she wanted to go back and find something about it to remember forever. His hands on her shoulder blades. The spicy scent of aftershave she'd picked out for him. The bright sun and his blue parka and his cold cheek. That was the last time, and she knew in a little while it wouldn't bother her so much.

"I'm sorry you choked," Jim was saying. "I am. But I've had enough of this. I won't give you a hard time, because I think you're jumbled up right now—"

"I am jumbled up right now." She was relieved to say so.

"But I won't act like nothing's happened either."

Fran studied the grit on the green doormat. "The only thing that's happened is you didn't do anything," she said.

"I see how you look at him," Jim said.

"He is in trouble, Jim."

"Like you can go back to being who you were."

"We need to do something," she said, but she could see Jim was too angry to hear her. On another day, he might come around, but for now he was too stuck on his own bruised pride.

"Nelson can take care of himself," he said, and Fran wanted to think she hadn't heard him right. She wanted to believe that love couldn't really turn a person so cold.

All at once, everything got much easier.

"I can do whatever I want," she said. "You can watch me."

"You don't know what I might have done if Nelson hadn't been there," Jim said back. "You'll never know."

"Oh, yes I do," Fran said. "I know." She straightened up, and Jim stepped out the door. He took the time to put his parka on, looking into the sun. He seemed to be leaving her the opportunity to back down or open up, but she already had him in his car and out the driveway, back to his house where he might or might not choose to throw out her pink toothbrush.

"Like I said, I won't give you a hard time," he said. "Just don't sit by me after bowling."

"I won't," she said.

"Things aren't like they used to be." He zipped his parka.

"That's the truth," she said, and then, though she hadn't planned it, she took his hand, still on his zipper, with his Black Hills gold ring glinting in the sun, and she squeezed it, and noted exactly how it felt.

CHAPTER 6

Nelson

Nelson had a bad feeling from the beginning. Not a sick feeling or a nervous feeling, but more like the feeling you got in bed when your pajamas twisted around your waist, except the feeling was in his head. Like things were packed too tight, so that breakfast sometimes seemed like dinner, socks like gloves, his daughter on the phone like his first wife, Lou Ann, who sometimes these days he thought of as still alive. Lou Ann had never bowled, but he caught himself wondering sometimes if he might see her down at Liberty. Yesterday he'd stopped in out of boredom—Sunday, no bowling—and even called Sandy "Lulu" to her face and couldn't explain why. It might have been the cold weather, the long winter, but things felt off. When he tried to paint anymore, he couldn't concentrate long enough to make progress, and the half-blank canvases in his spare room were starting to haunt him like lost thoughts. He wished some part of his life would keep humming along like usual, to reassure him. But even when he went to the alley's front desk earlier to pick up his bowling shoes, it turned out Sandy had accidentally rented them to someone. Not that his shoes were for rent: Nelson owned them and they were stored in a separate set of cubbies from the rentals, and Sandy must have returned them to the wrong place last time. She asked Nelson if it would be okay to let it go this once—to go with a pair of rentals. It was a busy day, what with this tour group come through from Coeur d'Alene, and they were only shoes, after all, she said. But the thing was, those were *his* shoes, *his* shoes with the tight new leather laces and the soles worn in exactly the way his big toes fit, and he wasn't sure he could bowl in a strange pair of rentals. Not with someone else in the alley bowling in his shoes. It didn't seem right. It seemed, to him, like another instance these days where things didn't add up.

"Who got my shoes?" he asked Sandy.

"I wish I knew," she said, and she looked at him like she felt sorry for him. "Just a paying customer."

Just a paying customer. Which apparently was all he was by now, anyway, after how many years? He paid Sandy to bowl. He paid Charla for his breakfast. He paid Doreen for his drinks. And today he would pay for Hailey James's drink, too, whatever she wanted. He couldn't forget that. He had a feeling she was really going to come. So maybe he was nervous after all. He had butterflies. It could have been also because Fran hadn't called him back with an answer about Rock Creek, and he was wondering if she was going to. He wanted to buy her drink, too, but he knew Jim would be there, as would Bethany.

It seemed like a lot of things all at once.

And all afternoon, he bowled poorly. He couldn't concentrate because he kept looking at other people's feet. But he never found his shoes. His score for the day was pot. Where he was normally the first person into the bar, today he waited around by the front desk to see who might return his shoes, but it seemed like this tour group was never going to quit. Sandy apologized and said his first beer was on her, which he accepted, even though he was mad. Then he ended up walking into the bar with Alastair, who was always the last one in because it took him longer to get everything squared away. Alastair could see shades of light—where there was a table versus where there wasn't a table, but not the peas versus the potatoes on his plate—and as they walked in together, Alastair's hand cupping Nelson's elbow, it occurred to Nelson that Alastair might be the only person he could think of right off the bat whom he still had one up on. The thought left a bad taste inside him.

Doreen came around and asked what they wanted.

"Miller Lite, thank you," said Alastair.

"An extra chair," said Nelson.

"On the rocks?" said Doreen, and everyone laughed.

"I mean it." Nelson sat down between Bethany and Fran. "We have a guest coming today, and she's going to need a chair, and I'm going to pay for her drink."

"You can get a chair." Bethany pushed Nelson.

"She's of age, of course," he said, and wondered what the odds were that the last free seat at the table would be between Bethany and Fran.

"Do you mean that reporter?" Clarette piped in and then clapped a hand over her mouth.

"Her name is Hailey James," Nelson said, irritated. "And I know you already bought her a beer at the Fivemile. She told me all about it." In fact, he remembered everything Hailey had told him about her encounter with Clarette, and he wished he could get a handle on why some things inside him went fuzzy while others rang up crystal clear.

"You go out to the Fivemile?" Stu Larsen had turned to Clarette.

"Back there last Monday," Nelson said. "If I'm remembering the day right." Which he knew he was.

"I live out that way." Clarette wrung her hands.

"Clarette's told you about Free the Fivemile," Fran said to Stu, though her eyes landed on Nelson. "Hasn't she?"

Again, he wondered how Bethany and Fran had arranged leaving the seat between them for him. Had they talked about it? Jim was sitting clear across the table next to Stu and Dale, and here was Fran wearing a black top with some lace around the edges, fancier than usual. The look of it excited Nelson but also made him sense there was trouble waiting just the other side of his beer.

Bethany sat with both elbows on the table like she hadn't heard Fran.

"We're protesting the teardown," said Clarette, stronger. "They're planning to put in a pizza shop and laundrymat and whatnot, and that's not right. The Fivemile is a landmark."

"It is *not*," said Jim.

"You don't have to be a part of it," Fran said to him, and Nelson took pleasure in her short tone. "I'm a team leader," she said. "I'm recruiting volunteers to get signatures to stop the teardown, so if anyone wants to—"

"I'd like to do that," Nelson said.

Bethany looked at him.

"I read Hailey's article in the paper," he explained. "About them tearing it down. I don't know if she said it was a landmark, but it's been there since 1938, which is good enough for me. You've got pizza parlors popping up on every corner. You don't have anybody leaving things alone."

"Bingo," said Fran.

"It's a dump," said Jim.

"It's a neighborhood place," said Clarette.

"I'll do it, too." Bethany's glasses were down at the end of her nose. "So how did you and this reporter end up having a beer?"

"Well." Clarette swirled her bourbon. "Now see. I go down there a time or two."

"She had a date," said Nelson, to show he was still in on something.

"With the reporter?" asked Fran.

"I don't know with who," said Nelson. What he knew was Clarette had bought Hailey a beer.

"For Free the Fivemile?" Fran wouldn't get off it.

"You'd have to ask Clarette," said Nelson.

Only no one did. Instead there was a hush around the table where probably everyone was putting together what Nelson had put together down at the *Free Press*, which was that Clarette had been leaving the alley early three Mondays running to go out to the Fivemile to meet who knows who. Five months after Dean passed on. Nelson saved the part about this whoever being sixteen years younger; he was ticked at Clarette, but not that ticked.

"I don't see whose concern it is who's dating who," she said.

Jim scoffed so hard a line of spittle hit the table. Clarette stared at the little bubbles until Dale wiped them away with his napkin, which Nelson thought just called more attention to the whole thing.

"You have something you want to say to me, Jim?" Clarette said. "As long as you know everything about everything, why don't you go ahead and tell me—"

"Hey," said Nelson.

"That's not it," said Jim.

"Thank you kindly, Nelson," Clarette snipped, then finished her drink.

Nelson held up his palms in surrender. Since when was everything he said wrong? "All I'm saying is what Hailey said about you buying her a drink." He turned to Bethany, who had leaned away in her chair, arms folded, and looked like she would rather ignore him. He felt bad for not telling Bethany he'd called Fran, but he also had to consider how Bethany had been leaving him out bit by bit for months now. Last week, he'd called up to bring her breakfast, and she'd said she was down with a headache, and then thirty minutes later there she was in the window of The Old Time with a friend Nelson didn't recognize—a female—and a bowl of oatmeal.

Since when was he the one to be left out?

"So now what?" Clarette leaned forward like she'd seen something in Nelson.

"Forgive me for living," he said.

"You're jealous I bought your reporter a beer," she said.

And, yes, the thing of it was, he was jealous. He wasn't going to say so, but that's exactly what he was. He felt one-upped, cheated, left behind.

"I think you are," she said. "And the fact of the matter is, it wasn't even me who bought her a drink, it was Louis—oh, shoot." Clarette went for her glass and it was empty.

"Louis McCormick?" Fran jumped in. "From the hunting outfit?"

"Never mind," said Clarette.

"He's got that gravelly voice," said Fran.

It seemed to Nelson everyone was talking very fast. He hadn't meant to start whatever this was, but now he couldn't keep up either. He was afraid whatever he thought to say, like everything he'd already said, would make someone mad.

"Listen," said Jim. "Hang on. I didn't mean to come down on you, Clarette. This has nothing to do with you, and nobody should be getting upset." He cleared his throat and glanced at Fran. Nelson clutched his beer. "I don't mean to make a deal out of this, either," Jim said, "but as long as we're talking about who's doing what with whom, it feels like a lie to sit here and not tell you that Fran and I aren't seeing each other anymore. So there it is. We've called it off and we're just friends."

Little gasps went up around the table. Alastair, next to Fran, reached out, found her arm, and patted it.

Fran turned a solid shade of beet. Nelson thought she looked ready to reach across the table and swat Jim.

"In light of everything," Jim said.

Nelson felt eyes shift to him, sitting there between Fran and Bethany. His mouth went dry, and his feet went cold like they used to on the floorboards of his parents' house. He thought of his mother's stern voice, Lou Ann's sweet dimple, Bethany's blue phone with the baggie of Power Pick money tucked beneath it, Fran's favorite joke about the little mice in Heaven, and a stranger walking around in his shoes. He felt his head twist up, and he was afraid Hailey was going to arrive in the middle of all this, right at the moment everything was coming undone.

"Nelson saved my life," Fran said then.

Which helped. It was old news, but it was the first time Nelson had heard Fran say it out loud, and it shut Jim up. It also suggested that maybe Fran was going to go one step more and say how she felt about Nelson—which wouldn't have been appropriate, but Nelson would have been interested to hear it. It had been four days since he'd asked her to Rock Creek, and she hadn't called him back. At the table now, with all those eyes on him, he wanted to clear up the fact that he and Fran weren't really lovers, that it was all a lie, that he had been turned around when he said it, and there was no need for anyone making a show of breaking up.

Only, there was a need. Nelson hadn't intended for his lie to end up in the newspaper—he hadn't intended to speak a lie at all. But now that it had, and he had, he wasn't willing to give up this new space it had cracked open in his life. It wasn't a space he would ever have known to ask for, but now that it was here—this unexpected sense of motion, of time and room where things continued to roll forward and everything was packed just right—he intended to hang on to it until he was gone from this world. When he sat with the crossword before dawn and gazed out the black window right into his own reflection, and now chose not to call Bethany, there were brief moments where he got clear on it all. He traced back to the first inkling of his own lie and found that it hadn't formed in the moments when he was saving Fran—hands on her pencil ribs, his heart all over their history—but while he was talking to Hailey, of all people. He was talking to this young girl, sitting almost in the dark, her hair wet from the shower, and he was giving her pieces of his past he didn't tell just anyone, that he might have told only a few people before. They were all women, Lou Ann and Bethany and Fran, who had the same complexion as Hailey back when they went out to Rock Creek and pulled their chairs half-in, half-out of the sun so Fran's skin might stay like Hailey's, smooth and fair, with just a touch of pink along the cheekbones. It was there that things got fuzzy. It was standing with Hailey where the bench was going to be on Main that Nelson had to keep straight that she was Hailey. She wasn't Fran. This was where a bench would be. This was not Rock Creek. This was Saturday, and no matter what Nelson wanted to do about it, he was not young.

Nelson knew he was in trouble.

Doreen showed up with an extra chair and said she saw his guest walking in.

There was so much all at once.

"Welcome," he heard himself saying as he stood up from his chair. "Everyone, welcome Hailey," he was saying as he turned to face the door, but his head was fuzzy. Things were packed so tight, but he knew there was something exciting happening. Something that made him happy—he held on to that—and then there she was, closer than he expected, her hair in a braid, loose wisps curling by her temples, her complexion the same as Hailey's—as Fran's. As Fran's. "Hi, baby," he said.

"Hi, Nelson," Hailey said, a smile breaking across her face. It was the biggest smile he'd ever seen on her, like she liked being called "baby" even though the instant the word left his lips he hadn't been sure. But, yes, it was the right thing to say after all, which felt so good to Nelson that he got twisted up and turned around in the moment, and he took her in his arms and with everybody watching he did the most obvious thing, at least what seemed the most obvious to him, and he kissed her. He kissed her and he kissed Lou Ann, and Bethany, and Fran, and all of the lovers he'd had and might have had, all the ones who made him feel like he said the right things, like he could hang on to this momentum for the rest of his life. He kissed them all right on the lips.

Which wasn't the right thing to do. He knew it immediately, as soon as Hailey tilted back from him and the table got quiet, and he realized it was Hailey he had kissed. Not that he hadn't known from the beginning, but more that he realized it wasn't Lou Ann or Bethany or Fran or any other lover; it was Hailey, who wasn't a lover at all. The rest was tangled in his head. Hailey was a young girl, so much younger than he, and he was old, and he had kissed her, hard, on the lips.

Bethany was guiding him to his seat like he was blind.

Hailey squeezed her chair in between Bethany and Nelson.

Nelson froze up, stiff in his chair, though what he wanted to do was tiptoe out the door and figure out who the hell had his shoes. He only half heard Clarette yapping away to Hailey, except he knew she was talking about the Fivemile, and then he heard her say, "His name is Louis Black, and while we're all putting it out there, you might as well know he's sixteen years my junior." Then, quick as lightning, she winked at Nelson, like she was saving him.

Clarette had never done anything like that for him before. She'd always been a person who would lift you up and cut you down in equal parts, and this made Nelson wonder what bad things she might say about him kissing Hailey if he got up to check on his shoes.

"Sixteen *years*?" Fran said. Nelson couldn't tell if she was horrified or jealous.

"Well," said Jim.

Stu was shredding his napkin. "I was seventeen when my son was born," he said, which Nelson thought was uncalled for. No, five months wasn't a very long time to wait after a person died—not that Dean had been anybody's favorite—but regardless, Nelson couldn't help feeling that, as ticked as he was at Clarette, he shared something with her, too. You could sit on your can and hope for the phone to ring, or you could get out of your chair and meet new people. Do new things. Grab ahold of this new momentum.

"It's not for anyone to judge," he said. "Unless you're going to walk a mile in the other person's shoes."

"Thank you, Nelson," Clarette said. "He's nice enough. And he treats me well. And I understand some of you probably have a thing or two you want to say to me, and that's fine, but the way I see it, I'm going to live my life."

"Beats the alternative," said Bethany.

Nobody said anything else. Jim ordered another beer—he shouted across the room to Doreen—and then Hailey said, "He seemed nice. Louis. He bought me a beer."

"*He* bought the beer?" Nelson asked.

"Yes," said Hailey.

The confirmation made Nelson feel better. "I'd like to buy you a beer," he said carefully. "Or whatever you want."

"I'd like a beer," she said.

"Okay, then," he said. "And I'm sorry about that before. I was wound up. I didn't mean anything by it."

"It's okay," she said. "I know what you meant."

"You do?"

Hailey patted his knee. "No harm done." She looked at him dead-on, and in her eyes and the wrinkling across the bridge of her nose, Nelson saw both a happiness and a sadness. In a way, it was the same kind of look the others had been giving him these days, like they were pitying him for not knowing a secret they knew. But in another way, it was different, like he couldn't say the wrong thing to Hailey if he tried—like they had crossed paths at this point in their lives for some good reason, and he didn't have to know what that reason was, exactly, to know that that mix of happiness and sadness came from the heart, and that it just about summed it up.

Whatever *it*, exactly, was.

"Thanks for having me here," she said.

"You bet, baby," he said. "You bet."

And then Alastair was leaning over the table. "It's nice of you to join us," he said in Hailey's direction. He cupped one ear. "Is there something more you're writing?"

"Oh," she said. "No. It was only that one article." She looked to Nelson like she was afraid she might have belittled his story.

"This is Alastair," Nelson said. And though he was afraid of getting too close to her, he whispered into her ear, "He can't see."

"You did a nice job of writing about us," Alastair said. "I can't read, but Bethany read the whole thing aloud."

"Thank you," Hailey said.

Nelson was going to tell Hailey about how Alastair had four big fish tanks in his trailer with all kinds of different fish you couldn't even pronounce—how she should write a story about those fish—but Alastair kept going. Normally, you couldn't get him to say more than one sentence at any time, but Hailey seemed to have gotten his attention.

Could you *smell* a young person in the room, Nelson wondered? Could you catch her energy on the breeze?

"I get tapes from the Library of Congress," Alastair was saying. "They get sent to me, and they're about anything. Right now I have ones on the Spanish-American War, diamond mines, and bees. But except for presidents, you never get ones about people like us."

"We're not in politics, last I checked," said Clarette.

"There must be one on bowling," said Nelson.

"Unless you count the Fivemile," Fran said. "That's politics. It's the first political thing I've ever done."

"People our age, I mean," Alastair said. "Where anything can happen."

"Is *that* what she wrote about?" Bethany had a bite in her voice. "Is that the story I read?"

Only then did Nelson realize how Bethany had been quieter than usual. He'd been worrying about Fran and about Hailey, but not about her. Then again, Bethany was always taking care of herself, and it didn't really matter that he wouldn't be able to find the right spot for his hands if she ever choked, because Bethany just wasn't ever going to choke in the first place. It wasn't in her nature.

"How *did* you get interested in us?" Bethany asked Hailey.

"I do think that's the story," Alastair said politely to Bethany. "That's what I got out of it when you read it."

"Well, Nelson was a hero," Hailey said. "That's how it started."

"Yes, but that was a while ago," Bethany said.

"Twenty-eight days," said Fran.

"And now you're here," said Bethany.

"Yes." Hailey sipped her beer, and Nelson noticed how her pinky stayed in the air as she did so. Like someone had taught her that. He wondered who. He wanted to know where Bethany was going with this.

"So I was just asking why," Bethany repeated. "Like you said to Alastair, you're done writing the story."

There was an uncomfortable silence around the table where everyone was looking at Bethany and Hailey. Even Alastair kept his eyes in their direction. Nelson watched him lick his lips as if he might have been preparing to say something but wasn't sure if he would be interrupting. Mean as it felt, Nelson was reassured by the fact there was someone else at the table who would have a harder time keeping up than he. But he'd barely finished the thought when Alastair said, "I do think it's a nice idea in your story. The idea that you never know."

"I think it's terrifying," Fran said.

"Am I right?" Alastair didn't stop looking in Hailey's direction. "I listen to a lot of stories, and I like to think about the main ideas. I was good at that in school, and it's something I can still do."

"You mean, the idea you never know what's going to happen in *life*?" Stu said.

"You don't," Clarette said emphatically.

"It was about *our* life," Nelson said. "That's it." And felt he'd nailed something there. But where he thought Hailey would nod at him, she was nodding at Alastair instead. How Alastair could have a connection with her that Nelson didn't, he couldn't understand. He couldn't figure out, either, how Alastair could tell Hailey was nodding. But somehow he knew because all she did was continue to nod, and then Alastair said, "That's what I thought."

Jim and Clarette nodded then, too. So did Stu, and even Fran started to. Nelson looked around the table at his old friends and his girlfriends and now his new friend, Hailey, and as frightened as he felt that half of him was somewhere else—was that because they were leaving him out or because he wasn't all there?—he also thought that life really was something. Alastair had a point: You never knew. Then, as usual, Jim raised his glass—but without saying a toast, which was unusual. Nelson watched Jim look at Fran, who was looking at Nelson, and so Nelson skipped looking at Bethany and just looked at Hailey, who raised her glass, too. Her braid was loose, and her pinky was in the air. They all raised their glasses, to their lives, to Hailey, to who knows what, and whatever might happen next, and the only one who said anything was Bethany.

"Beats the alternative," she said again, under her breath.

"Sorry?" Alastair said.

"To life," said Clarette. "To ripping and running." Nelson wondered what drink she was on. "And while we're still putting it out there," she said, even though she was the only one putting anything out there, "I'm not here next weekend because Louis is taking me to Flat Springs."

At that, Nelson felt a hand on his knee. He turned to Hailey, but Bethany had gotten her attention and was leaning into her, talking close, and so he knew that it was Fran. Fran's hand on his knee, and then it slipped right up his thigh. She pressed her light weight down on him, and as she leaned in, there was the smell of fruit either on her breath or in her perfume. He looked at her and was surprised to see that she was pale. White as tissue.

"Are you all right?" he whispered.

She closed her eyes and pressed her chin to her chest. There was still the slightest trace of rug burn on her chin. Nelson watched her chest rise and fall and wondered if he was going to have to save her again.

"I can take care of you," he said. In a way, the words sounded strange, but in a way they were the ones he'd been wanting to say for twenty-eight days. He put his hand over hers.

She took another breath.

"I'll take care of you," he said, and it made him feel good. It made him feel like he was able and needed.

One more breath and her color crept back. "I'm fine," she said. Her eyelashes flickered. Her skin was so clear after all these years, and, noticing this, Nelson wondered if she'd kept all the flowers he'd painted for her. Yellow tulips. Fuchsia bitterroots. That tricky red-orange of Indian paintbrush. As he glanced across the bar to his painting of the crumbling barn, the Missions' peaks towering behind it in a smoky sky, he wondered if he'd ever finish a painting again. He wondered why he hadn't ever bothered to learn faces. Fran's cheeks were bright as daisies, and she tightened her grip on his thigh again and whispered, "Yes."

Nelson didn't know what that meant. "What?" he said.

"Louis has a cabin," Clarette said louder. "He's taking me to his cabin up in Flat Springs."

"Rock Creek," Fran whispered in Nelson's ear. "I'm saying I'll go with you."

I'll go with you. The words went directly into his ear right to his brain. They were crystal clear, like he was ten. *Yes.* That was what he wanted to say to Fran, what he wanted to yell from the top of the movie house in Havre where he used to sneak up the fire escape and eat black licorice in the sun. But what he said to her instead was, "Oh." Which he knew wasn't the best thing to say. He knew the best thing would be to kiss her—to kiss her, and hold her, and take care of her, and, in his spare bedroom, practice painting faces before either one of them got one day older. But the best he could do at the moment was thank her. It sounded all wrong. But . . ."Thank you," he said. "Thank you more than you know." Then he bent toward her so that for a moment their cheeks grazed each other.

Fran perked up in her chair. "Nelson and I are going up Rock Creek," she announced to everyone.

Which wasn't the right thing to do.

Jim banged down his beer. "What is this, a circus?"

The table clammed up. Everyone sat fidgety and uncomfortable and, Nelson presumed, irritated by the refrain of "Singing in the Rain" coming out the bar's speakers at the same time the TV had on one of those murder shows. Everyone was waiting for someone else to do something—or at least tell Doreen to turn the channel—except for Bethany and Hailey. They didn't appear to notice anything. Bethany was still talking to Hailey, scrunched up in conversation, and appeared to have missed everything from Flat Springs on. Jim cleared his throat—like he was in charge, like he could *have* their attention—but not before Nelson caught Bethany say, in a low voice, to Hailey, "I'm glad we talked." Nelson also saw Bethany's hand on Hailey's knee. Fran's hand had been on his knee, only he'd thought it might be Hailey's, only Hailey had put her hand on Nelson's knee earlier, and now Bethany's hand was on Hailey's knee. And now Clarette was going to Flat Springs with Louis, who had bought Hailey a beer before Nelson ever had a chance himself, and now he was going to Rock Creek with Fran, who had just made a mess of the whole thing, spilling their secret like a schoolgirl. Only Bethany and Hailey hadn't caught it yet because they were hunched over in conversation, which Nelson took to be—and this was his worst fear—that they were talking about him.

Nelson knew he was in trouble.

"What," said Bethany, looking expectantly at Jim.

"I don't know if you heard," said Jim, "but Fran was saying she and Nelson are going up Rock Creek. She was just telling us."

Nelson closed his eyes. Could things come together and come undone at the same time? Sometimes dinner seemed like breakfast now, socks like gloves, but the happiest moment and the saddest? Could that be? Could Hailey show up, and Fran say yes, and he lose his shoes and now Bethany all at once? Or was it that things were fuzzy in his head? That he was missing something again, that he had all these roads but no map to put them on. The wrinkle across Hailey's nose was the happiest and the saddest all at once. It *could* happen—only for the life of him he couldn't tell you what *it* was. He opened his eyes and looked at Bethany. She'd pushed her glasses back up her nose.

"Rock Creek is nice this time of year," she said.

He would have rather she got mad.

Jim scoffed again, and Nelson wanted to tell him to keep his spittle to himself. "It's the dead of winter," Jim said.

Bethany nodded. Nelson looked at her, and on a different day he knew she would have scolded him for having that *let's-go-honey* look on his face. But today she didn't say anything. Today she looked into his eyes as if, whatever else she might rather have done, she pitied him. She used to get like this about other people—she would sit with him on the plush couch at her house and play cards and say how she felt sorry for Alastair for being blind, or for Stu Larsen with his wife up a tree, or even for Fran after she choked. Nelson thought she overdid it, but he'd gotten used to listening to her be sorry for everyone but him. He'd never considered, until now, what it would be like to have that attention turned on him.

He wanted to go up Rock Creek with Fran.

He wanted to not lose Bethany.

He wanted happiness to be happiness and sadness to be sadness and not have to live in this confusing new world where everything could be its opposite, given half the chance.

"You'll be all by yourself up there," Bethany said.

"Baby," Nelson said, but didn't finish.

"None of those fishermen from California," she said. "Who want to know all your business."

"Don't be mad," he said quietly, and there was Fran's hand on his knee.

"Don't worry," said Bethany.

Next to Bethany, Hailey was done with her beer and looking around like she had no one to talk to. Like maybe coming down hadn't been the best idea in the world.

"It's not always like this," Nelson said to her.

"Like what?" Hailey said, and he couldn't tell if she was egging him on, or if she was looking at him the same way as Bethany, like he'd shown up naked and now everyone was wondering what to do.

He could go get snowed in up Rock Creek and never come back.

He could stay at home and see when his phone might ring.

When the telemarketers called, they said, "Are you Nelson Moore?" and when you heard that a half-dozen times a day, you started to wonder. You started to say things like, "Beats being Elvis," or, "Let me go check," or, "You tell me." Once he said, "If you're not wearing panties," and the woman hung up. Another time, he said, "Only if he's winning," and that got a laugh.

Bethany nudged him.

"What?" He looked at her. She was pointing behind him.

"Nelson Moore?" said a man.

"That depends what he did," Nelson said.

The man was standing a few steps inside the bar. He was about Nelson's height but his hair wasn't as gray. He wore a shiny purple bowling shirt unlike anything they'd have at Liberty. "They said I'd find you in here," he said. "I wanted to thank you."

"I don't know what for," said Nelson.

The man held his fists up on either side of his ears and shook them. "I just bowled a 280, the best game of my life," he said, "and I hear I did it in your shoes."

"You're the one with my shoes?" Nelson shifted to the edge of his seat, to get a better look at him. The man had wiry legs and a belt cinched up tight on his jeans. His fancy shirt was tucked in, and Nelson couldn't make out the yellow stitching across the breast pocket that must have said the man's name. In any case, he was nothing like Nelson.

"They said there was a mix-up," said the man.

"Are they back in their cubby?" Nelson didn't want this happening twice.

"I gave them back." The man nodded.

"I better go check," Nelson said. The man didn't look shifty, but he did seem awfully thin.

"I'll come," Hailey said.

Nelson turned. She was already up, her eyes brighter, like she was looking forward to this. Nelson couldn't imagine why. "Okay," he said.

"My bus is leaving," the man said.

"As long as you don't have my shoes," said Nelson.

"I wanted to thank you, that's all," he said. "So," he added, actually doing a little bow for Nelson, "thank you much."

At the table, a few people clapped, but Nelson knew enough to know it wasn't for him. He knew it was for this other man making a show of succeeding in his shoes. The man was nothing like Nelson. In his flashy shirt and his cinched-up jeans, he disappeared out of the bar, waving and wiggling his fingers as he went.

Hailey and Nelson wove their way past the other tables to the lobby. Behind them, conversation bubbled up, but Nelson didn't try to listen. He took his steps carefully because his knees felt stiff, and he wondered if that could happen from bowling in a pair of rentals. He wanted to see if that skinny man had changed the shape of his shoes. At the front desk, he lifted up the part of the counter you had to lift up to get to the back, and he let Hailey walk through first. Then he squeezed past her, careful not to touch her as he went, so he could lead the way. The rental cubbies were right there behind the counter, but the other cubbies were tucked in behind the office, in the leftover space between the file cabinets and the back door that opened up to the lockers. There was a standing lamp with one light bulb, but that was it.

"Be careful," Nelson said to Hailey. Bill and Sandy sometimes left bowling balls all over the floor back there, and you had to watch it.

"Where did you get your shoes?" Hailey asked, behind him.

It seemed like an oddball question. "I had them made," he said.

Hailey moved next to him so they were standing by the cubbies. "Doesn't that cost a lot?" she asked, like she was suddenly in the market for a pair of shoes.

He didn't see why the price of his shoes was important right now. "They cost enough," he said. The number eighty came to mind, but that could as easily have been the cost of his last utility bill. He had no idea what he'd paid.

"How much?" Hailey said. "Does everyone else have their shoes made?"

All these questions, he thought, when all he had wanted was to get away from the table and know if his shoes were back in the right place. All he wanted was to be friends. "How would I know?" he said.

"Sorry," Hailey said. "I—"

"I haven't forgotten everything," he said, and then thought about saying sorry, but decided that might make things even worse. "My shoes are right here." He reached into a middle cubby—four up and six over, to be exact—

and withdrew his shoes. He held them toward the lamp for Hailey to see. They didn't look any worse for the wear, the blue leather still shiny and the new laces loose and tucked into the shoe the way he did it himself.

"They're handsome," Hailey said, reaching out to the shoes. "I've never worn bowling shoes."

"I've never heard a person call a shoe handsome," Nelson said.

"My mom called them germy," Hailey said. She ran a hand along the side of one shoe. "So we never bowled."

"That's why you buy your own shoes," said Nelson. He didn't tell her he thought her hands made his shoes look even better, her clear skin against the smooth leather like that. "Here you go," he said, handing her the pair. "Try them."

Hailey took the shoes from him and slipped them onto her hands so that they swallowed her wrists. Nelson thought that was adorable. She held her hands above the lamp so that the shoes lit up. Shiny blue leather and brown leather, and tight new laces, and clear white skin. There was a freckle Nelson hadn't seen before on Hailey's right wrist. He wanted to touch it. His shoes looked beautiful. Hailey danced her hands back and forth like there was music playing. It was a *rat-a-tat* rhythm that made Nelson feel like tapping his own toes, like anything could happen, like at the next moment Hailey might plant a kiss on his forehead or go bowling with gloves on her feet. He wanted to thank her for this bit of time and space. He wanted to apologize for kissing her on the lips. He wanted to tell her his life hadn't always been like this—it had been something else entirely—but before he could straighten out the right words, his shoes were back in his own hands.

"That was one lucky man," Hailey said.

CHAPTER 7

······ ★ ······

Alastair

Alastair knew what it was like to almost die. He'd been on his way into the Salem Federal Credit Union to open a savings account for him and his wife Shyla when the lumber truck had come through the stoplight and jumped the curb. They had moved to Oregon two weeks earlier, right after their wedding, to be closer to Shyla's family. Alastair was twenty-three then, Shyla twenty, and he supposed if someone had pushed him out of the way that instant, if someone had saved his sight like that, he might love them forever, too. But he wasn't sure this was about love—what was happening down at Liberty—if he could actually say what love felt like anymore. First of all, Nelson would have saved a stranger on the street. And Fran had never struck Alastair as someone whose loyalties ran very deep. Jim was a stand-up man, and Bethany was one of the strongest women he'd ever known. Alastair couldn't see the sense in any of them, at their age, rocking the balance they shared. Nelson had Bethany, and Fran had Jim, and Alastair had the whole group to help him out. When they bowled, they guided him to the piece of tape on his lane; when they drank, they walked him to his seat; when they ordered happy-hour specials, they cut his food. Until Bethany read Nelson's article out loud, Alastair hadn't considered there might be any ripple in their smooth routines. But now he had caught it: A flicker of motion. A crack in their hero's foundation. A shifting and stirring he'd felt before any of the rest of them, before Jim had come right out that afternoon and said he and Fran were through.

Alastair lay in his single bed, awake, listening to the gurgle and hum of his fish tanks, wishing there was one other person in the world to whom he could explain his take on it all. He no longer knew any women outside their league.

Really, he had no life of any kind outside their league. He hated to admit these things, but on this night he did. Sad as he knew it was, he told his fish. He told the balloon-pink kissing gouramis in the round tank on his bedside table, and the guppies in the twelve-gallon tank by the couch, along with the dwarf loaches and the barbs and the neon tetras. He spoke to his shiny silver dollars all the way over by the phone in the kitchenette, and to his angelfish, his red empress, his corydoras catfish, and his potbellied mollies in the fifty-gallon tank where the television used to be.

He told them about what Jim said—*in light of everything*—and about the loose, cool skin on Fran's thin forearm. He explained the electricity that afternoon between Nelson and Fran. Had anyone else paid attention? He could hear Nelson and Fran's low voices, and he pictured two animals grooming each other, like the orangutans in one of his tapes from the Library of Congress. Did anyone else know what he meant? Maybe Clarette. Did anyone notice that she'd bailed Nelson out, and did anyone consider that none of this was about who loved who after all, this talk of Jim's, this buzz between Nelson and Fran, this coming clean of Clarette's, this coolness from Bethany—those words in the paper?

Because that was the thing. It started with words in the paper. Not a chicken bone. Not a hero. Not a history or a future between any two of them.

Words in the paper, written by a girl a fraction of their age.

Did anyone see it but him?

She was in her late twenties. Alastair could tell by the bouncy timber of her voice, and he could tell by the way Nelson remembered her. She was old enough to drink a beer and young enough to jog an old man's failing mind, and, despite how the rest of them were so quick to see what had happened, the ripple she caused their group was not about love. It was not about Nelson kissing her, nor about Nelson doing something he shouldn't have done. Though that was what they would remember. It was what they had *seen*. Not that you *wanted* to be a blind man, but it did grant you a perspective. Alastair imagined the women going home and calling each other up and picking apart this kiss, getting into what was happening to Nelson, discussing what they should *do*. But Alastair saw things differently. When you lost your sight, you gained something else. When you lost your mind, you gained something else. Maybe Nelson had kissed Hailey because he'd found something inside him that the others thought they'd lost years ago. Did anyone think of that? Did anyone think about what Nelson might have seen in this girl who had done them a service by telling their story, by accepting what their stories might continue to be?

Did anyone else think of that?

His fish, of course, had nothing to say on the matter. They darted and swooped to the hum of their tanks. They nipped flakes from the water's surface, pellets from the pebbly bottom, algae from the glass walls. Alastair knew everything about them: the bright red noses of his male barbs, the slow, moony circles of the silver dollars. He knew the iridescent stripes of his neon tetras, and the way they dimmed at night. The way the potbellied molly's scales caught the light same as a pearl, the way the kissing gourami rasped algae off the aquarium's back glass like a child first discovering a mirror. He didn't know these things because of tapes from the Library of Congress. He knew them because before the accident, he and Shyla had always had fish, and recalling the shines and flickers and glub had become, ever since, his way of holding on. The swish and gurgle of the four tanks filled his trailer with a rhythm as familiar as his own pulse. He slept and woke and cleaned to their beats. Swish, gurgle, flow, whoosh. It was the closest he had come, again, to love.

Shyla had divorced him after the accident. She'd waited until he was on his feet, with a decent settlement. They had no children. Alastair didn't blame her.

But since he'd left Oregon he had always had fish, and they reminded him of what he had been *before*. One of his few ex-girlfriends, Mora Byrnes, had told him he couldn't live in the past, and he'd said she should try losing her sight. He'd told her something he'd never told anyone before; he told her he shared something with his fish. It was a sixth sense, he said. That fishes have. That blind men have. You can call it a fish's lateral line if you're the Library of Congress, or you can call it the part of you that feels the currents of those around you. The part of you that picks up on things. You feel vibrations running from one person to the next, electricities shifting inside someone else's heart. You see useless shades of light and dark, but you have *this* instead of sun and stars and stop signs, this invisible tether the seeing world goes without.

That was the last time he'd had dinner with Mora, and so Alastair had never tried to explain the phenomenon to anyone else. It was his secret. He had never tried to explain it to Shyla either. Only recently had he wondered where she might be anymore. He really hadn't thought about Shyla—really *thought* about her—in longer than he could remember, until Bethany read Nelson's article. He'd grown settled with his life—seventy-seven now—with his fish and his audiotapes and his four-dollar cab rides to Liberty, where he was fortunate to have such a warm group of friends.

When Nelson or Clarette or any of them came over, which was not often, all they talked about were his tanks. They asked a lot of questions, and because they stopped by so infrequently their questions were always the same. Why fish? Are they much work? Expensive? How do you know when one of them has died? Because they were his friends and he needed them, Alastair always answered. He'd always liked fish, he would say. The work was worth it. Everything worthwhile costs. But how did he know when one died? Was that the question? He didn't have an answer for that. He just knew.

There was a patch of grass at the south end of his trailer where he buried them, in bubble wrap and sandwich bags. Occasionally, he bought glass pebbles at the crafts store and included them in the baggies, too. He liked their cool, smooth feel. He knew his friends would think he was strange if they ever found out.

Lying in bed that night, he actually felt content that his friends did not stop by often. In the dark, in his bubbling trailer, he thought about Nelson with Fran, and Clarette with this man so much younger, and he thought of this new sense, shared by all of them, that things were up for grabs. He might be blind, but if having a shot at love again—really remembering what it felt like—was something that he wanted to do, maybe it was something he could try. In his dreams, Alastair could see everything, the rainbow coat of his red empress, Shyla's tiny rear tied tight with one of those waist aprons. Listening to the hum of his tanks, he thought about what it would be like to see again and fall in love again, and it came clear to him that if his sight were restored and he were to take back what he'd lost, there were things he would miss about this life, this quiet life as an old blind man. He would miss the intimate sound of the swish and gurgle, the sense of other people's vibrations on his papery skin, the light-dark dance of shadows that let him see things differently from everybody else.

⋆

CHAPTER 8

Clarette

Louis's idea was to go ice fishing on the way to Flat Springs and catch some dinner. Clarette had a fear of falling through ice and had been thinking more along the lines of cooking a roast while music played in the background, but she didn't want to make a big deal of it. After everything that had gone on recently, she mostly wanted to get out of town and not think about what would go wrong next. Because things came in threes, everyone knew it, and first there was Fran choking, and then Nelson kissing Hailey, and now who knew who was on deck. Clarette didn't want to stick around to address any of it. She didn't love the idea of being set up there on the ice with Louis, either, because she could almost see that headline—*Elderly Victim Perishes in Salmon Lake*—and she couldn't stand that word, *elderly.* Especially not when she was on her first weekend away with a man besides Dean in her entire life, a man sixteen years her junior, but who was so much bigger and slower that she felt even younger than he was, which put her, in her mind anyway, at sixty-two tops. That was a safe dozen years from Nelson's age, which was the age where all of them now had to admit things started to come undone.

She looked over at Louis, intent on his hole. When they'd first arrived, he'd drilled two holes in the ice twenty feet apart, which made it hard to talk and gave them both too much time to think. Louis had been so tense when he'd picked her up that she'd poured them each a glass of bourbon, and then added the bottle to her bag. Now she tried to tell herself no matter how old she really was or how young he really was, that bottle was big enough for them to get warmed up and lean into the weekend just fine.

Except for the fact she hadn't told Louis she was afraid of falling through ice. She'd had this fear ever since she was a girl, since her leg went through on her uncle's pond, and now here she was on her date, practically to the center of Salmon Lake, Louis weighing in the neighborhood of 350 pounds, and the day so mild she wasn't even wearing mittens. Louis had brought her boots big enough to bathe in, and as she stood heavy-footed in the sun, six inches deep in slush that Louis swore was supported by four feet of solid ice, Clarette held onto her dinky line, hoping to be distracted by something more substantial than the itty-bitty perch that, every few minutes or so, grabbed ahold of Louis's line but not hers.

And there it was again, what kept coming back to her: the fact Nelson was five years younger than she. She wished she could quit thinking about it and enjoy herself. But after he had kissed Hailey, you could feel it all at once, everyone prickling up at the realization there was no more doing nothing. Now there was just the question of who would take the first step. There was the question of why any of them, like one of those Power Pick balls popping out of the big tumbler on TV, would jump the tracks before another.

Clarette looked over at Louis, who was hunkered down like a bear over dinner. She bobbed her line and hoped the numbers were on her side, that she still had some room in this world to make up for lost time before she ended up with Nelson out there in left field with the dandelions. That was her intention, anyway, to go out living it up.

Louis lifted another perch out of his hole. Each time he did so, his body did a little hop.

"Are you hogging them all?" she called across the ice.

Louis was scowling into the sun, cupping his ear.

"I'm bored out of my skull," Clarette called louder, but Louis couldn't hear her.

He looked puzzled. Then he dropped the perch into his bucket and tilted it for her to see. He'd half-filled the thing, while she had none. "It takes time," he said.

"What?" she called.

He put his rod down, rubbed his head, and started taking big slushy steps toward her. "You cold?" he asked.

"I'm getting a sunburn." Clarette shook her head. "And I said I'm so bored I'm about ready to crawl into these boots and take a nap."

She hadn't intended for it to come out like that. What she'd meant was that

Louis was the better fisherman, that he was catching all their dinner while she was lodged in his boots like a scarecrow, but it was either her nerves or the bourbon that made it come out badly. Louis was still scowling.

"I have enough for dinner," he said.

"That's what I meant," she said. "You're doing all the work."

"It takes time," he said.

She had a brief image of the ice opening up and Louis dropping through silently. She pictured him not putting up a fight. "Don't *you* get bored?" she asked.

"Nope," he said.

"It must have to do with being a man," she said. And then it happened very fast—a bend of her line, a tug in her palm, a spring of action that made her throw her whole body behind that line. She hooted like a cowgirl.

"Easy," Louis said.

Her weight shifted against the back of her borrowed boots, her muscles snapping to in a way she didn't know they had in them anymore. Not that there was more than a little perch on that line, but what a feeling. She hadn't caught a fish since her honeymoon. Which brought her up short. She'd wanted to go to Mexico, but it was June and Dean didn't want to leave when the trout were rising, and so they'd camped along the North Fork of the Smith River instead, and it turned out to be a dream, in those canyons, with the prairie smokes blooming, and a new cookstove from Dean's father, and fish too big to fit in the pan.

When the perch broke the surface, Clarette lurched backward, and she saw how you needed that little hop to lift the fish out of the hole. Her line didn't have a reel, so she just shot her hands up over her head. Louis came up behind and reached his big arms around in front of her, pulling in that perch for her to see. It was yellowish orange, twitching in his big hand, without even a fraction of the meat Louis had in the pad of his palm. Dean would have never wasted his time.

"They're lean little buggers, aren't they?" said Clarette.

Louis picked up the perch with his other hand to judge for himself.

"We'll have to cook the bones," she said.

"No, we won't," he said. "I'll show you. Little fish are worth their trouble; you just have to have the patience."

"I have patience," she said.

And then Louis squeezed her in his arms and laughed the first big, open laugh she'd ever heard from him. "No, you don't," he said. "You're my wiggly worm."

Such a swell of raw happiness surged through Clarette that she thought she might shout. Fifty-nine years married and Dean's only nickname for her had been Thumbs because she wasn't particularly handy except with cooking. Fifty-nine years. Clarette looked at that tiny perch, motionless now, and thought she'd be crazy *not* to be out in the middle of the ice on a sunny day, anchored to a man who had the patience to catch a hundred fish for her dinner.

"Do you know what?" she said, pushing back into Louis's cushiony gut, just about daring the ice to open up and let them in.

"Nope," he said.

"I am scared to death of falling through the ice."

"You should of told me," he said.

"Then I wouldn't of caught my perch."

"We could of bought steaks."

"I'd like to catch a few more." She shook her line.

"We're going to have to go to the store anyway," Louis said. "For beer and ranch and whatnot."

Clarette turned around so she was facing him and could wrap her arms around him like she would an old tree. She didn't even try to clasp her hands on his backside. She looked into his serious face, at his low bank of dark eyebrows, and imagined he was doing a grocery list in his head.

"I am enjoying myself," she said to Louis. "I truly am."

Then she went back to it and caught two more perch, and soon it was time to trudge through the slush to the truck so they'd have a fighting chance of getting to the cabin before dark. Louis tuned the radio to a talk program about cars. Clarette had thought a country song would be nice, but a talk program made it comfortable for them not to talk themselves, and Clarette sensed that might have been Louis's idea. He didn't seem nervous to her anymore, and she guessed he was probably warding off the same two thoughts as she, which were that his wife had left eight months ago and her husband had bowed out just under six.

Dean had known everything there was to know about cars.

"I don't even know how to change the tires," she said to Louis.

He didn't know where that came from, of course.

"I think maybe I'll drink wine tonight," she said. "With those little fish."

Louis turned down the radio. "They have wine at the store," he said. "But

I can't say I know about buying wine." He took his eyes off the road to look at her. "I drink MGD."

Clarette gave his arm a punch, then rubbed the spot she'd punched. "Yes, you do," she said.

They wound through the Swan Valley, past Seeley Lake, with the peaks of the Missions and the Swans rising up on either side of them, into the dimming winter sky. The ground was covered in snow, minus some thin patches where the wind had blown hard enough to dust off the bent stalks of scrappy grass. The store came up on their left, and as Louis slowed down, Clarette noticed the few cars in the gas station/motel across the street had their headlights on, and the vacancy sign was already burning red. The sun would be gone within the hour, and she didn't want anything to go too fast. Louis came around and opened her door and helped her change back into her regular shoes. Then they went inside the store, each shopping with their own basket. Louis got his ranch dressing and his MGD, and also some frozen French fries and bread and juice and butter and chips and eggs and sausage and a sheet cake with chocolate icing, even though the cake said *Happy Birthday Marian.*

"They're giving it to me for a dollar," Louis said to Clarette at the checkout. In her basket, she had lettuce and tomatoes and oatmeal, and also eggs and bacon and toilet paper and a nine-dollar bottle of Merlot.

"Who's Marian?" she asked.

"It's supposed to be Mary Anne," he said.

They paid for their groceries separately, but Louis carried hers to the truck. The cabin was another fifteen minutes from the store—a right turn at a worn-out mini-American flag stuck in a tree, and then ten slow minutes down a woodsy dirt road that cleared out by the river and the cabin. Which was actually a singlewide with a log addition tacked on. Which was, even from the outside, a mess.

"There's some cleaning out I haven't gotten to," Louis said, cutting the engine. "But I don't get any bears. I don't keep any food in the house."

On the log porch, there was an array of rusting lawn furniture. There was also a rubber hose frozen in its coil, three empty propane tanks lying on their sides, a half-dozen cracked flowerpots with icy dirt leaking out everywhere, several empty beer bottles, and a black grill tipped over, exactly by bears, Clarette imagined, and likely licked clean of last summer's meat. At least Louis had bothered to drag it up onto the porch, and she was relieved to see a bright blue tarp pulled tightly over what looked to be a stack of wood that would be dry. But otherwise, the place appeared to be stuck in August.

"I haven't been here since summer," Louis said, as if he knew what she was thinking. He reached a key down from above the front door.

"Not by the look of things," she said, and he hesitated before putting the key in the lock.

"It looks like you have a good time up here," she said.

"We did," he said too fast, and there was no covering up the fact this was a place he'd shared with Nan, and now Nan was gone, and by the look of things Louis had up and left his own party and not looked back. Clarette had a hunch Louis hadn't been to the cabin since Nan left; only Nan had been gone eight months. August was five months ago.

"Well, as long as you can say that, then there's something good to hang onto." She reached out and rubbed his back and tried not to be jealous. "But that being said, we might as well get on with it."

Louis walked in ahead of Clarette and tugged the light string above a small yellow kitchenette set. Clarette hadn't seen the knickknacks Louis had taken to the pawn shop, but here were enough to give her an idea. There were little china roosters on a spice rack, salt-and-pepper roosters on the kitchenette, a band of china farm animals on the windowsill, a family of bunny-shaped baskets on top of the refrigerator, and the refrigerator itself. It was a wonder Louis could stay so fat with all those magnets about God and hips standing between him and a glass of milk.

But Clarette wondered why, in eight months, Nan hadn't gotten up here and collected her things. Maybe she and Louis were fighting about whose house this was, but Clarette didn't want to think about that right now. She just wanted to enjoy herself. And anyway, Louis didn't seem to be paying Nan's knickknacks any mind. He was moving through the house, flipping up lights and plugging in two space heaters in the living room, which was also crammed with dolls and stuffed animals and pillows like those refrigerator magnets. *A woman needs a man like a fish needs a popsicle,* said one centered on the loveseat, but again Louis wasn't looking. He was carrying their bags to the bedroom, and though Clarette didn't follow him back there, she could see the bedroom from the living room. When the light went on, she saw the one bed with a yellow quilt and more pillows she didn't even want to read, and it wasn't the fact of the one bed that startled her so much as that the bed was Nan's.

Then again, it wasn't like she'd bought new sheets since Dean died.

"I put our bags in the closet," Louis said, coming out.

"Does it feel funny being here with me?" Clarette asked.

Louis stopped in the center of the living room. He looked around like someone had just taken off a blindfold. "A little," he said. "Not much."

Clarette rubbed her hands together. "All right, then," she said. "I just wanted to get that out of the way."

In the kitchen, Louis knew what he was doing. First, he started a fire in the wood stove. Then he put the French fries on a pan in the oven, and cleaned and stripped the perch and piled their slippery bits of white meat on a plate. He got his Fry Daddy out from under the sink and rinsed it while Clarette was washing the lettuce and chopping tomatoes and pouring the ranch into a rooster-shaped creamer. She also got the bourbon out of her bag and opened the wine and cracked Louis a couple of MGDs. When he added the perch to the fryer, the Fry Daddy's hiss was satisfying to her, and the smell of potatoes, even frozen French fries, always made a place feel like home. She would have liked some music going, too, but she didn't ask Louis if he had any out of fear he'd have a whole stack of love songs between him and Nan.

"Have you ever fallen through ice?" he asked her then. He was pausing to take off his boots, and Clarette did the same. "I was wondering how you got afraid of something like that."

"Well," she said. "Think of anything you're afraid of and how you got afraid of it."

"I can't think of anything," Louis said.

"You didn't try."

He started to protest, but when he looked over at her she winked at him.

"I'm cooking," he said.

"My leg went through once." She picked up her wine. "On my uncle's pond."

Louis watched her sip wine. Clarette felt him looking at her legs in particular, probably because he was trying to imagine one of them sunk through ice. Clarette wanted to add that she was afraid now, too, about Nelson, though what she really meant was that his going downhill made her own decline seem not too far off. But all that did was bring up her age when she'd rather keep Louis looking at her legs and thinking of them as strong enough to push that recliner out the door.

"I met Nan in the hospital cafeteria," he said then. "In Billings."

Clarette wasn't expecting that.

"Her father had a heart attack, and my neighbor sliced off his thumb," Louis said. He didn't give the circumstances of either, but it made Clarette think of Dean. Dean was slumped in his recliner when the paramedics arrived, then stretched stiff as a bean in the ambulance.

"Dean had a heart attack," she said.

"Who?" Louis switched off the Fry Daddy, and the room got quieter.

"Oh," she said. "My husband."

"Oh," he said.

"I never told you Dean's name?" That didn't seem possible.

"Not that I can say." Louis checked on the French fries but then stopped and wrung his hands in a dish towel instead, like this new information made him uncomfortable.

Clarette was rattled herself. "I must of told you somewhere along the way," she said.

"I don't think so." He checked the French fries. "Almost," he said, and then there was a silence so thick it made Clarette want to go ahead and ask Louis if he might have any old love songs to put on. Instead she took a seat at the kitchenette only half-facing him and checked if the rooster shakers were full. They were, enough. Louis put his hand on her back. Before she could turn around, he added, "It's a good thing you didn't go all the way through." His one hand was like a hot pad. "It's too bad I ever went for lunch in that cafeteria," he said.

Clarette pushed the shakers aside and stood up and put both her hands flat against Louis's chest. "No, it's not," she said. "They're both good things."

They sat at the kitchenette, picking up the perch with their fingers and dipping them in ranch. Louis was right—the little fish made a tasty meal. After all the meatloaf and onion rings they'd split, this felt like their first real meal together. Louis poured Clarette's wine for her, and he didn't complain when, for dinnertime, she poured his MGD in a glass. Unlike Dean, Louis even picked up on the salt she sprinkled on the tomatoes and said he liked it though it wasn't something he'd had before. Nan wasn't a cook, he said. She liked the frozen pizzas. That, and she wore a T-shirt he hated that said, *It was a man's world. Then Eve arrived.* Clarette thought that was a kick, but she didn't say as much. You got farther in this world if you kept some thoughts quiet.

For example, her and Louis. Even sitting at this table warmed up with his big hands and the wood stove and her wine, Clarette knew it wasn't going to last. For one thing, she wouldn't be alive by the time he was her age. But more than that, she knew they were at this messy time in their lives where they both needed something good to happen. What was the point in talking about it? Given the circumstances—and here, Clarette was thinking not of Dean or Louis, but of Nelson—why bother being gloomy? The bottom line was that Clarette needed Louis same as he needed her, and there was no sense ruining it with a bunch of words. For her part, she was going to enjoy herself and love this man and take the whole adventure with her once it was through.

Louis reached over and clinked his beer glass against her wine.

Clarette leaned in and kissed his big mouth.

That was the beauty of your own choices, good or bad: Once you'd lived them, there was no creature on this earth or otherwise could take them away.

They sliced the birthday cake and ate it with ice cream and another drink in the living room. Then they watched a TV program about great whites and had one more drink. After that, when it seemed like there was nothing else to do but change into their nightclothes and get into that yellow bed, Louis stood up and said he was going to check on the springs out back, see if they were hot. Clarette took this as his way of giving her the privacy to change into her nightclothes, and so she quickly carried their dishes to the sink and then got her toothbrush out of her bag and brushed her teeth. She double-checked that the tags were off the lavender nightgown she'd bought, then put it on and draped the new, matching lavender robe over a corduroy chair beside the bed. She took two pillows off the bed without reading them and slipped between the sheets. She couldn't say they felt crisp or clean. They did smell like Louis, though, like sawdust and perspiration, and she left it at that. She wished she'd taken a minute, in her nightgown, to look at herself in the mirror, but she would have been embarrassed if Louis had walked in and found her looking at herself the way she would a stranger.

"There's too much snow," Louis said when he finally came in. He didn't make eye contact with her there in the bed, and he sounded just about miserable. "The water's cold."

Clarette was relieved. "I had half a thought it would be," she said.

Louis eyed her nervously there in the bed.

"I know I asked you this already," she said, "but does it feel funny having me here?"

Louis's hands were white, either from being outside or clasping them so hard. "A little bit," he said, sitting on the edge of the mattress. "This part." He found where her ankles were under the covers and held on to them.

"Well, I can close my eyes or you can turn off the lights, or whatever you like," she said. "It's not like this is an everyday thing for me either."

Louis moved his hand from her ankles to her toes, and pinched them gently, and didn't say anything.

"I'm closing my eyes," she said, and she did. A moment later, she felt the mattress rise up, free of his weight, and she heard the jangle of his belt buckle and the thump of his jeans hitting the ground. She pictured him fumbling with his shirt buttons, and then, no harm done because he'd never know, she peeked. Just a little squint. And there he was at the end of the bed, facing sideways from her and pulling off his shirt to reveal a soft white barrel of flesh, a giant belly you just about had to rub your hands all over, with some wispy gray chest hairs but not too many, and then below that belly, the most thrilling part of all, a pair of red plaid boxer shorts. She'd never seen a man wear a pair of those before. Dean believed in briefs. It was almost like Louis was still dressed.

"All right," he said, not in a way that suggested it was okay for her to open her eyes, but more that he'd gotten himself through this first step. "I'm just going to brush my teeth."

Through her squinty eyes, Clarette watched how his body moved toward the closet—big rolls and jiggles—and then squeezed inside to get his toothbrush out of his bag. He leaned over, and Clarette got a downright fascinating sight of his enormous rear, and that's when the bat appeared. It flew straight out from the closet, right over Louis's rear, and swooped around the room. It wasn't a big room, and Clarette didn't have to hate bats to wish it wasn't there. In fact, bats were handy to have around some of the time, but not when you were on your first real romantic getaway in almost sixty years, and not when the man you were with turned out to run for the hills at the sight of one. Then there was a second, and maybe a third—it was hard to keep track. But Clarette knew one of them flew out to the living room and another one was still figuring out the bedroom when she threw back the covers, grabbed her lavender robe, and scrambled after Louis.

He was in the kitchen. He'd shut the door tight—which she did behind her as well—and was already in his coat, bare-chested, and tying up his boots.

Clarette started laughing. "Where do you think you're going?" she said. She'd never seen a man in boxer shorts and a parka and boots before.

"I don't like bats," he said.

"I just saw that," she said.

Louis grimaced at her from his chair and kept his body balled up. Clarette did her best not to laugh anymore.

"I don't think I can go back in there," he said.

"Well, how do you know they're not in here?"

"I got here first," he said, and Clarette couldn't help letting a laugh go at the thought of big old Louis flying through the house quicker than a bat.

"I'm sorry." She clapped one hand over her mouth. Her eyes were wet with tears.

"Bats have rabies," he said.

"Sometimes," she said. "But their aim in life isn't to bother you."

"I'm not going back in there." Louis sat straight enough to zip his coat. Some wispy gray chest hairs poked out the top.

Clarette sat down with him. "How did you get so afraid of bats?" she asked.

He didn't answer. He was glancing around the room like a robber looking for cameras.

"I said how did you get so afraid of bats?" Clarette had her eye on the bottle of bourbon there on the counter by her purse. They might as well at least have another glass.

Louis wrung his hands. "I don't think I'd be able to sleep," he said.

"Enough bourbon and you would," she said.

"It hasn't been eight months," he said then. "It'll be four next Friday."

"What?" Clarette straightened up in her chair so she almost had a bird's-eye view of Louis. His squashed hair showed the beginning of a bald spot she hadn't seen before. Dean had gone bald by forty.

"Nan," Louis said, and he cupped his hands around the sides of his face like a bat might be after him. "She left four months ago. I've been saying eight."

Clarette stood up. She stayed quiet at first. Sometimes you got farther in this world if you stayed quiet and made your plan. Louis looked like a melting snowman. A sad, lying, scared lump of a man. Clarette took her time to think about this. She started out furious, but that wasn't where she landed.

"You've been lying," she said. It was a fact, not an accusation.

"I've had a hard time," he said so quietly she almost asked him to repeat it.

"Oh, well I've never had one of those," she said.

"Clarette," he said.

It was funny, she thought, how rarely lovers spoke each other's names. Maybe *Honey* or *Baby* or *Sweet Cakes*. Lovers. The word was right there at the front of her brain, as if it had been there forever. As if there was anything in this world lasted that long.

Clarette didn't say one more word. She'd made her plan. She turned and walked back to the living room and closed the kitchen door behind her.

"Clarette," Louis said, louder this time.

First she unplugged the heater by the bedroom, then the second one by the TV. She wasn't worried about the bats. She was thrilled. She thought for a second about getting her and Louis's bags out of the closet but decided that would change the momentum of the whole thing. She quickly turned out all the lights and knocked a mushroom-shaped night-light out of the wall. Then she went back to the kitchen, where Louis hadn't budged, and dumped a pot of water over the glowing embers in the wood stove.

That made Louis stand up. "What are you doing?"

Clarette clasped Louis's upper arms, grinning now, and did her best to shake him. She was so excited inside, she wanted to tell him everything was perfect, that age was just a number, and her mind was sharp as the day she got married. "You're right about those bats," she said instead. "They could have rabies."

"So what are you doing?" Louis sounded distressed.

Clarette was putting on her shoes. "I'm getting us out of here." She grabbed the bourbon and her purse. She took the keys from a turtle-shaped ceramic dish. She'd never done anything like this in her life. "I'm taking us to that motel."

"What?" Louis said, staring at Clarette in her lavender robe and shoes, while she stared at him in his parka and boxers and boots.

"You can go back in that closet if you want." Clarette opened the front door. "But this bus is leaving." Then she was out into the night, the cold air straight up her nightie, and Louis, as she knew he would be, right behind her.

"I'm driving, anyway," he said.

"It's your ride." She tossed him the keys. "Gun that heat."

He did. He got the heat cranked and the radio onto a music channel that was neither love songs nor rock 'n' roll, but somewhere in between. The radio was up so loud it wasn't easy to talk, and they bumped down the dirt road listening to a young woman belt out something about the sun in Texas. She was singing about bugs in the headlights and beer in the back, which wasn't so different from their own circumstances, Clarette thought, except that in Flat Springs it was below freezing, in the middle of the night, and she and Louis had bourbon. They were going to drink it out of those plastic cups that came in plastic wrapping by the motel room's sink. They would get ice from the machine outside the office, they would sit on the king-size bed, on top of the clean sheets, and watch a murder show or a Western in their nightclothes. They'd drink as much as they wanted to, and watch as much TV as they wanted to, and sleep as late as their own jitters would let them. In the morning, Clarette might run a bath in the tub with those little wrapped soaps, or she might stand on the cement apron outside their room in her lavender robe, in the sun. If there was sun. In the winters, sometimes it was all clouds and gray. Either way, Clarette, for her part, was going to stand in front of that motel room mirror and take a look at herself before the night was through.

"You doing okay?" She put her hand on Louis's knee. They were off the dirt road onto pavement, and he still hadn't said a word. Now he turned his head out the side window, away from her.

"Louis?" she said.

He didn't say anything, and Clarette wondered how hard it might be to be a man, brought up your whole life to swallow your feelings. "I'm not mad, you know," she said. Women were expected to say practically everything that crossed their mind. Clarette took in the black night speeding past them, the motel lights coming up, the music going, and the truck's heat sending out a toasty burnt smell. "I'm having the time of my life," she said.

She loved it when Louis smiled. It didn't happen all that often, but when it did she just felt like something was right with the world, and it happened right there in the truck, with the vacancy sign burning in clear view. As Louis made the wide turn into the motel lot, he smiled and said, "You need to think up a nickname for me."

"Is that what you've been thinking?" Clarette asked.

"Just when you said my name."

"Okay, then," she said, because she knew what he meant. "I'll think of one."

Louis kept the engine going but turned down the music. "Only it can't have to do with bats."

"Only if you go in there and get our room." Clarette pointed to the office. It was lit up, and she could see a TV on, and also a pair of boots, coming out of blue jeans, up on a table.

"I'm not going in there," he said seriously.

"I know you're not." She pushed him. "I'm the one's going."

"You're a woman," he said.

"Not a day over sixty-two," she said, and slinked her way out the door.

The man in the office looked to be about her age. He dropped his boots to the floor when she walked in and took his time getting behind the front desk. He was probably trying to see if his eyes were playing tricks on him. Clarette pulled herself up close to the front desk so he might not see as much of her. The man was taller than she was, with comb lines through his silver hair and a lot of sun splotches on his skin, but also angular cheekbones like you might find in a Western.

"Well," he said, his voice higher than Clarette expected and his eyes wide open. "Look what the cat dragged in."

It was something Dean used to say under less flattering circumstances, but this man sounded tickled.

Clarette blushed. She'd never had one of those nightmares everyone else talked about where you're back in your grammar school undressed, but the thought crossed her mind now. Only this felt closer to a dream than a nightmare, with the bright office lights beaming down the way she'd heard people on TV describe how it was before you went to Heaven, everything going bright white and your life marching before your eyes. Only Clarette was just going into a motel room with Louis, and a king-size bed and a bottle of bourbon.

"I'm looking for a room, please," she said. "With a king-size bed and a television. Just for the night."

The man was either in awe of her or about to call the cops, she wasn't sure. He slowly shuffled some papers around on his desk, and she wondered if it was true what she'd heard, that these motel owners always kept a gun in their desk drawer to take care of crazies. She looked over her shoulder to Louis, who was keeping an eye on her. She'd never done anything like this in her life. The man placed a key on the counter, along with some papers to sign if she was paying with a credit card.

"I'm paying cash," she said.

"All right," he said.

She wondered if Louis would pay her back half, or the whole thing, or if this one was on her. He'd caught all the perch, after all. She opened her wallet and took out two twenty-dollar bills. It was thirty dollars for the night, and the man made change. He took away the paperwork and lifted a big black book onto the counter.

"If you could sign our book," he said, opening it. There were a handful of names above the empty line he pointed to. He handed Clarette a pen. There was Ronald Baker from Polson, Martha and Conrad Stevens from Alberta, Mitchell Something-or-other from Deer Lodge, Chap Warner from Darby, Mr. & Mrs. Karl Simmons from Priest Lake. Clarette had never liked the way you didn't include the woman's name when you wrote Mr. & Mrs. So-and-so, like on an envelope. Mrs. Simmons had a name. It could have been Kathryn or Grace or any number of things, and you wouldn't know. *It was a man's world,* Clarette smirked to herself and thought about what to write.

"That's a nice color on you," the man said then.

That caught Clarette off guard. She looked up at him. He had dark eyes and a straight back, and he really was handsome for a man about her age who worked all night running a motel.

"I thought you might think I was losing it," she said.

"Not me," he said.

"And I'm not planning to," she said.

The man waited for her to sign the book, but Clarette wasn't sure what to write. First she wrote the date and then, slowly, she wrote *C. Luther* in careful cursive. But then she crossed it out. She didn't want to leave her real name, but then she was thinking how Luther hadn't always been her real name anyway. Her maiden name was Farrity. She married Dean three days after she turned nineteen. That was a long time ago. She tried writing out *C. Black* for fun, in all capital letters. She liked the look of it enough, except it sounded angry, *see black.* As she crossed out that second signature, too, the man said to her, "Running from something?" and she said, "You bet your life," and that's when it clicked inside her. She wrote quick and hard, and then she slapped that book shut and zipped out of the office with the key in her hand. *C. What the Bat Dragged In,* she had written. She wondered what the man would think of that, a woman about his age in a lavender robe, in the middle of the night, paying for a king-size bed in cash and putting down a name like that one. She loved everything about it. It was something she'd only ever heard the movie stars had done.

CHAPTER 9

★

Nelson

The Rising View Cabins up Rock Creek rented April through October, and there was nothing Nelson could do about this being January. The ground was coated white-gray, and the sky was blotched gray-green, and the clouds wove through the lodgepoles like webs. Nelson waited until half past ten to pick Fran up so enough trucks might have headed east by then to warm up the black ice on I-90. He stayed in the right lane, in the grooves of those trucks. Fran sat beside him, smelling like lilies and reading aloud headlines and horoscopes from the *Chronicle*. It was Saturday, which meant the crossword was out of the question. Nelson had a feeling Fran was disappointed they were only making a day trip instead of spending a whole weekend away, but it wasn't his fault it was January or that her family had sold their place up Rock Creek twelve years ago. They could still drive a good portion of the Rock Creek Road and have a meal at the Rising View Lodge, whose restaurant was open year-round, and be back in town before the roads got dark. They could be together without having to share a cabin that went for tourist prices anyway, and that, as Nelson recalled, had the sink right there in the bedroom.

He white-knuckled the wheel. Every few minutes, he eyed the gas gauge. He'd hoped he would be excited about this trip, but now he felt he'd ended up in this position more by accident than desire, and a part of him wanted to explain as much to Fran. He told her he didn't want to rush things, but the truth of it was he no longer enjoyed being away from home. When he was home, he didn't necessarily like being there either, but when he was away all he thought about was getting back. And now here was Fran smelling delicious and reading to him about his future, and all Nelson could think about was what a relief it would be to be back at his kitchen table by nightfall, alone.

"If we were Virgos, we would have to swallow our pride tonight and let someone else shine," said Fran.

It struck Nelson as an unattractive quality, to always want the thing you didn't have.

"Because you can't live in the spotlight without losing your glow," she added.

He felt guilty, but he thought that he might be happier if Hailey were there instead of Fran, because then he wouldn't have to worry about being anything more than friends.

"The hospital got the okay to take down the old Marwick Building." Fran pointed at an article. "For a parking lot."

Or maybe it was that he had pictured this differently. In the first place, all his memories of himself and Fran were from summer or early fall. They were in bright colors, with flowers and leaves and sun.

"I don't know where people are coming from," Fran said, "who need all these parking places."

He remembered them heading to a square dance at the Eagles in Hamilton and blowing a tire on the way and ending up drinking beer on a picnic table outside the 4&4 Café. Fran was wearing a blue-and-white skirt with a lacy white blouse. The beer went straight to their heads and the café owner's son gave them a ride to a nearby motel where they spent the night.

"They're the same people who are building all these houses," he said.

"Did you hear about them doing condos on the old Keeough Ranch?"

"Which ones?" he said, wondering if he'd be more or less comfortable if they were talking like lovers instead of people who might have been passing time at the bus station.

"It says right here it's off," Fran said. "It's a floodplain."

"I guess I don't know those ones." Nelson glanced at Fran. He could tell she'd had her hair done for the occasion; it was standing up higher than usual, in big waves. It might have been the weather, or it might have been the difference between wanting a thing so badly and all of a sudden having it, but Fran looked older to him, peering through the paper.

"Oh my gosh!" she said, smashing her hand into the paper's crease.

"What?" Nelson hit the brakes.

"They've set the date for the Fivemile demolition," she said. "Why are you slowing down? Is there ice?"

Or maybe it was his own faulty mind. "You shrieked," he said. "I thought something was happening." It was just that he'd twisted things around, so now he remembered Fran as young as Hailey, when in fact he and Fran had both been in their forties when they'd started dating. Fran was twenty-seven and he was twenty-nine when they met—right at Hailey's age—but they'd both been married. By the time they were going up Rock Creek, they were already so much older. They must have had crow's-feet and joint aches by then, but Nelson only remembered them with energy and possibilities, not at all like they were already halfway done with their lives.

"Something is happening," Fran said, holding out the paper like she might catch a piece of falling sky. "The demolition date is set."

"I thought it was always set," said Nelson.

"The point is we're fighting it," she said. "But now here they're saying it doesn't matter. They got the go-ahead for Friday, February 9."

"That's a few more weeks." Nelson was unfamiliar with this new tone of Fran's. Her voice had a bossy, hard-edged ring to it he didn't remember.

"I hope you're still interested in helping," she said.

"I am."

"Because some things you can help, and some things you can't, so you have to at least fix the things you can."

Nelson looked to see if her expression might give him a clue what she was talking about, but it didn't.

"Do you know what I mean?"

"I think so," he pretended.

"Good," she said. "I thought you would." She touched a big wave of her hair with one hand, then reached out to Nelson's shoulder. "I am here for you, Nelson."

He felt an uneasy prickle run through his chest. He knew the whole point behind this drive was romance, but he wasn't comfortable putting it out there like her. She was sitting there waiting for him to respond, though, and so he said, "I'm here for you, too."

"I know," she said, squeezing his shoulder. "You've showed me that, remember?"

For a second it sounded to him like Fran was suggesting he could have forgotten saving her life, and he wanted to tell her that he remembered more than she and the others thought—more than Bethany gave him credit for, anyway. He had all kinds of memories of him and Fran, for example, only in those memories the two of them were so much younger; and he hadn't realized until that moment that it was impossible, no matter what they wanted, to return to where they'd been.

"Are you with me, Nelson?" Fran was touching his thigh.

He put his hand over hers. "I am with you," he said. "And I'm watching this road."

It was twenty miles from town to the Rock Creek exit, but winter made it feel longer. The inversion socked in the valley and didn't burn off until the afternoon, so you might not see the sun until two o'clock, and it was on its way down by three. Meanwhile the clouds were sinking low enough to meet the snow, which left you with this tunnel vision, especially on the road, like you were in a winding gray tube running from one steamy-windowed place to the next. Nelson himself sealed his windows at home with plastic to keep the heating bills down. He also warmed up his car ten minutes before driving, and he always drove in the right lane because he trusted those truck grooves. He took the Rock Creek exit so slowly Fran started rocking in her seat like she was pulling the car along.

"You can't see black ice," he said.

"Can we drive up to the old place first?" she said.

"That's what I was thinking." He turned the heat up. "The road should be clear to there, and then we could go eat at the lodge." He said this even though he knew it was unnecessary to repeat the plan; he'd already laid it out over the phone, and again when he'd picked her up.

"I hope the owners aren't there." Fran looked sideways out the window. Nelson thought she meant the owners of the lodge, until she said, "I want to sit on the porch."

Which was what they used to do at her family's place. They'd sit on the porch, or the lawn chairs, and eat peanuts or drink whiskey coffees or vodka lemonades, depending on the weather. Nelson could still see the silver thermos they poured coffee into.

Nelson had been thinking they would drive by the house, see if it looked the same. "We don't want to trespass," he said.

"What are they going to do?" she said, and he thought she sounded annoyed. "My family owned that place a hundred years."

"But that—"

"Let's just see." She patted his leg, and he drove on. First they passed the lodge, a piecemeal log structure with the letters RISING VIEW LODGE

FISHERMEN WELCOME propped up on the roof. The lights were on in front. There was one car parked outside, and smoke chugged out the chimney. Up ahead, the road went from pavement to gravel, and though they weren't planning to go this far, Nelson knew that twelve miles up, past the suspension bridge, the road would turn to rocky, knotty dirt—now under feet of snow—and stay that way as it wound along the creek and through the trees to Philipsburg, where the valley opened up on the Sapphire Mountains and the John Longs. As they drove, the creek stayed to their right, and Fran kept her head turned sideways—probably, Nelson imagined, catching glimpses of the icy water.

"It looks empty, doesn't it?" Fran said, not specifying anything.

They hadn't seen any other cars except the one outside the lodge. "It's more of a summer place," Nelson said, and saying so made him wonder why they'd both been so hooked on going here in January.

"It's very private." Fran's tone softened noticeably. She shifted her knees toward him, and Nelson bristled. If he could tell her how he really felt, he would tell her that right now he was only looking for someone to listen.

"We're about there," he said, and they drove a few more minutes in silence, up a straight stretch of road with fields on either side, then around a bend to the left away from the creek and into the trees, then back to the right toward the creek and another field. There, on the left, with its deep front porch and log front steps and oval window centered in the second story—the same stained-glass eagle spreading its wings in blues and golds—was Fran's old family house.

"They got rid of the fire pit," Nelson said. He recalled a substantial ring of rocks to the left of the porch.

"No one's home." Fran had already unclicked her seatbelt. Nelson watched her trudge through the snow. Her arms swung at her sides the way they had when she'd demonstrated power walking around the perimeter of Liberty's bar. Nelson had thought she'd looked like a soldier minus the gun. Now she went right up the steps—slower on the steps, both hands on the banisters—and pressed her nose to all the windows before making her way around the back side of the house.

Nelson got out of the car himself. "Fran," he said. "Frannie." But she was out of earshot. He went up on the porch, nervous about the footprints they were leaving in the snow, and found Fran's nose smudges on the windows. He wiped them off. He didn't peer in the windows himself. Instead, he looked at the view off the front porch—the same view that had always been there, of the crossbuck fence and the ponderosas and the creek snaking along the side of the road—and thought that maybe the reason people changed and places didn't was that people knew, every day, they were going to die. It wasn't something he'd thought about before, but the moment the thought hit him, it struck him as unfair.

"Look what I found," Fran said, coming around the corner. She came up the steps and gave Nelson what she was holding, then brushed off the top step but didn't sit.

It was a heart-shaped piece of flint. You could find them along a river's edge or on the bald top of a mountain. They had sharp points, and some of them were thin enough to snap in two. Nelson used to find them all the time. He'd give them to Fran. He turned over this one in his palm.

"How'd you find it?" he said. "In the snow."

"There's a screened porch now, too." Fran thumbed over her shoulder. "They have a collection."

"You went in?"

"It's just a screen door."

"You took this?"

"For you."

"That doesn't make a diff—"

"Nelson—"

"I'd like to give it to Hailey then," he said.

Fran stopped and looked at him like maybe she'd known him once. Then she reached over and took the flint out of his hand. "I'm giving it to *you*," she said.

"I don't need it," he said, which wasn't exactly what he meant.

"This isn't about need."

"Hailey could use it," he said. "She's—"

"It's a *rock*," Fran said.

"She's still got it all ahead of her," he said, which was more what he was getting at.

"Are you in love with her or something?" Fran held her hands out to her sides like Nelson better fill her up with an answer. That, or she was going to chuck the rock into the snow. He said nothing. Yes, he was in love with Hailey, you bet. A part of her. Same as he was in love with a part of Bethany and a part of Lou Ann and a part of Fran—the part of Fran that had crossed his path when they were more or less Hailey's age. The part of Hailey that saw there was more to him than a regular bowling game and a rusting brain. A part of each of them that had, at one time or another, listened to him.

"Are you going to give it to me or not?" he said.

"So now you don't care that I took it?"

"I'd like to give her something," he said.

"I'd like to give *you* something, Nelson." Fran held up the flint the way the priests in Havre held up Communion wafers—the thought of which felt dreamlike to Nelson, since he hadn't gone to church in decades. "Did you ever think of that?" Fran said. "I'd like to give you something for saving me."

"I didn't do anything anybody else wouldn't of," he said. Hailey had quoted him saying so in the paper.

"Yes, you *did*, Nelson," Fran protested. "Stop saying you didn't *do* anything when you're the only person who saved my life—"

"Frannie, I'm not—"

"This is about you and me, Nelson. It's not about anybody else."

Nelson looked at her blankly. He felt guilty for leading them to this point and then finding himself in such a different place from her. For an instant, he wondered if it was only possible to fall in love with a person—to really fall in love—when you were too young to know any better.

"For this whole day, anyway," she said.

He wondered if God gave people who died before their time a special wisdom. But Nelson was one of the few in their group who skipped church Sunday mornings. He preferred to cook eggs or do a painting. The crossword was out of the question, and the church in Havre was always chilly, even in the summer.

Still.

"Do you think you can, Nelson?" Fran was saying. He'd missed wherever she was coming from.

"Do you remember Nichol Aiken?" he said then.

Fran stopped. She squinted at the flint in her hand as if, even though she didn't want to, she had to give up. As if you couldn't keep on talking about love and fun once someone else brought up tragedy.

"Of course," she said.

She handed Nelson the flint and sat down on the top step. He went and sat beside her. The porch was cold but not soaking. It was a whiskey-coffee day. Nichol Aiken was the boy who'd gone missing up Rock Creek the summer Nelson and Fran started dating. People had searched for him for days, but all they found were bears, and Nichol Aiken's drop point knife, and a mountain lion. Though Nelson doubted anyone had actually *seen* a mountain lion. You knew they were there, but . . .

"Was he in his twenties?" Nelson said.

"Nineteen," Fran said.

"I knew it was something like that."

Not that plenty of people didn't go missing every summer—hiking alone, swimming a river too high, some of them *trying* to disappear—but only Nichol Aiken went missing practically out their backyard the summer he and Fran were head over heels and searching the woods without proper shoes and only a handful of chewing-gum wrappers to trace their path.

"Do you think he died?" Nelson asked.

"They ran his obituary in the paper," Fran said.

Nelson had always held out half a hope that Nichol Aiken was one of those ones who wanted to disappear. Not that Nelson knew the first thing about him, but it had always seemed to him a possibly perfect ending, to find your own crack to slip through.

"They spelled his name wrong," Fran said. "Remember? They spelled it like the coin?"

"Newspapers don't always get things right," Nelson said.

"They get if a person's alive or dead," she said.

"The part about you and me," he said. He didn't regret saying it. It was something he needed to say. "I don't know why I said that part."

"I do," she said.

"Listen," he said, but then stopped.

She put her hand on his back. "You're mixed up right now, same as I am. Neither one of us has ever been through anything like this before." She was rubbing his shoulder blades. "I've been so mixed up, I've been afraid of everything."

"You have?"

"You don't know," she said. "I won't go near any meat on bones, or the phone if there's a storm, or railroad tracks—"

"Railroad tracks?"

"What if those red bulbs went out?" she said. "What if they forgot to put the arm down?"

"That's not what I mean," said Nelson.

Fran looked to the ground. "Should we try to enjoy ourselves?" she asked uncertainly. "Before we freeze?"

And, sure, that had been the original idea, but now it no longer seemed simple to Nelson. Now he doubted that any two people ever really understood each other, and yet he couldn't bring himself to give up trying. There was this twisting inside his brain, and he thought maybe if he could tell someone else about it, he might loosen up enough to breathe easy a minute and remember who he was. Not that Fran was his perfect audience, he knew that, but she was his only audience. She had been there for his best, and now she wasn't off base—they were in this thing together. And even if they were in this thing on their own, sometimes in life you needed help from a person, even a total stranger.

"I'm not sure I knew what I was doing," Nelson said. "When I said that to Hailey. I think I might of thought it was a long time ago."

Fran nodded gently. "I know," she said. She reached out and held onto his arm. She squeezed it three times—*I. Love. You.*—like she used to when they were together. "I know." Then she let go of him and let out a sigh that sounded like she was going to cry. "I do wish you thought those things today," she said. "That's what I was hoping." She closed her eyes and took two deep breaths. "But we'll get through this, Nelson, whether we can fix it or not."

Nelson nodded, though he didn't feel much better. "Okay," he said. He felt embarrassed for not being the person Fran had always known. "Sometimes things get fuzzy," he said, in apology.

Fran let her chin fall to her chest, and the way she didn't meet his eyes, he saw that he was repeating something she'd known all along. He felt his cheeks flush hot. He remembered the day she'd worn a new denim skirt when they'd hiked Kootenai Canyon. Nelson had worried she would get it dirty, but she hadn't even blinked when they crossed the creek and got it soaked at the hem.

"I am here for you," Fran said again, and Nelson didn't know what to say. He felt silly for worrying that she'd been thinking about romance, when all this time she'd been wondering if he was fixable. How many of them had been wondering this, and for how long? It was too embarrassing to think about. And the best he could backtrack through what Fran had been saying, he realized her thought was that he couldn't be. Fixed. That this was the way it was going to be.

"I'm okay," he said to her, because suddenly the thought of being anything else was unbearable.

"We can do anything," Fran said. "If we think about what's best. I could come stay with you—"

Nelson squared his shoulders so abruptly, she stopped.

"Or come by some days," she said more quietly. "Maybe for dinners. Or errands. Or—"

"Stop," he said sharply, shaking his head. "Just stop." He didn't mean to sound stern, but he was mortified. He was scared. The whole group must have been thinking about this for some time: Jim passing off Nelson's lie in the paper as a joke he'd intended; Bethany whispering to Hailey after he'd planted that kiss; Hailey telling Bethany about Nelson in the newspaper office on a Saturday. Would she have told that? Would she have done that to him? And had one of his friends asked Fran to talk to him, or had she decided to on her own? When Nelson looked at her, he could see he'd hurt her feelings, and all he could think was that he should have spent the day at home, alone.

Then Fran was prying the piece of flint out of his hands. He had gripped its rough edges so hard there were purple indents in the palms of his hands.

"I'm sorry that I started all of this," he said. "I should of said no to the newspaper in the first place."

Fran smiled a sad smile and pressed the flint between her own palms. "It's okay," she said. "It's all going to be okay." Then she gave a small laugh like she honestly was happy about whatever had just occurred to her. "Whatever you said and whyever you said it," she said, "it came from inside you."

Nelson didn't smile back. "I suppose," he said. He recalled the morning of his interview, his own awkwardness and Hailey's calm voice telling about her mother's perfume. And then he said, "I think she liked it. What I told her."

Fran waited with her mouth half open, and even though Nelson could see he was saying the wrong thing for this moment, it seemed preferable to talking anymore about how far gone he might be. It made him consider, all things being relative, that talking to Hailey was one of the last best things he had done.

"I might of known she would," he said.

"Hailey?" Fran lost her soft tone.

"Frannie," he said.

"I wish you'd been thinking that *I* would like it."

Nelson cringed. He looked out to the lodgepoles and the ponderosas, their limbs sagging—but beautifully, he thought—under the snow.

"You *kissed* her," she said.

"I didn't mean it like that," he said.

"What did you mean it like?" she said.

Which was what he'd been trying to explain, if she'd been listening. If she hadn't been so wound up with horoscopes and heart-shaped rocks and now getting her ruff up about a girl a fraction of their age, who shared no history with him. It was Fran who shared his history. She was the one who kept him on the dance floor when everyone else went for the buffet, who burned a hole through a can of peanuts while they talked all night, and who thought they might find Nichol Aiken over one more hill. Nelson had a whole history there in Fran, a million stories that had almost wrapped up with a chicken bone, a nonsense ending, and that's why he'd kissed Hailey, with the whole group watching, with Bethany and Fran and Jim, and Sandy out front who looked like Lou Ann, and Alastair gazing in the wrong direction, and none of them talking about how many days they might have left, not when they're all together at the same table having a good time. He kissed Hailey because they were all together at that table having a good time, even if they were each going to end up packed too tight with their own stories, even if kissing Hailey didn't make any sense. His head was getting tighter all the time. Tighter and fuzzier at once, and he didn't know how you explained that. How could you tell this beautiful woman beside you that as much as you loved to dance with her, and hold on to her, you could see into the future to a day when her skin wasn't clear and creamy? When you'd lost your own ability to take care of her? How could you tell her you knew that even though you were having fun today, in the end you were going to end up looking past each other, talking in different directions, on your own?

There was this day right now, though.

"Time for whiskey coffees," he said, standing up. He went for the door.

"Nelson?" Fran watched him.

"You want the thermos?" he said. He was startled to find the door was locked. Fran's family always left the door open, usually ajar. Suddenly he felt the cold air all over him, like something waking him up. "Oh," he said, staring at his veiny hand on the knob. "That's what we used to do," he heard his own voice saying. "I was joking."

"Come sit with me," Fran said. "Come sit."

And when he sat, she stopped talking about Hailey. Her voice became soft. "Let's sit here. Let's stay here a few more minutes," she said.

Nelson moved in so close his hip was touching hers, and after a minute

Fran leaned into him and rested her head in his lap. She closed her eyes, and Nelson was comforted by the weight of her head. It made him feel like he was trusted. He stroked Fran's hair and was surprised, happily, when she didn't stop him. From what he understood, it cost a fair amount to have hair done. He ran his fingers from her forehead to the base of her skull, and her hair was so fine it almost made him sad. He noticed that her face had a sad look about it, too, resting there, but he decided that was because her eyes were closed. Except, the longer he sat there looking out to the crossbuck fence and the gravel road and the churning creek, the sadder he felt himself. And so he tried Fran's trick. He closed his eyes, and he took two deep breaths, and he stopped his mind at the point it had traveled right then, which was to where he'd figured out that Nichol Aiken must be dead, because at some time or another you always returned to the place that you were from, even if it wasn't the way you remembered it, and Nichol Aiken had not done that. He had never turned up anywhere.

Nelson opened his eyes. It was the same view it had always been, but nothing felt the same. "I bet they make a whiskey coffee at the lodge," he said.

Fran opened her eyes, too. She looked up at Nelson like she was working her way out of a dream. He ran his fingers along Fran's cheekbones to her temples, then down along her jaw and her throat to her collarbone under her sweater. She felt thin as a bird, but she was all there. Bone for bone. With him. When he ran his hand back up to her cheek and cupped it, she smiled a slow smile that pressed into his palm, and Nelson decided right then that he would learn to paint a face if it was the last thing he did. Fran gave a happy sigh, like she approved of the idea, or like she was letting him know that some packed-away part of her still loved some packed-away part of him.

If a crack had opened in the earth right then, Nelson might have taken it.

When Fran offered to drive to the lodge, Nelson let her. She drove even slower than he had, right down the middle of the road. There were no other cars, so he didn't say anything. He looked out his window and wondered if it had been hard for Fran to see her parents' old place, and how many other people had lived in there since her family had sold. Then he wondered how big Nichol Aiken's family was, and if they had kept their house or sold it after he disappeared. Nelson couldn't remember. He started to ask Fran if she might know, but decided it didn't make much difference either way.

"What?" she said.

"I was just thinking," Nelson said. "Nichol Aiken would be in his fifties by now."

"Oh," she said, and she sounded put off.

"Remember the card table his parents set up in their driveway the first day? Remember the coffee and the lemonade, and those cinnamon pastries someone said they brought all the way from Clinton?"

"It was terrible," Fran said.

"There was that big map on the table that Mrs. Aiken kept going over and over with whoever came by, and she was handing out flashlights." Not that it would change anything, but Nelson felt like he was on a roll. "And the other children were in the house, but you could see them looking out the window. Do you remember?"

"Nelson." Fran's voice was flat.

"We were all standing around in the driveway trying not to say what was on our minds, trying to come up with something good to say. We'd been out hiking since before breakfast. Do you remember how hungry we were?"

"Please," Fran said.

"And the look on Mr. Aiken's face?"

She didn't respond. She picked up speed.

"I'll never forget that," Nelson said. "He was sitting in the lawn chair holding his knees, and he had a look in his eyes like he wasn't there. His body was just sitting there, and he still had on his shirt from work."

"That's enough," Fran said. "I don't want to think about it, Nelson. It's a horrible thing to think about."

But Nelson felt energized, if anything. "I haven't thought about it in so long, I feel like we could get out of this car, and Nichol Aiken could still be out there. We could find him and all go back to the house for pastries, and Mr. Aiken could get back to work." Nelson nodded, like he saw it all unfolding. He was talking fast. "Nichol Aiken could be sixty by now," he said. "He could have a family of his own." He looked out the windshield, then craned behind him, looking out the back window in time to see a plume of smoke rising up from a chimney behind them. The last bit of RISING VIEW lettering disappeared out of sight. "Oh," he said, and for a moment time stood still. The gray sky wrapped all around him. He wasn't sure if what he felt was loneliness or confusion, or just the last bits of something precious slipping between his fingers. Then he looked at Fran and nodded. "That's okay," he said. "I'm okay. I'm not that hungry anyway. It's probably best if we get home."

Fran looked at him nervously. "I think so," she said.

He didn't blame her. He wished the day had gone differently, but like she'd said, some things could be helped and some things couldn't.

"I could come home with you, though," she said. "I mean it."

Nelson nodded, not to say yes but to acknowledge that he understood what she was offering. It had nothing to do with romance. It was about being friends, and the fact that if something happened to him—if he got lost or keeled over and they were way up Rock Creek in January—Fran wouldn't be equipped to save him. Nelson understood that, and also how he must be worrying her.

"Just say so," she said.

At home, she could at least be quick to call a doctor, or call the police, or get him the help he needed. He knew that was how she was thinking, but he didn't want to talk about it. He wanted to be home at his kitchen table with the crossword. In the dimming winter light, he reached out and touched Fran's hair, and he wondered what good he might still be to her. He wondered if the world would be any different if Nichol Aiken had lived to be sixty, and if he himself would be found, should he one day wander off.

CHAPTER 10

★

Bethany

Bethany got the call at half past three. She was driving Alastair back from Carmine's Classic Haircuts and almost didn't answer. Only her daughter Lonnie and Nelson had her cell number—Lonnie had given her the phone last year for emergencies—and most of the calls she got were from teenagers who'd dialed wrong. They never said hello, just started talking, as if they existed inside her phone chatting around the clock. Bethany disliked the very idea of cell phones. She didn't think of hers as something that even belonged to her.

"Yes," she said into the receiver.

She heard a breath on the other end of the line. A hesitation.

"Lonnie?"

"Excuse me?" It was an older woman's voice, but not one Bethany recognized. "Is this Bethany Lane?"

"Who is this?" she asked.

Alastair turned in her direction.

"My name is Pearl Armstrong." The woman's voice was trembly.

"I don't know any Pearls," said Bethany.

"No," the woman said. "I don't know you either. But do you know a Nichol—I'm sorry, a Nelson Moore?"

Bethany pulled over.

"Is something wrong?" Alastair asked.

"I don't know." Bethany shoved the transmission into park. "I think so."

"Excuse me?" came the woman's voice through the phone.

"Yes," Bethany said. "I'm sorry, I'm—" She was furious at herself, is what she was. "Yes, I know him."

This was what she got for looking the other way. For letting Nelson go to Rock Creek. For not keeping him under her thumb every second of the day.

"I have him here," the woman said. "At my house. He was coming around with a clipboard, and he's out on the front stoop. He looks all right, but he doesn't seem to know—"

"I'll be right there," Bethany said. "Where do I find you?"

Pearl Armstrong told her 112 Fitch, a blue house with a white front door and a piece of farm equipment in the yard. It was a decorative piece, she said, and Bethany nearly laughed at the absurdity of what people chose to say and not to say.

"You'll see a big wheel," Pearl said.

"I know the street," Bethany said. As if she wouldn't be able to find a house anywhere in town after forty-three years. As if she would need a piece of farm equipment to locate 112 Fitch when Nelson was planted on the doorstep, worrying himself and Pearl Armstrong to death.

"And there's a boy with him," Pearl added.

"A *boy*?" Bethany leaned into the gas pedal, and adrenaline spiked through her fingertips.

"A young boy." Pearl's voice was wary. "I have him with me. I don't know his name."

"Tell me he's fine." Bethany didn't recognize her own voice, it was so low and rough with fear. "Please tell me that."

"Yes," Pearl said. "He's fine."

"Okay," Bethany said.

"But there must be people looking for him." Pearl took a deep breath, like she was short of air. "They don't seem to know each other."

"I'm almost there," Bethany said, and she snapped shut her phone. She tossed it into the passenger seat, forgetting Alastair was there, and he flinched as it landed in his lap.

"Oh, Alastair—"

"Don't worry," he said. "I'll hold onto it." He clapped both hands around the phone and squeezed it between his palms. "It *is* Nelson."

Bethany nodded and then realized her mistake. "Yes," she said. "It's Nelson."

Alastair nodded, too. He turned toward his window, and for a moment Bethany imagined that he could see their surroundings—the shoveled sidewalks and the lined-up bungalows painted all different colors, but looking their shabbiest in winter. What a coincidence, she thought, that Alastair should be the one with her when this call finally came. Again, she felt ashamed for believing that telling a blind man a secret was less of a betrayal than telling a seeing person the same thing, and yet that remained her thought: A blind man was more likely to keep the secret, because he already understood what it was like to live every minute with the consequences of loss.

But then Alastair said, "It's probably for the best. To get it out in the open."

Bethany's grip slipped on the steering wheel, and she realized her palms were damp with perspiration. She dried them one at a time against her thighs, digging her nails into her wool slacks as if she were punishing herself for being the kind of person she was, the kind of coward who said nothing until it was too late. "I can't—" she started. "She said he is all right."

Alastair kept nodding slowly. "That's good," he said. "He was getting signatures for the Fivemile?"

"That's what he said this morning." Bethany's voice wavered. "He called me first thing. He always calls me first thing."

"It's not your fault," Alastair said.

"He has a *boy* with him? My god, Alastair—"

"And she said he is okay, too, didn't she?"

Bethany was crying. She didn't actually feel herself crying, but there were tears on her cheeks, and so she knew she was. "It *is* my fault."

"No." He fumbled for Bethany's shoulder. "This is something that happens."

"I didn't want to go behind Nelson's back," she said. "I only told you—"

"Any of us could have said something," he said.

"—and Hailey."

"It's okay," Alastair said.

"I mean, my god, he *kissed* her." Bethany clenched her slacks.

"Bethany," said Alastair.

"Yes?"

"Any of us could have said something."

"Is that right?" She looked to him, sadly hopeful. Suddenly she wanted to know exactly what everyone else had been thinking about Nelson, and when. She didn't want to think things might have been different if she hadn't brushed Fran off that day at the alley. "I wanted to be good to him," she said, but she heard how that was giving herself too much credit. She tightened her grip on the wheel. "I didn't want to face it," she admitted. "I didn't want this to be happening."

"No," Alastair said. "Of course not." His hands were in his lap, and Bethany noticed he was wearing his black dress pants with a crisp white collar poking out from his navy sweater. He looked proudly put together. "You want to do your best," he said. "But sometimes it's hard to know what that is."

Bethany wanted to ask if he was speaking generally, or about her. She *did* always want to do her best by Nelson, but she had other lives to juggle, too, including her own. She looked at Alastair. His head was cocked and his brow creased as if he were in fact seeing something, and it crossed her mind that maybe he *was* catching something she didn't see—that maybe he knew something about what was going to happen to Nelson that she didn't. She appreciated the sense it gave her that she didn't have to be the only one, right now, coming up with all the answers.

She turned left on Fitch, drove two blocks, and there was the blue house and the white door and the big old rusted farm gizmo. And there, on the front steps with his back straight and his knees pushed together, was Nelson.

She pulled up to the curb outside Pearl Armstrong's house. Alastair sat quietly beside her. Bethany was hollow. She was flat-out sad this day had come.

The worst part was, Nelson lit up when he saw her get out of the car. "Hi, baby," he said. It was what he always said, and there'd been a time she'd loved to hear it, but this time he sounded like he was only trying to be brave. His eyes looked bigger than usual, like he was seeing something extraordinary.

"Hi, Nelson," Bethany said. She glanced at his bare hands holding on to the clipboard. "Aren't you getting cold out here?" Her own voice trembled.

"It's cold," he said. "I'm sorry you had to come all this way."

"We're right in town," she said. "You'll be in the tub in fifteen minutes." It was something she might have said to one of her children, decades ago.

"Okay," he said. She was in front of him, but he didn't stand up. "I don't know what happened," he said. "I'm a little turned around."

"Why don't you get in the car," she said.

"Okay," he said, but he didn't move. He held the clipboard stiffly a few inches off his knees, while Pearl Armstrong appeared in the doorway. First she looked at Bethany through the screen door, and then she pushed the door open. She was a tiny woman in a green sweat suit and brown slippers. Bethany counted five purple clips in her white hair, like she'd brushed past a lilac bush and knocked off the blossoms. Behind her, on the floor, sat a small boy wearing a striped sweater and dungarees. He was playing with one of those beanbag draft stoppers in the shape of a dachshund.

Pearl looked from Bethany to Nelson with a frosty attentiveness. She was so tiny, Bethany could see how this whole incident must have frightened her.

Bethany herself felt frightened.

"I'm Bethany Lane," she said to Pearl. "Thank you very much for calling. I'm very sorry about this."

"He doesn't know where he is," Pearl Armstrong said, like Nelson wasn't there.

Bethany nodded. "Yes," she said, though she was resisting the moment. The boy *did* look fine to her.

"And we need to find the boy's parents," Pearl said.

"Yes." Bethany felt numb. She was having a hard time thinking what to do. "Do you mind if I ask how you got my number?"

"From the sign-up sheet." Pearl pointed at Nelson, then checked on the boy. "He's getting signatures?"

Bethany had forgotten that when Nelson had pestered her into putting down her name to save the Fivemile, she'd written her cell number specifically so no one would call her at home. She'd omitted her address altogether. Now she looked over Nelson's shoulder and saw he had a full page of names. He must have been wandering around for some time, and the thought brought her almost to tears.

"I called some others first," Pearl said.

Bethany looked at her. She wondered if Pearl would invite her in, but Pearl didn't seem to have the inclination.

"None of them knew him," Pearl said. "That is, they didn't know him personally. They remembered him. They all had different stories."

"About Nelson?" Bethany bristled.

"One of them called the police."

Bethany glanced down at Nelson. She knew they shouldn't be talking like this, right here, but Nelson appeared to be vacant. He appeared to be focused on sitting straight, on pressing his knees together.

"We should get you in the car," she said to him, but he gave no response. She didn't want to ask Pearl when or where these police had been called, or at what point along the way Nelson had found this boy. She wondered if Hailey, as a newspaper person, might know anything about getting around the cops.

"What did they say?" Bethany asked, meaning all these *people*.

"My husband went the same way," Pearl answered.

"He's not my husband."

"So I didn't call the police." Again, Pearl looked to the boy.

Bethany felt her throat tighten. "Thank you," she said. She let her arms go limp at her sides and looked at Pearl in surrender. "I'll take care of this," she said. "But—could you explain to me what happened?"

Pearl nodded. She waved Bethany inside the door, folded her arms across her chest, and bowed her head so Bethany got a better look at those purple clips. They were actually butterflies. Then she told Bethany she had started with the top name on the page, Dennis Frank. He was a nice man who didn't know Nelson but had enjoyed the Fivemile enough to sign the petition and agree to attend the protest. He told Pearl that Nelson had seemed like a stand-up guy to him. A little distracted, maybe, but it was no easy task to knock on a stranger's door. And so Pearl skipped a few names down. Andrea Mason and Dot Livingston both agreed Nelson was polite, though Andrea said she'd been confused when he'd asked how to get to Maple Street, when Maple was the street he was on. Pearl kept on calling, and it was near the middle of the list where things went wonky. She got ahold of Marybeth Short and asked her if a man had recently stopped by to save the Fivemile, and Marybeth said no, but that was funny, some man had come by about a missing boy. She was still calling around to learn more about it. She asked if Pearl knew who this missing boy was, and what on earth her signature had to do with anything. Then Pearl made two more calls, no answers, before finally reaching Deanna Young, who remembered the boy's name—Nichol Aiken, a name Pearl didn't know. Deanna said the man was looking around a lot while he told her some kind of freak camping story, and not that it mattered, she said, but she herself would never set out camping this time of year. You'd have to be crazy. So Pearl went on down the list, reaching a young girl who signed up to find Nichol Aiken. Then the next woman Pearl reached said, no, what had happened was a man had shown up and introduced *himself* as Nichol Aiken, but she hadn't gotten a good feeling about him, there was something funny in his eyes, and she'd shut the door. For a moment, Pearl *had* considered calling the police herself. Only just as she was debating it, her phone rang, and it was the young girl's mother. She'd gotten Pearl's number off caller ID, and she wanted to know what Pearl was doing, calling her daughter, talking about Nichol Aiken, who'd been dead thirty-some years. She told Pearl she had called the police on Nelson. She wanted to know—in a rude tone of voice, mind you—exactly who Pearl was and what this man had said to her. And that was the strange part, Pearl said to Bethany. She unfolded her arms and opened her palms. Nelson had never mentioned the Fivemile to her. He'd never mentioned Nichol Aiken either. He'd just told her his name was Nelson Moore, and he was lost, and this young boy had found him.

"Could we have a moment?" Bethany asked Pearl when she was through.

"Of course," Pearl said, touching the clips in her hair.

"None of them mentioned the boy?" Bethany added. "Who you called?"

Pearl shook her head. "They must have met up right at the end. His hands weren't too cold when I brought him in. But those parents—"

Bethany stepped back outside and put her hand on Nelson's shoulder. He reached up and put his hand over hers. "You ready to go, handsome?" she said.

"Not yet," he said.

"How about very soon, though?" she said. "Before my behind freezes over."

Nelson smiled but said nothing. Bethany joined him sitting on the doorstep. She tried to take the clipboard from him, but he wouldn't let go.

"I'd just like a few more minutes," Nelson said to all of them. He lifted his clipboard. "A few more minutes and I should have it all added up."

Bethany put her arm around Nelson. He was staring at his clipboard. She was wondering if she should ask him what, exactly, he was trying to add up, but decided not to. She decided that the real Nelson, the old Nelson, wouldn't want her to. He'd rather they told some jokes, or talked about the headlines, or went for milkshakes at the café in Ravalli. Nelson would take a milkshake anytime. He was a good driver, too. And he cared about the people around him, about who was warm enough, and who had a full beer, and who might need a little boost. Those were the things Bethany liked about Nelson, and she knew that Nelson wouldn't want to talk about any of this. Bethany would have done anything to be able to call that Nelson up and tell him to come on home.

"I am sorry," he said.

"I don't know why," she said right back.

He rolled his eyes at her, something she couldn't remember him ever doing before.

"Nelson," she said.

"No," he said. "Hang on a minute. You came all the way out here, and I mean it. Some things are clear and some things aren't, but what I want to say is I've been thinking it over, and I don't believe I've treated you well."

That wasn't what she expected. Certainly she hadn't expected Fran to announce their Rock Creek trip to the whole table, either, but who cared about any of that now. She wondered if Nelson even knew there was a little boy inside.

"That's not true," she said.

"We've known each other a long time," he said.

"Yes," she said. "And sometimes I haven't done things the way I should have done either. Alastair and I were talking about that in the car. That's the way it goes."

Nelson grew quiet, and Bethany thought maybe she shouldn't have mentioned Alastair. Maybe that made things more confusing than they needed to be. "We've treated each other fine," she said.

Nelson scanned his long list one more time, and, when it was apparent he couldn't find what he wanted, he handed the clipboard to Bethany. "I hope so," he said.

Bethany turned the clipboard upside down in her lap. She moved her hand from Nelson's shoulder to his back and rubbed some warmth into him. Then she leaned over and kissed him on the cheek—his cold red cheek—right as the police car pulled up.

"Oh, no," Bethany said under her breath.

"Did I do something?" said Nelson.

"No," she said. "Don't say that. You haven't done anything at all."

"I'd like to go home," he said.

And at that, Bethany felt a real chill run through her. Assuming they got past this cop part, what was she supposed to do—what were they all supposed to do now—about returning Nelson to his Burr Street house, alone?

"Good afternoon," the officer said. He walked toward them, his whole uniform clanking with gear.

"It is," Bethany said quickly. "It's nearly evening, and we don't even need gloves." Which was an out-and-out lie, of course, but why else would two old people be lounging on a stoop, at the end of January, with the sun going down?

The officer was staring at Nelson. Bethany wished Nelson would wipe off that wide-eyed look; it did make him seem up to something. The officer wore gloves that they probably made all police officers wear. All police officers were exactly alike, Bethany thought. The state trooper who came to tell her about her daughter's wreck had the same look as this one, close-cropped and clanking and stuffed tight into his clothes, except with a different color uniform. They probably got haircuts every day, these cops. If the one who'd come to her door in the middle of the night had at least sounded like he was talking for himself instead of reading off a form—that might have made a difference. Then she might have thought cops came with brains in their heads, like human beings.

As it was, Bethany didn't warm up to any of them.

"Is this your home?" the cop asked.

"No," Bethany said, all smiles. "This house belongs to our friend Pearl Armstrong. We're here—"

"I'm Pearl Armstrong," Pearl said from behind them. Bethany had assumed she'd stepped inside, but instead Pearl remained there on the threshold. "This is my house." She stepped outside to meet the officer and pulled the door mostly shut behind her. "Who's that?"

Bethany looked up to see Pearl looking past the officer, across the lawn to Alastair, who was getting out of the car. He looked sharp in his black pants and his navy sweater, his white hair neatly combed.

"It's okay," Bethany called nervously to Alastair. "You can leave the heat running."

"Is everything all right?" he said across the lawn. "Do you need a hand, Bethany?"

She wished he hadn't used her name. She didn't have an easy answer to either of his questions, and so instead she whispered to Pearl and the officer, "He's blind."

"He's been in the car?" Pearl let go of the doorknob.

"We'll just be a few more minutes," Bethany called to Alastair.

The officer was staring at her.

"This whole time?" said Pearl.

"That's fine," Alastair said.

"Wait right there." Pearl came down the steps and crunched through the snow in her slippers. "I'm Pearl Armstrong," she said as she approached Alastair, and Bethany prayed the little boy inside was sitting contentedly and wouldn't follow. "And this is my house," Pearl was saying. "There's a curb right there." She took his elbow. "We're drinking hot chocolate in the kitchen."

At that, the officer looked to the front door. He raised his eyebrows, and as he turned his back on Bethany and Nelson, he lifted a radio from his belt. He spoke into it too quietly for Bethany to hear, but when he turned around and eyed the clipboard in Bethany's lap, she knew they were in trouble.

As Alastair and Pearl approached the stoop, the officer stepped back to make way for them. Bethany figured she had one breath, maybe two, to make a decision.

"Hello," Alastair said to all of them, though he found Nelson's shoulder and tapped it. "Come on inside if you get cold, old boy."

"I've got on my lined flannel under this," Nelson said.

Bethany thanked God Alastair hadn't used Nelson's name. She wasn't sure what the penalties were for lying to an officer, especially one who most likely assumed there was a little boy attached to that hot chocolate in the kitchen, but she also knew you couldn't waffle in moments like these. She wasn't free of blame that they'd ended up here, and now her number-one concern was that Nelson get out safely. By which she meant that he get out with his pride.

"We're visiting from Coeur d'Alene." Bethany went ahead. "Pearl's late husband and my husband worked together out at the mill before you were born," she said to the officer. "But we sold our house after he retired." She nudged Nelson.

"I was a saw sharpener," Nelson said.

Bethany glanced at him, her wide-eyed husband, and thanked God a second time that Stu Larsen had worked as a saw sharpener in the seventies and, to this day, sat around talking like it was the best job going.

"Is there something we can do for you?" Bethany asked. "Is there something going on?"

For a second, the officer acted amused, the way some people got around old people—which wasn't the way Bethany thought of herself, as an old person, but sometimes you had to play that card.

"We're looking for an older gentleman—excuse me," said the officer. "We have a report of a man approaching homes in this neighborhood."

Bethany looked appropriately alarmed.

"We also have a report of a missing boy."

She sat up straight as if to look around. She stared blank-faced at the officer. "Well, which one is it?" she asked. "Which one is true?"

The officer looked irritated.

"Those are two very different reports," she said. "Aren't they? A man on the loose. A boy on the loose."

"Ma'am, kidnapping is a serious—"

"*Kidnapping?*" Bethany felt a surge of nausea in her belly. She never would have thought of this as *kidnapping*. She couldn't decide if this officer was laughable or terrifying, but she knew she needed to keep talking lest Nelson try to defend himself. "I suppose crime's up since we left," she said and worked to keep her voice even. She rubbed Nelson's knee. "You don't really hear about crime going down."

The officer didn't respond. He was staring at the clipboard in Bethany's lap. He'd said nothing about it, not yet, but she knew these police didn't just hit the streets looking for a man or looking for a boy. They went searching for a certain height and a certain hair color and certain clothes and whatnot. Sometimes they had a sketch.

Nelson had been marching all over creation with that clipboard.

Who knew how long he'd been marching around with this boy.

Bethany imagined she would check in with Hailey when all of this was said and done, for what it was worth.

"We have a granddaughter in town, lives in one of these first-floor deals," she pressed on. "Half the time you go over she's left the door unlocked. It makes you wonder."

"Everyone needs to lock their doors," the officer said. Was he entertaining her or listening to her? She wasn't sure.

"She works for the newspaper," Nelson said.

"Our granddaughter," Bethany said. She couldn't tell, either, if Nelson knew what he was doing. "You should see her." Her words were coming out as fast as she could make them up. "The way she talks to all these different people. She's getting married in July. Her mother is up to her ears in the guest list and she drug us into the whole thing." She raised the clipboard without turning it over.

The officer moved forward like he was going to have a look himself.

Bethany dropped the clipboard back in her lap and planted her elbows on it. "When we got married, you went on down to the courthouse and people brought over casseroles."

"She's going to make a knockout of a bride," said Nelson.

"He's a lucky young man," said Bethany.

"I'm working on a painting for her, but I don't want to talk about it." Nelson pushed a hand dismissively through the air.

Bethany looked at him, wary. Nelson shook his head, but Bethany thought she saw him smile.

"Did you hear about the married couple speeding down the interstate?" Nelson said then. He was addressing the cop. Bethany felt a thread of hope course through her. She had heard him tell this one before. It wasn't one of her favorites, and she was pretty sure the officer wouldn't love it, either, but she couldn't have cared less. She wouldn't have cared if Nelson was telling the one about the Hooters waitress to a priest. All that mattered was that Nelson was back from Lord knows where, telling one of his jokes.

The cop looked over his shoulder.

"It was their twenty-fifth wedding anniversary," said Nelson. "And they'd had their candlelight dinner down at the fancy restaurant, and now they were in a rush to get home, if you know what I mean."

"Honey." Bethany rubbed her shoulder into his. It was all she could do not to say his name.

"He knows what I mean," Nelson said. "This guy." He winked at the cop. "And then a siren comes on behind them, and they get pulled over, and the officer asks the husband for his license and his, you know—"

"Registration," Bethany said.

"Registration," Nelson repeated. "And the husband says, 'But, officer, I didn't do anything wrong.' And the officer says, 'Unless you call going a hundred miles per hour in a fifty-mile-per-hour zone doing something wrong.' And the officer starts to write the husband a ticket, and the husband starts running his mouth. He starts shouting and saying how he wasn't speeding and how the officer would be better off spending his time catching real-live criminals instead of harassing tax-paying, law-abiding citizens like his wife and himself, who are just out to celebrate twenty-five years married. 'Cops today,' he says. And the officer gets red in the face and leans down to the window. He's about to give the husband the third degree when the wife pipes in and says, 'Please excuse my husband, officer. He gets this way when he's been drinking.'"

Nelson looked the cop dead in the eye like he was sticking up for this couple, trying to live their lives.

Bethany wanted to applaud.

The cop didn't laugh. He bowed his head as if he was trying to conceal his pity, and if Bethany hadn't been holding the clipboard she would have stood up and poked her finger into his chest and said it was *she* who felt sorry for *him*. Poor Mr. Freshfaced Clanky Pants couldn't say he had any of what they had—so many years being there for each other you didn't blink about a bad joke or a trip up Rock Creek or a freezing afternoon in January when it was all you could do not to cry on a stranger's doorstep. You just bucked up and bullied on. You stood up and gave a goddamn standing ovation for every joke told start to finish.

Not that anyone in their group talked that way. More or less, they kept it clean.

"We've been married forty-five years," Nelson said.

"Well, I don't know about you," Bethany cut him short. "But I'm going to go warm up." Then she did stand and look the officer in the eye. She gave him her sweetest smile. There was no question to Bethany he didn't believe them, but what was he going to do? Challenge two old people who were telling him about their lives? He didn't know the first thing about being old. "Would you like something to drink?" she asked him.

Before he could answer, a second police car pulled up. And then, within seconds, from the opposite direction, a third. Their sirens weren't on, but their lights were flashing, and somehow the absence of sound, Bethany thought, made the moment more sinister. Also, it made it seem like things were happening in slow motion. The cruisers' doors all opened, and Bethany counted one, two, three, four officers get out. Three of them started across the lawn, while the fourth turned to give a hand to someone else getting out of the last cruiser. A woman in baggy sweatpants and a baggy sweatshirt scrambled from the car—her hair in a messy black ponytail, only sandals and socks on her feet—and it was her screaming that broke the silence. It was her yelling and her pointing at Nelson—*Is he the one? Where is my son?*—that made Bethany realize how real and terrible this was.

"Bethany," Nelson was saying to her.

"It's okay," she heard herself saying, the greatest lie she had ever told.

"Nelson Moore," the first officer said to him then.

"Bethany, I found him," Nelson said.

"My son wasn't *lost*," the young woman yelled. "Who *is* this man?"

"Can we talk to you?" the officer turned to Bethany as the other three gathered around. One of them held the woman as she continued to yell.

"Quiet," another officer said to her.

"*Don't* tell me to be—"

"That's enough," the officer said.

Bethany felt light-headed. Alastair came to the door. Pearl Armstrong followed. At her knee was the young boy. His mother lunged at him, crying and yelling at the cops. There were four of them. They were talking to Pearl, and Alastair, and the boy, and his mom. They were talking to her, too, but she had no idea, anymore, what to say. She was staring off to the street, to the three cruisers, two with lights flashing. The sun was setting, and the snow was rock gray, and the old piece of farm equipment looked like a skeleton propped up in the yard. She was freezing. Nelson must have been, too. He was standing still as stone, dazed, while the first cop was talking to him. As the time passed— so slowly, like clouds with no wind—Bethany was thinking that there was no way, ever, she would be able to erase this day from her mind.

Suddenly Nelson said, "Whitfield," out of the blue. Bethany turned away from the flashing lights. The cop stopped talking to Nelson and pursed his lips. Nelson was waving across the lawn. "What are you doing here?" he said.

And sure enough, coming across the lawn was someone else. A young man in canvas pants and a wool hat, a good-looking young man who definitely wasn't a cop. He was smiling, and Bethany wondered how the hell he fit into this picture.

"If you could hold off a minute, Nate," said another of the officers. "We're still sorting things out."

"Mr. Moore," the young man said to Nelson. He nodded at the cop who'd spoken to him. "It's nice to see you. A surprise to see you, but—"

"I'm not sure what's happened here, Whitfield," Nelson said. "I'm not sure how you tracked me down."

"You know him?" Bethany elbowed Nelson.

"No problem." The young man stood at the bottom of the stoop and held his hand out to Nelson. Nelson shook it. "I'm not going to get in the way of these officers," the young man said. "I get calls sometimes. It's part of my beat, so I came."

"Your what?" Nelson kept a grip on his hand.

"Just hang in there," Nate said.

"He took my *son*," shouted the woman.

"This is Nate Whitfield," Nelson said to Bethany. "This is Hailey's boyfriend."

Bethany looked at Nate, baffled. But in his navy parka and his leather boots, he appeared so normal, she thought, compared to the rest of them. The woman's sweatshirt was decorated with an airbrushed wolf, and a line of hair on her upper lip needed shaving. The boy stood beside her, his hands pulled up into his sweater.

Bethany watched Nate look at Nelson, then at the cops. For a second, Nate chewed his lip. Then he took a step toward the woman. "Where were you?" he asked her.

"*What?*" She took a step toward him, too, and put her hands on the elastic waist of her sweatpants. "What are you saying, where was *I?*"

"I don't know." Nate shrugged. "You tell me. He looks about three?"

"I found him," said Nelson. "Singing a song."

"Who *are* you?" The woman pointed a finger within a few inches of Nate's face.

"I'm Nate Whitfield," he said. "I'm a reporter with the *Free Press.*" He slid a pad from his back pocket. "So, were you at home, or—?"

"I don't have to talk to you," she said, taking her son's sleeve. "I don't have to say anything to any of you. This is a joke. You're all standing around doing jack shit." She waved an arm angrily at all of them. "This is a fucking joke," she said, and she pulled her son to follow her as they trudged toward the street.

"Ma'am." One of the officers went after her and caught a piece of baggy sweatshirt in his fingers. The woman batted his hand away. "Don't *touch* me," she snapped. The officer put both hands up by his chest, then slowly dropped them to encourage her to lower her voice. He lowered his voice, too, and Bethany could hardly make out what he was saying—about charges, about a ride home—but it didn't matter. The outcome was clear. After the officer had said his piece, the woman scooped her son into one arm and thrust her free hand high above her head, her middle finger jutting into the gray light for everyone to see. Like that, she disappeared down the sidewalk, her socked-and-sandaled feet skidding in the snow.

There was an embarrassed silence afterward. The officers shuffled around with a few more questions, and one made a couple of calls on his radio. By then it was dark, and with everyone safe and no harm done—at least on paper, at least as far as they were concerned—everyone was standing around exhausted. Except for Pearl and Alastair, Bethany noticed, who had disappeared some time ago. Nelson had stayed quietly beside her, holding her hand, and Nate had lingered, too, talking to Nelson about the Fivemile and other everyday things, which Bethany was grateful for. The officers were flipping pads shut and adjusting their clanking belts to get going when Nate asked,

"What song was he singing? Just out of curiosity?"

Nelson furrowed his brow.

"The boy," said Nate.

"Oh." Nelson lightened. He swung his head side to side like the melody was still in there. "It didn't have words," he said. "He was too young. It was just one of those tunes that goes up and down and up and down, and no one else will ever know what it's about except you could probably bet it involved a dog."

Nate laughed. Nelson did, too. The officers looked at Bethany and tilted their heads sympathetically before they turned to leave. One of them said something to the effect of, if she was in charge she needed to see that something was done so that nothing like this happened again—that this was a warning. It was all she could do not to say to him, Tell me something I don't know. Lucky for him, she was so tired she just thanked him and wished all of them a good night. As they disappeared into the darkness, Bethany listened to their clanking and their engines, and she watched the harsh, final flash of their silent lights before they were gone. A moment later, the small overhead light went on inside Nate's truck, and then he climbed in and gave a wave as he drove off. Bethany wished it was him she had thanked.

She drew in a long breath. She felt the cold air burn in her chest, and the hot tears nip at her eyes, and she blew the air from her lungs in a slow, easy twist of steam. In her mind, she was deciding between whiskey and wine.

"They were after me," Nelson said then. "Weren't they?"

Whiskey, she thought. A double.

"I got turned around," he said. "But I didn't do anything wrong to anybody." When he took the clipboard from her, she was astounded she still had it. "Did I?"

"No," she said.

He nodded. "That boy was in the street."

"You didn't do anything wrong."

"Okay." He knocked on the clipboard. "I got enough names, anyway," he said. "For that bar way out there." He ran his hands over his face, then cupped them over his mouth and blew warm air. Once. Twice. A third long breath. "We're right in town," he said. "I know that. I just needed some time."

Bethany doubted he'd been adding up the names all this time, but it was a possibility. How many did he need, she wondered, to save the Fivemile? Would it make a difference to any of them if they did save the Fivemile? Bethany couldn't say she cared. She was so sad from the whole awful afternoon that now she simply felt drained. Like there wasn't enough whiskey at the Fivemile or anywhere to set them all straight.

"Bethany," Alastair said.

She turned around, and Alastair was behind her, talking through the screen door.

"Where did you go?" she asked.

"Would you like a glass of wine?" he said.

Pearl sidled up next to him, purple blossoms in her hair, both of their faces blurred through the screen.

"Pearl and I were talking and—"

"I'd like a glass of wine," said Nelson.

"We were saying we could all go to my house. We were thinking maybe getting away from here and having a drink—"

"Yes," said Nelson.

"You read my mind," said Bethany.

"That's because Alastair has a sixth sense," said Pearl. "Like fish."

······ ★ ······

CHAPTER 11

Hailey

The editorial meeting hadn't gone well. Nate had forgotten to bring the weekly police blotter, from which he generated story ideas. Craig had told Hailey he was giving her one more chance with the Fivemile story before handing it over to a freelancer who had a tip that the county attorney had been seen having triple-drink lunches there before returning to work. The point was, Craig had told Hailey in front of the staff, she was once again being too soft. This was about politics, not heartstrings. *Newspapers aren't for lovers,* he'd said, and Hailey wondered how long he'd been waiting to use that line. The rest of the staff had laughed—except for Nate, that is—and so Hailey had gone ahead and said what she shouldn't have said, which was that there were no lovers in the articles she'd written. That part was a lie. Craig had gotten quiet, trying to see if she was kidding. But the arts editor Pitt had chimed in, "I could write a correction." He'd cleared his throat for effect. "Further investigation has shown that, contrary to earlier information, these two old timers *can't* get it on. The *Free Press* regrets the error." Craig had cracked up, and Nate had put his hand over Hailey's, and Hailey had thought, for the first time, about leaving the *Free Press.*

Outside, leaning up against the frosted front window of Loggers with Nate, she wondered if she would make it another year.

"You didn't really forget the blotter," she said to him.

He shook his head. "I threw it away."

She looked to the sidewalk where she and Nelson had stood a few weeks earlier. The blue chalk had almost completely faded.

"Thanks," she said, sliding toward Nate so that their hips touched. "Did it mention his name?"

"No," he said. "They only use names if there's an arrest. But it said, 'report of a man blah blah blah,' so—"

"Thanks," Hailey repeated.

"I thought Craig might get interested if he saw it. The way they ran Nelson's report back-to-back with the one about a missing boy, it didn't look good."

Hailey jammed the toe of her boot against the sidewalk. "It makes me sad," she said.

"It wasn't happy," Nate said.

Nate had told Hailey the whole story after he'd left Pearl Armstrong's. They'd ordered pizza at his place and talked their way through two bottles of wine. It was the most they'd ever talked outside of work—about Nelson, about getting old, about good parents and bad parents and who those cops should have been after in the first place—and though the one night wasn't enough for Hailey to go so far as to say she loved him, the accumulation of recent events did make her feel aligned with Nate in a way that she didn't care to hide. On his futon in front of his wood stove, they'd talked until the sky was lightening, and then they'd slept through Nate's alarm and shown up at work together, late.

"Craig was pissed, wasn't he?" Nate said about the meeting. It had been one of the shortest editorial meetings they'd ever had.

Hailey smiled. "He was."

"He's got one reporter showing up with almost no stories, and the other announcing she lied in hers." Nate cupped his hand over Hailey's head. "I guess he could fire you," he said.

Hailey shrugged. "If the story mattered to him." She pictured the cardinal walking in the street as she and Nelson ate their donuts. She lowered her voice to imitate Craig. "But what do I care about two old people screwing?"

Nate laughed, then sighed. He jutted his jaw forward for his own Craig imitation. "I only care if it's my reporters who are screwing," he said.

Hailey looked up at him. Broad cheeks, alive eyes. Maybe if she'd never met Nelson, she never would have felt so comfortable with Nate. "Let him wonder," she said. "I'm sick of him. The whole attitude in there." She chewed her thumbnail. "But I can't believe I really said that."

Nate looked at his watch. It wasn't unusual for any of the staff to end up at Loggers for an afternoon beer. "One?" He pushed off the front window and opened the door for her. "Craig can't afford to lose you," he said as Hailey walked past him. "But he probably knows you're going to quit."

She stopped short and Nate collided with her. "Whoa," he said.

"What do you mean?"

"There they are," a man's voice called from across the bar.

"You are thinking about it, aren't you?" Nate looked toward the voice.

Hailey grew quiet. Was she?

"Your whole *attitude*." Nate smiled at her.

"Hailey. Whitfield. Over here."

Hailey looked to the near end of the bar, and there were Nelson and Bethany sitting at the two stools closest to the wall. Nelson was waving to her. He was wearing a green cardigan over one of his plaid shirts, which made her think that Bethany had helped him dress. But otherwise he looked just like himself, like nothing was wrong with him at all. He was another man at the bar with his girlfriend. Bethany wore a paisley-patterned sweater with a brooch near the collar, and the two of them looked a little bit spiffed up, like they might have been on a date. For an instant, Hailey wondered if she had overblown what was happening to Nelson. He appeared so normal sitting there, which made her think that you never really knew, seeing a person, what was going on inside.

"We were looking for you," Nelson said as she and Nate got closer.

"The receptionist said you were in a meeting," Bethany said.

Nate smirked. Their "receptionist" was a high school intern whom Craig had recently asked to stop snapping her chewing gum in the office.

"And this seemed like a good place to wait," said Nelson. "I never come in here."

"You look great," said Hailey.

"Well, I'm moving out of my house." Nelson made a clucking sound with his cheek.

"Oh." Hailey gripped the high back of his stool.

"Because of all of this." He raised a hand toward his head but could have been gesturing to the world in general as much as his own mind.

Bethany leaned in. "We're having a party," she said, opening her purse. She withdrew two envelopes and handed them to Nate and Hailey. "At Nelson's house. To celebrate. We wanted to invite you."

"She won't call it a good-bye party," Nelson said.

"Because you're not leaving," Bethany said.

"Thank you," Hailey said, and Nate nodded, holding up his envelope. Hailey ran her finger around the edges of hers. "You're moving?"

"Bethany says everything leads to something else." Nelson sipped his beer and fiddled with the cocktail napkin below it. "And this is something else. She's taking care of everything. I don't know."

"Where is it?" Nate pulled around a free stool. "The new place?"

"Something else," said Nelson, and Hailey noticed his nose wrinkle. "It's that Mountain Mews." He creased his brow. "Out there on Highland."

"It has views of the Bitterroots." Bethany smiled gamely. "And supper included every night." She put a hand on Nelson's back.

"It's a straight shot in to the alley." Nelson looked off down the length of the bar. "If you take Highland down to 93." He caught the bartender's attention. "Two—four beers," he said, and then he looked at Hailey. He put his hand around her wrist. "It's good to see you," he said. "I'm buying you a beer."

"It's good to see you, too," she said.

"Are you working too hard up there?" he asked, and she wondered if the pained feeling inside her was showing on her face.

She looked at Nate. "I'm thinking about quitting."

Nelson frowned again.

"I'm not sure," she said. "But it might be time for the next thing."

The bartender set their beers in front of them, and Nelson passed one first to Hailey, then another to Nate. "Well, I hope you don't quit before Friday." He sipped the foam off the top of his beer.

"Thank you, sir." Nate raised his glass.

"The Fivemile demolition," Hailey said.

Nelson nodded. "We've got the whole group going out there. We've got signs made up, and a couple of lines to yell, and we've planned out who all's going to bring the coffee and whatnot."

"You are going to be there, aren't you?" Bethany said to Hailey.

"It's important to us," Nelson said.

Hailey concentrated on the beer cold in her hand. She felt suddenly jittery, but the cold feeling in her palm grounded her. Every day, her phone rang with new people insisting she print their names in the paper. Every week, Craig waited for her to deliver hard news that would get someone in trouble. Craig thought it was funny—they'd all thought it was funny—to make jokes about the idea that two old people might be in love. Hailey looked at Bethany and Nelson waiting for her answer. She wanted to tell them that what she wrote wouldn't make a difference—the Fivemile was coming down no matter what any of them did—but the way they were watching her, so openly, she saw they weren't angling for her to *do* anything for them. They just wanted to be part of what was happening.

Hailey sipped her beer. No, she decided, she would keep her job for now. Then she wished she'd waited to drink her beer, because Nelson was holding his glass up to hers.

"Of course I'll be there," she said. She clinked her glass against his.

"To the Fivemile," Nate said. "And to your new place." He tapped Nelson's glass. "When do you move in?"

"No, to *you*," Bethany interrupted Nate.

Hailey turned to him expectantly.

"If it weren't for you," Bethany said, "we wouldn't be sitting here like this."

Nate bowed his head.

"She's right," said Nelson, and Nate waved his hand dismissively.

Hailey looked to Bethany. "What—"

"The way I understand it," Nelson added, "if you hadn't stepped in, things might not have wrapped up so neatly."

"Stepped in?" Hailey glanced at Nate. He'd told her he had been down at the police station on another interview—the cops were his beat—when he'd heard the call come in on an officer's radio. An older man, either disoriented or disorderly, soliciting homeowners. The area the officer had called in was roughly Nelson's neighborhood. Nate had thought he'd heard the officer say something about the Fivemile. It was just a hunch he had acted on, Nate had told Hailey, showing up at Pearl Armstrong's like that. He'd told Nelson the police sometimes called him in such instances. He'd told the cops that Nelson was a friend.

But he hadn't said anything to Hailey about stepping in.

"Nothing would have happened," Nate said. "Except maybe to that woman." He had told Hailey that the boy's mother had that stale-beer-and-cigarettes smell all over her.

"What did you do?" Hailey tugged Nate's sleeve. "Why didn't you tell me?"

"She's flattering me," Nate said.

"Don't listen to him," Bethany said. "That woman busted out of the police car going haywire, and the police held her hands back behind her so she wouldn't—" She looked at Nelson, who was squinting, and chose to tone it down. She pointed at Nate instead. "And he stepped in right when things could have gone south. He slipped in there and asked that woman about where she'd been, since she apparently hadn't been around to see her boy wander off with a stranger, and then, very calm, he mentioned that he was with the newspaper." Bethany reached over and gave Nate a warm rub on the shoulder. "He could have not done anything," she said. "But it would have been a very different day."

"He saved the day," said Nelson.

"*Nate*," Hailey said, smiling.

"You should have seen that woman run," said Bethany.

"I probably saved *her* by scaring her off," Nate said. "Not you." He turned to Nelson. "You kept that boy safe."

Nelson shrugged and bit his bottom lip. "I'm afraid I'm not sure what I did. I'm afraid that's what this is all about." He looked down the bar again, like he was frightened by something he saw in the distance. "Would you all have another beer?"

"Yes," Hailey said.

"You talked me into it," said Nate.

And as sad as Hailey felt about Nelson—as difficult as it was to watch him there, working hard to be himself—she also felt real happiness. Nate had acted on a hunch so he could keep Nelson out of trouble, and in telling her the story he hadn't thought to include the parts that would have made him look best. He was who he was, and he made the good choices he made. He didn't have to think about putting other people first, he simply did it. Hailey watched Nate bend down to Nelson so that Nelson would be able to hear over the bar's afternoon drone, and she felt overcome by her own good fortune to have ended up in Loggers, on this day, with them. Was it love that she felt? She was so content in that moment, she didn't see what else it could have been.

"You're a good man, Whitfield," Nelson was saying. He reached out and took Hailey's wrist again. "I'm glad you have him."

It was the kind of thing she had always imagined a parent would say to a child before dying—or maybe it was something she'd heard enough in movies to think so—though she could never imagine either of her parents saying anything like it to her. They were more inclined to think about their own lives, what they needed to make themselves happy, but Hailey didn't care to expend energy on the thought right then. She was happy. And Nelson wasn't *dying* anyway. He was moving across town. She put a hand on Nate's shoulder. "Me, too," she said. "I'm really glad."

"So, invite us to the wedding," Nelson said, and Hailey stiffened.

Nate hooted a surprised laugh, but Hailey wasn't sure how to respond. She tried to read Bethany's still face.

"Get a dog and have a couple of babies," said Nelson.

"I have a dog," Nate went along. "She's my first—"

"And let them know how much you love each other." Nelson looked serious.

Nate didn't finish. Hailey stayed quiet. Bethany moved forward as if to consider Nelson more closely, and he rolled his eyes at her. "Yes, I know what I'm talking about," he said. He looked at Hailey. "And so does she. Right, Pennsylvania?" She didn't jump in right away, and Nelson didn't wait for her. "This is the worst part of it," he said, looking at none of them, and he took a long drink of his beer.

"Right," Hailey said. She touched Nelson's back, his soft green sweater.

"That's all I'm saying," Nelson said.

"Yes," she said, and Nelson set his beer down. He patted his front pocket like he was getting ready to take out his wallet. But she didn't want him to go quite yet. "When—when do you move?" she asked.

"A week from Saturday." He clasped his hands together on the bar. "They had a spot open up. Which means that someone died, but they won't tell you that."

Of course he was right, and so none of them said anything in response.

"And the party?" Nate asked.

"This Saturday," Bethany said. "The day after they tear down the Fivemile." She raised a hand to her mouth quickly, but she'd caught herself too late. Hailey didn't think any of them truly believed they were going to save the Fivemile, but still. She figured you hit a certain point—and she imagined they were just about there—where if you gave up believing, there wasn't a whole lot left. "We're all going to be there," Bethany said.

"We will be, too." Nate put his hand on the small of Hailey's back.

"We would like you to come to my party," Nelson said firmly to Nate. "To show our appreciation."

"I'll be there."

"You'll bring Hailey." Nelson turned to her, and his eyes looked watery, tired out.

"I will carry her over the threshold," Nate said.

Nelson raised his eyebrows. He winked at Hailey. "Watch out," he said.

"You started it." She smiled at him.

Nelson paused, like he was weighing the truth of her words. "Maybe I did," he said. "I used to be good at things like that." Then he reached for Bethany's hand and held it between both of his. He squeezed her hand as if it might have been cold, but the heat was pumping in Loggers. Bethany bent forward on her stool until her forehead almost touched Nelson's, and she didn't say anything. At first Hailey thought she should look away, like she was intruding on something she didn't fully understand. Nelson and Bethany seemed to be waiting for a moment to pass. Or having the same thought. But Hailey didn't look away. She watched them until they straightened up on their stools and looked each other in the eye. They didn't seem unhappy. They looked like they had come a long way to sit there together and have that beer. Then Hailey heard Nate say they should probably think about getting back upstairs. She felt him move his hand to her waist, and then she felt an empty space she hadn't even known was there fill up inside her.

CHAPTER 12

Fran

By 10:00 a.m., Fran had lost her voice. In all of her team-leader planning over the past few weeks, it hadn't occurred to her this might happen, but now she considered the frog in her throat the latest way in which her thunder was being stolen left and right. First there was Jim showing up in the Fivemile's parking lot at 7:00 a.m. with his ex-wife, Marcie. Then there was Clarette choosing this day of all days to show off her fat boyfriend half her age. And worst of all was Bethany, who hadn't unlinked her arm from Nelson's since the Nichol Aiken incident—which only Fran herself was calling it—and who now, with everyone gathered together for the protest, was making a point of not looking Fran in the eye. Fran wanted to tell Bethany that if she had something to say to her, she should come on out and say it, but she also wanted to stay focused on the day. It was four more hours until the demolition, and there weren't any indications yet that their yelling was doing any good. Fran had been leading the cheers—*Gooden is bad! The Fivemile is best!*—for nearly three hours, and the most she could say so far was that they had attracted a good-size crowd. The whole parking lot was full of cars and people, and out by the road, where two police cars had set themselves up, people were arriving with camping chairs and coolers, like the demolition was going to be a decent show.

Fran wished she could say she felt proud. That's what she had been hoping for. But all she had been feeling since the Nichol Aiken incident was guilty for not telling anyone about Nelson's confusion on their trip up Rock Creek. When she'd first heard about what happened with the boy, she'd worried Nelson would say how he'd gotten to thinking about Nichol Aiken while he was up at her family's old house, and then everyone would trace what had gone wrong back to her. The fact was, though, that she was the one who'd tried to say something to Bethany weeks and weeks ago, back when she herself was still dealing with her own mortality, and Bethany had brushed her off. And now, here was Bethany, parading around not even letting air come between her and Nelson, like she was the only one capable of taking care of him.

And there was Jim again with his ex-wife.

And Clarette with her new boyfriend.

Fran didn't mean to be selfish, but she couldn't help feeling that she deserved more attention than she was getting.

And to top it all off, there was Shoe Sanders, who was holed up inside the Fivemile and wouldn't come out.

"Jim," called Fran, though her voice didn't carry. "Jim, can you come over here?" She waved her hand. She needed to stay focused and get their group going on the next cheer. Jim had a booming voice, and she was down to nothing. She waved again, impatiently. No, she couldn't change that she and Jim had split, or that Bethany and Nelson looked by all accounts to be back together. And she wasn't going to be able to turn herself, overnight, into a person who didn't get jealous. But this Fivemile fight she could do. She could push all her frustrations—and her own fears, for that matter—in its direction, and she could let this be the first situation she approached as the new Fran, the Fran who looked outward instead of getting caught up with herself.

"You come here," Jim said to her. He was standing beside Hailey, who held a recorder in her gloved hand. Beyond Hailey, outside the Fivemile's front door, two more cop cars faced each other. The demolition was set for two o'clock, and Fran figured the cops in those cars were probably letting Shoe have the last few hours inside the Fivemile to himself.

All the cops in town knew Shoe. Fran wouldn't have known him if she'd collided with him outside his bar. It bothered her now more than ever that she'd never, ever been inside the Fivemile.

Fran lowered her sign and marched over to Jim, who was speaking into Hailey's recorder. Fran didn't want to say in front of Hailey what was on her mind, which was that they were slipping in this fight and needed to dig deeper. They were losing this one, she wanted to say, only those weren't the words a team leader ought to have on record.

Jim was telling Hailey how he and Marcie used to come to the Fivemile for the elk burgers Shoe cooked up after hunting season.

"What do you think Shoe's doing in there?" Fran said instead.

"You sound awful," Jim said.

"The thanks I get," said Fran.

Jim gazed off to the Fivemile. "This must be the hardest day of Shoe's life."

Fran thought that was probably true. She wondered how they were going to get him out of there—if it was going to turn into a scene. "He's all alone in there," she said, though she had no idea if he really was.

Jim shook his head.

"Do you know Shoe?" Hailey was asking.

"They have a policeman at the back door, too." Bethany appeared alongside them with Nelson. Her arm was looped through his, and he looked, for the moment, just fine to Fran. He even winked at her like he usually did, and for the first time all day, Fran felt like she could relax. She felt how good it would be if Nelson were the same old Nelson, and if it were all the rest of them acting like fools.

She would throw in this whole Fivemile fight for that to be the case.

"I'm asking everyone for their memories of the Fivemile," Hailey was saying. "Does anyone want to add one?" She raised the recorder.

Nelson eyed it.

Alastair and Stu Larsen came up behind him, and Alastair put his hand on Nelson's arm. "I'm sneaking up on your side," he said to Nelson. "Right here."

But no one answered Hailey's question, and Fran couldn't tell if that was because they were all gauging Nelson, or because Hailey herself didn't sound fully behind the task. She seemed preoccupied, and maybe tired, and was looking at Nelson and no one else.

"You know who'd have a story," Bethany said, "is that big fellow Clarette's running around with. Have you seen him?"

"He's bigger than a house," said Fran, who couldn't believe Clarette had managed to hide anything so big for so long.

"Louis," said Jim. "His name is Louis Black."

"Can you believe it?" Fran said.

"I met him," Hailey said. "On my first story about the Fivemile. He bought me a beer."

Fran caught Nelson rolling his eyes. She couldn't remember him ever doing that before.

"I don't know what his name is, except he looks young enough to be my son," said Bethany.

"No, he doesn't," Nelson said finally. "He's sixteen years Clarette's junior, and you're seven years younger than her. That's only nine years."

"That was an exaggeration, Nelson," Jim said. "She wasn't being serious."

"I know that, Jim." Nelson rolled his eyes a second time. "But Clarette is old enough to do what she likes." He sounded miffed. "He makes her happy, and that's the end of it."

See, thought Fran. Nelson still had the good sense to be irritated about a bunch of people blithering at a time like this. In some ways, he *was* fine. He might have been about the only one with his head screwed on.

"How long have they been running around?" asked Jim.

"Beats me," said Bethany, "but I bet he's one of those ones who sweats just sitting."

"He doesn't like reporters," Hailey said.

"And Clarette's a string bean," Fran added, though she didn't like to admit as much. She herself had put on a few pounds since the chicken-bone thing. Too many carbs.

"I hear he's friends with Shoe," Bethany said. "I hear they're the same age."

Marcie had put on a few pounds. Fran had seen her only a handful of times —Marcie didn't care for bowling—but even through a parka and snow pants you could see Marcie's rear and tummy had spread themselves out. "Extra weight doesn't bother some people," she said.

"Dean would come out shooting if he was here," said Bethany.

That made Fran wonder if Shoe might, too. She wondered if their whole protest might go up in smoke.

"There they are." Jim pointed. "Clarette!" he called. "Louis!"

Fran turned to see Clarette and Louis making their way through the small crowd toward the Fivemile. They stopped at the sound of their names. Clarette had on a puffy yellow hat, and Louis had a baseball cap perched high on his head, and they each were carrying a sign. From a distance, they didn't look so different in age, Clarette nimble as ever and Louis dragging his own weight side to side. Watching them approach, Fran almost thought she was witnessing something miraculous, but then she figured it was only that Louis was one of the biggest men she'd ever seen.

"There you all are," Clarette said, tapping the back of Jim's head with her sign. "I was thinking you'd gone off for whiskey coffees somewhere."

Fran looked at Nelson to see if he'd made the connection, but he hadn't. He was staring at Louis with fascination. Louis looked miserably cold.

"Nope," said Fran. "We were just gearing up for our next move."

"Our next move?" challenged Bethany, and because Fran had no ready answer to that, she was glad when Hailey spoke up.

"I'm gathering stories about the Fivemile," she said. "Louis, I hear you know Shoe Sanders."

Louis did nothing but adjust his cap.

"I don't have to record anything." Hailey shut off her recorder.

"I don't have to tell you anything," Louis said, and Clarette gave him a solid elbow in the gut.

Nelson and Bethany's eyes went wide.

Fran wondered if she would ever do what Clarette was doing, dating a man who was so much younger and so fat. And also not so friendly.

"Tell the one about the goat," Clarette said to him.

Louis scowled.

Fran didn't think she could.

"Or was it a bat?" Clarette squeezed a handful of Louis's great side, and he swung his rear her way.

"It wasn't a bat," he said, and there was maybe the first bit of a smile they had ever seen on Louis. "It was a pig."

"What happened?" said Hailey.

"Go on." Clarette swatted Louis's belly. It was like she couldn't resist how big he was. Fran found herself envying Clarette's enthusiasm. "Tell about the pig," Clarette said.

But Louis said nothing. He shifted his weight. He looked at the ground and then raised his head and stared off in the distance. It was like being at the zoo, Fran thought, the way they watched him. Would he roar? Or go to sleep? It hardly mattered. To them, he was a brand new creature, deliciously taboo. Fran actually got excited when he cleared his throat. Then he looked at his audience—Clarette and Nelson and Bethany and Jim and Fran and Hailey—and right at that moment a young man appeared by Hailey's side. He was carrying two cups of something hot, and he handed one to Hailey. Fran willed him not to speak. He looked so healthy, he could have flattened Louis in an instant.

"Thank you," Hailey said quietly to the young man.

"Whitfield," Nelson said to him too loud.

"Shhh," Fran said to all of them.

The young man shook Nelson's hand. "Nelson," he said softly as he looked at Fran.

"I'm telling a story here," said Louis.

"While the iron's still hot." Clarette clapped again.

Nate was rubbing Hailey's shoulder. "By all means," he said, and it was right then Fran crystallized how she was all alone. There was Nelson with Bethany, and Clarette with Louis, and Hailey with this young man, and Jim with Marcie who was floating around out there somewhere, and Fran left holding her own, flying solo, fighting her own fight that she knew she wasn't going to win. The thought made her both strikingly lonely and also curious to know what the hell Shoe Sanders was doing inside the Fivemile all this time on his own.

"There was a time Shoe got a pig," Louis started then. "And he kept it in the back room in there." He looked off to the Fivemile. "And he was never going to kill it or eat it. It was his pet pig, and you could go feed it slop or whatnot if Shoe was in the mood." It must have been evident to everyone that Louis was no storyteller, but no one interrupted. "And then when the cops found out, they told Shoe he had to get rid of it for health reasons or they were going to shut him down."

Louis grew quiet then. That appeared to be the end of his story, though everyone waited a minute to give him a chance to come up with more. A punch line, maybe. If Louis was going to become a part of their group, Fran could hear everyone thinking, he was going to have to polish his storytelling.

"So," said Jim, "did he get rid of it?"

"No," said Louis. "He kept it back there for a while, and him and the cops went back and forth like this, and then one day he got rid of it."

"He killed it?" Fran asked.

"No," Louis said impatiently. "He took it home."

"Hmm," said Nelson.

"I wouldn't put a pig in my house," said Bethany.

"You don't have to," said Louis. "She was asking for a story."

"Did it have a name?" Hailey was jotting notes.

Louis looked like he had no interest in sharing any more with this group. He ran one big gloved hand over his face and erased whatever trace of emotion he might have shown. But when Hailey started to ask a second time, he cut her off and said, "Porky," and right there everyone burst out laughing. Maybe it was hearing that word out of Louis's mouth, or maybe it was the bad way he told the whole story, or maybe it was how unoriginal the name Porky was for a pig, but the sound of it got everyone laughing. And when they started laughing, Louis couldn't hide his own big smile, which was the fleshiest smile

Fran had ever seen. Jim and Nelson looked a bit suspicious, like maybe they didn't need a younger man in their group making the women laugh, but Clarette appeared to be the happiest of them all. Fran was suddenly glad Louis was there. In the midst of this Fivemile thing, he was a decent distraction.

"What about you?" Hailey was asking. "What are your memories of the Fivemile?"

Fran didn't catch, at first, that Hailey was addressing her.

"You're an organizer here, right?" Hailey said. "With Free the Fivemile?"

"I am, too," said Clarette.

"I'm a team leader," said Fran.

"She's never been inside the Fivemile," Jim went ahead and added.

"Of course I have," Fran clipped. She could have smacked him. "Good Lord," she said. But in the gap where she was supposed to offer up a story—maybe the story she was keeping to herself about waiting outside the Fivemile the day Clive went in to fish out Jesse—she said nothing. She glared at Jim for being too small a man to credit her for being team leader, to let her have this day. Really, what great harm would that have done? "I'm sorry," Fran croaked to Hailey. "I've lost my voice."

"Nelson, what about you?" someone asked. Fran turned away from Jim and saw it was this young man with Hailey. "I bet you have some stories about the Fivemile," he was saying to Nelson.

How could she not have been inside the Fivemile? Fran was wondering. What else had she been so busy doing?

Nelson was standing with his fists deep in his front pockets.

Was Shoe Sanders in there adding up the years he'd spent in his own bar?

Bethany's arm was pinned under Nelson's elbow, against his side.

"Oh," Nelson said, a drip forming on the tip of his nose. "I don't know." He turned to Bethany, who took the opportunity to shift her arm. "It's been years," he said. "I don't know, but I hope they don't tear it down."

"It's not looking good," said Jim.

"That's the spirit, Jim," Fran said.

"I hope they don't tear my house down either," Nelson said. "Bethany thinks they will."

"Now, Nelson." Fran could feel their focus slipping, and it was her job, as team leader, to keep everyone on the up and up. If you started dwelling on the possibilities, you were done.

"Or they'll make it a rental," Bethany said. "That's what they're doing to all the old places."

"We're going to have a big party in your house." Fran strained her raspy voice. She needed to keep things light.

"I'll miss having the second bedroom," Nelson said. "For painting."

"Let's start the next cheer." Fran couldn't bear the idea of losing this fight. She looked to Hailey and noticed that she'd crossed her arms so the recorder was lost up in her armpit. The girl looked a shade paler, watching Nelson.

"I'll always remember that house," Nelson said.

"Please," Fran tried.

"Nelson—" she heard Hailey say, but that was all. Then Fran was moving out of earshot, marching for the Fivemile, anger rising inside her. She couldn't have explained why she broke away like that, but she was suddenly mad all over. She couldn't believe that she had never been inside the Fivemile, or that Nelson was leaving his house, or that she was all alone. She didn't know exactly what she was going to do. All she knew was that nothing was like it used to be, and under no circumstance was she going to let two sleepy cops stand between her and whatever came next.

"Ma'am." They both climbed out of their cars at the same time.

Fran dropped her sign, but that was her only concession.

"Hey." One of them grabbed her by the elbow.

The best part of all this anger, if she had to pick something, was it flushed the fear right out of her. "What?" She turned to both the cops like she'd never, ever choked on a chicken bone. "You can let go of me," she said.

"Not if you're heading in there," one of them said. "No one's allowed."

"Shoe Sanders is in there," she said.

"He shouldn't be," said the other one. "But . . ."

"But?" she said. "He is. And there's a parking lot of people waiting to see him. Look around." She flung her free arm.

The officer must have had enough time to get a look at her and decide she was too old to pose a threat, because he released his grip.

"You with Free the Fivemile?" the second cop said. He studied her team leader sticker. Both cops looked the same to Fran—young, mustachioed, the beginnings of tires around their guts.

"I'm his mother," Fran said right back. Somehow skipping Shoe's name made it less of a lie.

"I'm sorry?" said one officer.

She did, in fact, have two sons not so much older than these two. Of course she didn't look old enough to be Shoe Sanders's mother. But at the same time, she was an aging person wrapped up in a hat and scarf and parka, and what did they know? For once Fran wouldn't have minded coming off older than she was.

"I said I'm his mother," she repeated.

"Ma'am," one of them started again.

"You don't think I am?"

"I think—"

"Who do you think gave him that pig?" she asked. That bought her a second. "You're four hours from tearing down his whole life."

They got quiet then. Not that they were going soft so much as they saw that she was losing it before their eyes. There was no sense slowing down.

"And you're going to go home tonight and sit in front of your TV," she said. "Honest to God, what have you done for us lately?"

Both officers had quizzical expressions, like maybe this whole episode was worth the price of entry. What was she going to do, anyway, nail herself to the Fivemile?

"Make it quick," one of them said.

Fran didn't respond. She just went. She blew past those cops and threw open the Fivemile's front door for the first time in her life. For the first time in her life she smelled its heady mix of grit and beer and cigarettes. She felt the slippery sawdust under her feet and the dark walls wrapping around her. She imagined the stools filled and the bar three deep with drinkers from the mill and the railroad and, heck, probably the police station, unbuttoning their top buttons, or getting down to their undershirts altogether, bellying up and readying to lose themselves. She pictured the bar lined up with every bottle you could imagine, and a juke box going with whatever honky-tonk was in fashion, and her own self, a hundred years younger, daring to sit down and order a beer.

For the first time in her life, she saw everything she hadn't done.

Not that there was any point regretting what might have been.

Not that there was anything left inside the Fivemile anyway.

There were no bottles and no music and no pictures hanging on the walls. There was only the warmth, and a little bit of yellow light coming through the front window, and Shoe Sanders, at the bar like a customer, hunched over by himself. He perked up when Fran walked in. He pushed back from the bar, revealing a bottle of brown liquid on its way to empty.

He didn't say a word to Fran but only watched her walk toward him. With the light from the window behind her, she realized he couldn't see her face. But she could see his round face clearly, the deep folds his ruddy skin made below his eyes and in the corners of his mouth. He hadn't combed his hair. Or maybe he had, but he'd been tousling it as he drank. He wasn't dressed badly. He wore a denim button-down with blue suspenders, and blue jeans. His cheeks were so round his eyes seemed incidental, but when Fran got closer she could see that they were blue. A light blue, like a wild dog's, but again, Fran was anything but scared.

"My name is Fran Murray," she said to him. "I've never been in here before."

"Impossible," he said, like he wasn't surprised to see her. Like he was drunk.

"And you should be out there," she said.

He lifted a small glass from between his legs and placed it on the bar. There was a sip left. "They sent you in for me?" He squinted at her.

Fran hadn't considered that. "No," she said. She thought of Nelson and Bethany, Jim and Marcie, Hailey and that young man. "I came in here for me," she said.

Shoe finished his drink and turned to her. She pulled off her hat and fluffed her hair.

"That's refreshing," he said, but Fran didn't know what he meant.

"I'm with Free the Fivemile," she said. "I'm a team leader."

"I'm Shoe Sanders," he said. "I've sat here thirty-five years."

"I know that," she said, but somehow his saying so was endearing. "I'm a friend of Clarette Luther's," she said. "I've never been in here before."

"That's what you said." He showed no recognition of Clarette. "Is that your real voice?"

"What if it was?"

"It's sultry," he said.

"Careful," Fran said, though she couldn't remember the exact meaning of sultry. She knew it could be used along the lines of sexy, but was that in a good way or bad? It was uncomfortable and exciting, being alone in the Fivemile with Shoe. "I've been shouting my head off," she said to him. "Since 7:00 a.m. And you should be outside thanking everyone. There are a lot of people out there shouting their heads off for you. Running around in the cold getting in trouble for you."

"Who's getting in trouble?" Shoe seemed to find that interesting.

Her intention was to tell him about Nelson, and how she'd known something was wrong up at her old house but said nothing. Then she'd somehow lay it on Shoe for Nelson's going over the edge getting signatures for him. Then on the whole world for getting behind a strip mall instead of a landmark.

But what she said was, "I think it's better to knock a place down than keep it up." She took a seat beside Shoe. "As long as you have to hand it over either way." The stool was very high. It had a wide, smooth seat and arm rests. It was fixed to the floor. She twisted slowly side to side.

"Do you want a drink?" asked Shoe.

"That way you don't have to see anybody else with it," she said.

Shoe didn't respond. Fran thought of Nelson's house with its bowling-ball pyramid in the backyard and his easel set up in the spare bedroom. She thought of her and Nelson drinking out of jelly jars on her parents' porch, and she thought there were a lot of things she could have done differently.

"Did you read that article in the *Free Press*?" she started.

"About today?" he said.

"No," she said. "About Nelson Moore."

"Who's that?" he said.

"Oh," she said—or maybe she didn't. Maybe she didn't make any noise at all. It might have just been the shivery feeling working up her arms. Did Shoe Sanders see her flinch?

"I meet a lot of people," he said.

Nelson's the one who saved my life, she didn't say. He's the one who wouldn't be leaving his house, not yet, if I hadn't sent him out for signatures. *He might be okay, if not for me.* That was what she wanted to say, except in the Fivemile's yellow light, with Shoe pouring himself another glass, Fran knew saying as much would be selfish. Because the thing was, this whole deal was not about her. Best she could pinpoint it, it was about a person she loved, a person the whole group of them loved, and it was about figuring out how, now—even though she more or less wanted to clock Bethany and Jim—how, now, to put everything else aside and protect him. Fran wondered if anyone in particular was doing the same for Shoe Sanders.

Shoe had never heard of Nelson?

"It was the article about the group of us down at Liberty," Fran said. "That's the one I meant."

Shoe shook his head. "I guess I don't know that group."

"You don't?"

"Why?" he said.

She didn't answer. She looked around the bar, at the dingy ceiling fan and the bare nails in the walls—the last remnants of Shoe Sanders's whole world—where she'd never been before. "Never mind," she said.

It wasn't like every person automatically knew about every other person who'd been saved or come undone.

"I don't read the *Free Press* unless it's about me," Shoe said.

"Me neither," she said.

"There's been a bit recently about me," Shoe was saying. "Except they didn't take my picture."

"They took Nelson's picture," Fran said. "He was on the front page."

Shoe shrugged like this didn't help him.

"Do you know Louis Black?" she asked then.

"Good man." Shoe nodded.

"Fat," Fran said.

Shoe laughed a rich laugh that made Fran want to laugh, too, that made her picture a whole bar contagious with laughter, a whole world of men and women she would never sit with at the Fivemile, feeding off Shoe's laugh. She imagined photographs tacked to the walls, and people with nicknames for each other, and birthday drinks and anniversary celebrations and slumped-over, dead-drunk heartbreaks. And smoke so thick everyone looked good, and her own son, square-shouldered, with a tin of chew burning a circle in his back pocket. She could see why he would have wanted to be here. Alongside the sadness overtaking her, she felt a surge of excitement from being in the right place, even though—or perhaps because—that place was the very thing that was about to disappear.

How, she wondered, could Shoe bear this?

"How did you get in here?" he asked her.

"I would like a drink," she said.

Shoe knocked on the bottle. "This is what I've got," he said.

"That's fine," said Fran.

Shoe apparently didn't have another glass, because he went behind the bar and rinsed out his and poured her a drink from his bottle. He put the glass down in front of her, and the way he stared at it, like it might talk to him, Fran knew they were both thinking how it was the last drink he was going to serve.

Fran took a sip. Was it whiskey or bourbon. What did she know? Was there a difference? Had either one of them ever tasted so good? Fran didn't normally drink hard alcohol, she stuck to wine, but now this brown liquid burned through her like the return of something familiar, something you couldn't believe you'd ever lived without.

"Whoa," she said out loud, the word clearer and stronger than any she'd spoken all day. She touched her throat. "My voice."

Shoe swigged from the bottle and made a smacking sound with his lips. "This is the water," he said, whatever that meant. "It'll make you do a goddamn opera standing on your head."

But Fran just wanted to talk.

"Excuse me," he said.

She liked that.

She took another sip, and crossed her legs, and settled her elbows onto the bar. The dim light was nice. She felt like she could talk and talk. Like, for a few minutes, she could stop worrying about Nelson and their group—Shoe didn't know them—and so she started telling him about how she stood outside the Fivemile the day Clive went in to fish out Jesse. About how she should have gone on in herself and not bothered chiding Jesse for wanting to have some fun. About how it was funny you kept on thinking you were as old as you were going to be, and yet you kept on getting older, seeing things better, and how maybe one of the best things that had ever happened to you was choking on that chicken bone. That, and getting in on this Fivemile fight. Getting right past the cops and in the door for the first time in your life and sipping from this glass in the dim light of this big, old rattly space that, my God, was practically like you were in church.

Shoe erupted at that. He laughed hard, and his whole face went red, and then he laughed again when he told her his version of the Porky pig story, and the time Louis Black danced on the bar—yes, Louis Black—and the time a guy in pink pajamas sleepwalked in and ordered a Manhattan, neat, and the time there was a wedding in the Fivemile, and a bike rally, and a fundraiser whenever one of the regulars ended up in the hospital without insurance. And then he told her how his son Laine was supposed to take over the Fivemile but went to Portland instead. He had a girl there, Shoe said. This girl didn't want a small-town life—he sneered *small-town*—she wanted *opportunities*, except when the opportunity arose she found another boyfriend who wanted to be a lawyer, and Laine found another girl who wanted to have a baby, and so that's what they were doing, having a baby in the spring in Portland, and Shoe supposed he should move to Portland, too, except he was never going to. He was going to fix his cabin up the Blackfoot and do all the fishing he'd always said he would do.

"That sounds divine," Fran said.

"Another," Shoe said, but he didn't make it a question. He refilled Fran's glass, and she didn't even care that he'd been drinking straight from the bottle. She was thinking how the first drink he'd poured her hadn't actually been the last drink he would pour, and how you didn't know when you were doing something for the last time. Except for this afternoon in the Fivemile, which Fran was pretty sure about. Because whether Shoe came out today, or whether he got stubborn and came out tomorrow, or even if he had a real standoff and came out the next day, the thing was, he was going to come out. He wasn't going to let a building fall on his head. Neither were the cops.

"They might tear down my friend Nelson's house," she said. "He's the one I was starting to tell you about."

Shoe knocked back another sip himself. "Why?" he asked, swishing the last of the bottle, judging how many sips were left.

"He has to leave it behind." Fran rubbed her eyes to see if it was the drink dusting up her vision, or if it was the mustiness of the bar. She thought it was the bar. "He got sixty-four signatures to try to save this building for you," she said.

"I'm sixty-three." Shoe planted the bottle on the bar, and Fran figured he was blotto. She thought it might be time to leave, but then he leaned down on his elbows and added, in a hushed voice, "Thank you."

Fran nodded. "I asked him to," she said. She leaned forward and pressed her forearms against the bar, too. There was dusty light seeping in the windows. There was the low hum of protesters cheering without her. And out of nowhere, Fran remembered something. It was a story she'd heard on a history program about Native Americans years ago. It was all done in reenactments, which Fran never cared for. A tribal leader was telling a young girl that if you kissed the walls of a place you loved before you left—north, south, east, west— then you would be back some day. Fran herself was superstitious. She didn't go under ladders or anywhere near thirteens, and so the story had stayed with her. Why it popped into her head right then she couldn't say, except maybe the combination of the strong drinks and her wanting to have something more to say to Shoe.

"We're having a party at my friend Nelson's house before he moves," she said. "The whole group of us from Liberty."

Shoe raised his eyebrows like he was waiting for her point.

"Do you want to come?" she asked. If she had heard her own voice on a tape recorder, she wouldn't have believed she'd said it.

"Why would I want to come?" Shoe lifted his chin so he was looking down his nose at her.

Fran shrugged. "You could thank him."

"I'll be fishing," he said.

Fran's head was buzzing, and she started to laugh. "This is February."

"I'll be fishing every day," Shoe said plainly.

Fran cleaned the smile off her face. She thought of that, of how Shoe had been running the Fivemile every day for thirty-plus years, and how now he was going to be not-doing that every day going forward. He was going to have to go somewhere else, same as Nelson. "Why didn't you have a party?" she asked Shoe. "To celebrate this place?"

Shoe pushed his bottle with one finger. It hit the thick, rounded edge of the bar and teetered. "This is my party," he said.

Fran looked around. Of course. There had already been a million parties inside those walls, and she felt silly for suggesting Shoe needed one last one to acknowledge all the rest. She shifted on her stool and almost apologized for showing up uninvited, especially after all these years, but she blew warmth into her hands instead. She gazed at those dark, damp walls that she bet would flake off right under your fingernails if you scratched them. She thought how badly she would like to touch those walls before she left, and then she told Shoe about the television program she'd just remembered. She swept her hand through the Fivemile's dusty, yellowed air as she told him to kiss all four.

Shoe listened as he picked at a callus on this thumb. Then he looked at her very seriously. "Do you know how much crud is on these walls?"

Fran laughed. She sipped her drink and watched Shoe look at his walls as thoughtfully as she'd ever seen anyone look at anything. When he was done with that, he turned his stool so it was facing hers. He sighed and narrowed his eyes, like he was in on an important conversation. He was lost, Fran thought. She was feeling blurry herself. She thought she might ask if the powder room was still in working order, and then Shoe was leaning in giving her a wet, boozy kiss on the lips. For a split second, she thought about fighting him off, because that would have been the appropriate thing to do. But in the same instant she had the good sense to ask herself what would have been better, right that second, than kissing Shoe Sanders, in the Fivemile, on the lips? Nothing, she told herself. Not one thing. She took in his kiss along with all the smoke and the sawdust and the stories she had missed, but before she could make too much of it either way, Shoe straightened up and turned back to his bottle. He took her glass to pour himself a last drink and didn't offer her any more. It was his way, she figured, of saying good-bye.

"Okay," she said, like they had reached an understanding. There was the antsy side of her that wanted Shoe to ask her to dinner now, to tell her she was pretty—but that was the old Fran at work. This new Fran looked around and saw things differently. Shoe didn't know her. As it turned out, he didn't know a lot of them out there fighting for the Fivemile. He met so many people. And, anyway, she'd come inside for herself.

"Thank you for the drinks," she said.

Without shifting, he turned his head toward her, his wild-dog eyes gone lazy. "Thank you for the drinks," he said.

"I'm going to go out there." She thumbed to the door. Her body felt woozy, but in a good way.

"I'm not," he said.

The yellow light reached almost to her ankles. It lit up the dust and grit and sawdust on the floor. "You're the one they came to see," she said.

"I'm staying right here." His chest was against the bar.

She nodded and pulled on her hat. "I know," she said. But she didn't step toward the door. Instead she thought about how you never knew what might happen next, and how you got just the one shot at everything. Then she stepped farther into the bar. She walked past Shoe to each of the Fivemile's filthy walls, and kissed them—north, south, east, west—and then, nothing doing, she walked out the door.

CHAPTER 13

Alastair

Alastair was bringing bread. He had a bread machine, which dinged when the bread was done, and he bought bread mixes that came in dense paper sacks, like sandbags. The baking itself was easy. The only tricky part was making sure the kneading paddle was in place in the bread bucket at the beginning, and then that it hadn't gotten stuck inside the loaf during baking. Alastair used hot mitts and eased the loaf from the paddle with a wooden spoon. He had a letter opener, too, that he used if the loaf seemed particularly stuck. But that wasn't the case today. Already, since early morning, Alastair had baked two loaves, one wheat, one raisin nut, that both lifted smoothly from the bucket, their sides tall and even, their tops billowy. Normally he would have been thrilled with such results, but today his happiness was dampened. As he was daydreaming and waiting for his loaves to bake, he imagined Nelson puttering around his house with Bethany, preparing for a party that, no matter what any of them said, wasn't a celebration you would choose. And yet, Alastair had to admit, he himself *was* happy. He felt guilty that his own excitement coincided with such a good friend's hard time, but he had had his hard times, too. Now he opened his trailer's door and felt the icy air hit the toasty warmth of his kitchen and thought, *Here is a day I hadn't thought would happen.*

He wanted to hear Pearl's car pulling up. He sat on a kitchen chair he'd pulled to the edge of the open door. He kept his hands on his knees. Once he got ready for going out, Alastair found, it was always best to stay still. That way there was less chance for his pressed shirt to get wrinkled without him knowing, for his black pants to brush up against floury bread mix along the kitchen counter without him realizing. He hadn't been on a date of any sort in years. He hadn't had a date pick him up, ever, except for Shyla and Mora Byrnes, and that was only after he'd known them better. Otherwise, he'd always had the money to pick up his dates in cabs. But again, it had been years.

It would have been better if they were going out to dinner, or to one of the parties Nelson used to throw on St. Patrick's Day or Memorial Day. This was going to be a melancholy party—and the day after the Fivemile came down, no less—but at the same time, Alastair had met Pearl under these imperfect circumstances. For someone who didn't know his friends, she was in on what had happened even more than some of the rest of them. She had been there with him and Bethany. She had chosen not to call the police. She and Bethany and Nelson had come back to his trailer for wine, and they'd spent an hour just talking about his fish. Alastair had almost invited Pearl to the Fivemile's demolition with him but had decided that might be *too* grim. And also too cold. At least Nelson's would be warm, with all of them together in that front room, and the group of them could do a good job of keeping each other happy. They always did.

He heard her car on the gravel, crunching slowly into the space next to his trailer that stayed empty. Pearl gave a light honk like she had said she would, and Alastair stood up. He was nervous, and so lucky.

"Hello," he called to the sound of her door opening.

"I'll be right there," said Pearl, which he knew was her way of saying not to try the few steps down without her, even though he'd lived with those steps for decades. Pearl was no-nonsense and kind at the same time. She wore a gingery perfume that Alastair found daring compared to the rosy scents of so many of the women at the alley.

"You can help me with the loaves," he said, and she rubbed her hands on his arms as she led him inside. "They're on the counter."

"The *smell*," she said.

"The raisin nut has cinnamon," Alastair said. "I add a tablespoon of honey to the whole wheat."

"I would keep the door closed." Pearl inhaled deeply through her nose. "I wouldn't let this smell go."

"I wanted to hear you coming," he said. He could sense himself blush, but he had a feeling Pearl missed it.

"Which ones are these again?" she asked. Her voice came from near the big tank, not the counter. "With the feathery fringe? I think I like them best."

"The angelfish," Alastair said, but he turned to feel for the bread. As much as he would have loved to walk Pearl from tank to tank again, maybe this time taking her hand as he told her about each of his fish, he also wanted to go. He wanted to arrive at a party with Pearl, and *be* at the party with her—but, most of all, he wanted to be there for Nelson. On this day that was number one.

Pearl took the loaves from him, and they went down the steps together to the car. Inside, the seats had a caramel scent that almost disguised the smell of smoke in which the previous owner had pickled the cloth. He could tell she didn't have many passengers because there were no crumbs in the seams of the seat, and the seat itself was too far forward. He had to lean over the loaves in his lap and feel around beneath the seat for the adjustment lever.

"Do you need—"

"All set."

"Well, okay." Pearl started the engine. "I'm wearing black slacks and a purple sweater," she said. "You look very handsome."

"Thank you," he said, and he didn't have time to tell her how nice she smelled before she was talking again—maybe she was a little nervous, same as he was—telling him she didn't go out all that much, telling him she was a people person when she was around people she knew but not as much when she'd never met the people before. She could be a bit reserved, she said, but today she wanted to make an effort to be outgoing. "So, tell me about them," she said as he felt the car turn out of the trailer court's gravel driveway onto 93.

Alastair turned his head to her.

"Your friends," she said.

"Oh," he said. In his mind, he had been planning to spend the drive telling her about what had happened during the Fivemile's demolition. He had thought about how he would tell her what a shock it was to feel the heat of the fire and the smell of smoke—like an itchy wool blanket all the way to the back of his throat—when Shoe Sanders burned down his own place. He wanted to tell her how everyone was on Shoe's side for not letting W. W. Gooden have the final say, how they'd cheered so loud that Alastair thought his feet were going to lift off the ground.

But Pearl said, "Tell me about them so I know something about who's who when I walk in."

Alastair shifted in his seat. This wasn't what he'd had in mind. "Okay," he said, only he didn't know where to start. One of the things about being blind, he'd found, was that he liked to think about important conversations before he had them, because so often it turned out that his way of expressing a thought wasn't clear to someone else. He saw things in his own way, and sometimes that left him feeling alone. So, he thought, his friends . . . He ran his hands over his slacks. "Well, I think there will be about twenty of them," he said. "Fifteen or twenty."

Pearl turned the heat up a notch and then down a notch. "I'll know Bethany, anyway," she said, and so Alastair started there.

Bethany was the sturdy one in the group, he said. She'd lost three husbands. She drank regular beer, never light, and she'd been with Nelson almost three years. Also, she was a straight-ahead kind of person, if that made any sense, and she was the one who would do favors without wanting anything in return. Then there was Fran. She was more like one of those sparklers on the Fourth of July. Sort of whiz and pop, with sparks going in all these directions, but at the end you weren't sure if it added up to anything or just fizzed out. There was Jim, who was like an old oak planted in the same spot at their table every Monday, Wednesday, Friday, and Stu Larsen who neither drew you to him nor repelled you, like a radio program you listened to because it didn't make you happy or sad. Alastair went on to Clarette—she was either a tight wire or the busy bird that every now and then touched down on it. The more he talked, the more he realized that talking about his friends wasn't so different from talking about his fish, except he hadn't learned about his friends from the Library of Congress. And, what he'd learned about them weren't facts at all. Really, what he had inside him was a collage of abstract visions—yes, visions—that made all the sense in the world to him, that actually defined his world. Did his friends have this, too? Did they think like he did when their eyes were closed? He wondered how they would describe him if they were in his shoes and couldn't say, *white hair, square chin, about yay high.*

"What about Nelson?" Pearl said to him.

"Oh." He turned to her quickly, as if he'd forgotten, for a moment, she was there. In black slacks and a purple sweater. He had his hands on his knees. There was the caramel smell, the smoky undertone, the ginger air wafting off of Pearl. Had he not mentioned Nelson? Alastair could feel the rise and fall of Pearl's breath. The dip and swell of the wintry road. "Well," he said. "You've met him. This is his day."

Some things, he thought, there was no need to talk about. Some things, you were better off just closing your eyes and seeing for yourself. Of course, Alastair didn't have to close his eyes. He just saw the group of them, stones in a wall, with parts getting ready to crumble.

"Yes, but I don't know him," Pearl said. "I just met him that once, and—"

Alastair didn't fill the silence.

"How would you describe him?" Pearl said more quietly. "How he used to be?"

Alastair liked having Pearl in the car next to him. He liked that she was interested in his fish and his friends. But he didn't want to talk any more about Nelson, or about any of them. Then again, he didn't want to seem difficult either. And so he said, "He was funny. He made sure everyone was having a good time. When he patted you on the back, his hand was—" Alastair stopped himself there. Nothing he was saying felt right. "Well, you'll see," he said. "He's right up here."

Then he gave Pearl directions for the last few turns. Left on Elm, right on Hickory to Burr. Past the closed-down corner store and the firehouse. It was the third house on the right after the engines. He'd told cabbies plenty of times. Nelson had thrown all sorts of parties over the years. Birthdays and Super Bowls and Veterans Days. Besides Mora Byrnes, Alastair had never brought a date, and he'd brought Mora only twice. It had been years and years since he'd pulled up to a party like this, with someone to arrive with and leave with, like everybody else.

Bethany was the first one to greet them. She took Pearl's coat and said what a happy surprise. She gave Alastair a long hug and whispered in his ear, "You sneaky dog." Then there was Clarette—she pinched Alastair's side and did a couple of soft punches against his chest. "Yes," she said with each punch, "Yes," and there was no need for her to explain. Alastair heard Clarette's date Louis introducing himself to Pearl, and Pearl saying what a colorful room it was, which Alastair would have loved to see. He let her guide him across the room—there was Jim slapping his shoulder, Stu letting out a whistle, Fran falling in step behind them: "How did you meet? How long ago? Which church does Pearl belong to?" Alastair noted that Nelson must not have done much packing yet, because the same old armchair and side table and standing lamp and potted tree were where they had always been. The card table Nelson used for parties was also in its usual spot, where the second armchair normally was except when Nelson moved it into the spare bedroom. At the card table Alastair let Pearl pour them each a glass of wine.

And there was Nelson.

"I'm Pearl Armstrong," Pearl was reminding him a little loudly.

"Well, I don't have any fish," Nelson said. "But it looks like you found the Merlot right there." He sounded at ease in his own home. Merlot was what Pearl had liked in Alastair's trailer. The four of them had drunk two bottles Alastair had kept in a cupboard since last Christmas.

"Good to see you," Nelson said to Alastair, taking his hand. It was a strong, extended handshake, like Nelson was trying to impress something upon him.

Nelson's hand was warm no matter the season, Alastair thought, like a nectarine or a pillow left in the sun.

"Good to see you, too," he said.

"It really is," said Nelson. "Everyone is here." He let go of Alastair's hand. "There are some seats behind you. I need to open another bag of chips."

So, it wasn't exactly the entrance Alastair had envisioned—at a different kind of party, he would have liked to hear his friends roar as he entered with Pearl on his arm—but in a way, it was even more than he had expected. He was so happy to sit with Pearl on the couch, to sit with her and know she didn't want to be somewhere else. Together, they drank their wine, and he listened to her tell him about the party. Pearl described the colorful streamers above the card table, and the good food—the onion dip and the Jello salad and the potato casserole and the deviled eggs and the beef Stroganoff. It was only the hummus she didn't care for. She talked about Nelson's well-kept furniture. Such a comfortable couch, she said. Alastair listened to her clear voice—she enunciated carefully, perhaps for him—and he also listened to his friends. The roomful of them. Their voices swirled around him, and though he was accustomed to sitting on the couch like this, he also saw himself moving among them, filling in the spaces between them, catching pieces of their conversations rather than being in on any one. There was Stu with his same stories about the mill; and Bethany with her take on what Shoe Sanders had done; and Fran with her concerns about which quote the *Chronicle* might use from their interview in the parking lot, in all that smoke; and Charla bossing Fran over how many cubes to use in one drink; and Clarette with her jokes; and Jim with his jokes; and Nelson with his jokes; and the sense that none of them was going to act any different today if they could manage it, like there was no difference today at all.

Only, there was a difference. Among Nelson and Bethany and Fran and Jim and Clarette and Louis. And Hailey. She was there, too. And her boyfriend. Alastair could hear them, if he concentrated, the youngest and least familiar voices in the room.

"Are you?" Pearl was saying to him. "Are you listening?"

And he had his hand on her knee. "Yes," he said. Yes, of course he was. And it was true. He was listening to all of them. He felt slightly guilty enjoying himself, but more than he had in years, Alastair felt like one of them, sitting there with Pearl beside him. No, it was not his day, but it might as well have been. He was that happy. He was the same as any of them, keeping things going, pushing trouble out of the way.

A word in the paper.

A boy on the loose.

A building lying in its own shambles.

Alastair on the couch with Pearl.

And then it was time for the slides. Nelson's daughter Marny had driven from Sidney and picked up his other daughter, Carol, in Miles City, and together they'd put together a show with Bethany's help. The girls had said they were going to bring along Nelson's sons, too, but then there was something about bosses and shifts and how the boys couldn't get the time off work. Now Marny stood before them and thanked them for coming. She asked them all to gather around, and Alastair felt Pearl squeeze closer as they made room for two more people on the couch.

"I want a minute, too," Nelson said, and Pearl whispered to Alastair that he was making his way to the front of the room. "I want to thank you all for coming to my house," he said. To Alastair, he sounded mostly like his old self, but also a little stern, like he was thinking hard to get this out. "Not that this is anything to celebrate, but all things being equal, I am lucky."

There were a few sighs of acknowledgment around the room.

Clarette called out, "We love you, Nelson," and did a whistle through her fingers.

"Well, I love you, too," he said seriously. "And by that, I mean all of you. Don't get me in any more trouble with words."

No one laughed at that, but no one made a comment either.

"And while I'm up here I wanted to take a minute to think about the Fivemile," he said. Alastair hadn't anticipated that, and he wished he could see the looks on everyone's faces. "It may be gone, but we did our part, and that's something to be proud of. We'll always remember what it was like, and we were there to see something no one knew was going to happen, and there was a beauty to that." Then Nelson took a breath. Alastair could hear it. He imagined what it must have looked like, the flames rising into the dark sky as Shoe Sanders walked out the front door of his building, and he could feel all of them taking a breath together.

"I just wanted to say that," Nelson said, and then he didn't say anything more. The lights went down, Pearl told Alastair, and the back wall was cleared of everything so it was like a screen with a bright white box of light.

The first slide was black-and-white, Pearl said. She was whispering in his ear. It was of Nelson, in dungarees, as a boy. Not a teenager. The next one was Nelson in an army uniform with his hair cut short, she said. Then there was one where Nelson was on a motorcycle in a short-sleeve shirt, and he had a bit of a tummy and also a tattoo. There were more where Nelson was with a woman, and then one where they were getting married, and then another picture right after where Nelson was getting married to a different woman, and everyone laughed some at that. Alastair wanted to ask Pearl questions. What would the look in Nelson's eyes be, if his eyes were more of a sound? What sort of posture did he have, if posture was more of a feeling? What mood was in the picture, if you had to close your eyes and say? But the room was mostly quiet — bursts of laughter and a smattering of side comments — and Alastair didn't want to be the one making noise. He let Pearl keep whispering. The group of them at the bowling alley, she said. The group of them at Nelson's house. Bethany and Nelson on a deck. Nelson and Jim and Clarette with bowling pins in their hands. Nelson and Fran dancing. Nelson outside a truck, looking trim. Nelson in a big lineup of couples and babies that must have been family. Nelson by a river. Stu and Jim and Nelson at a shooting range. Bethany and Nelson in armchairs. Fran and Nelson dancing again.

Alastair told Pearl that was enough. That's okay, he said. She didn't need to tell him about any more. It was fine with him if she sat quietly and watched, he said, though the truth was he didn't want to hear more descriptions. He felt he could do better on his own, sitting quietly on the couch, his hands on his knees, just listening. There were the bursts of laughter. The wisecracks and the shushes, the pops of surprise and the drawn-out breaths, and his own breaths, too. There was the swishing and fidgeting, the ice clinking, the napkins rustling, the whoops, the yawns, and a couple of sneezes. Alastair listened to it all, the sounds of his whole world. He wouldn't have changed anything. He listened to the click-clunk of the slides, and the sigh of the projector shutting off. He listened to the exhalation all around him and to the sound of the bright screen going dark, the white box flickering to nothing, and the group of them waiting there, in the dark, like a roomful of blind men. Their hands on their knees. Their eyes straight ahead. Their bodies shifting and sighing in tune with each other. Hush, swish, flow, yawn, breath. It was a song Alastair would keep on hearing—hush swish flow yawn breath—long after the lights came up.

CHAPTER 14

· · · · · · ★ · · · · · ·

Nelson

Nelson sat at a two-person table in the dining area of the bowling alley at 7:00 a.m. He wore a green flannel shirt tucked into his blue jeans, and on the table he had everything he needed—the syrup and the jellies and the margarine. And Charla was trying out a new system where she left a small pot of coffee on the table, so you didn't need to keep asking her to come around. Hailey would be arriving any time. At the party on Saturday, she'd joked she would skip Sunday dinner so she'd have more of a breakfast appetite this morning, but Nelson had told her that wasn't a good idea. You needed three squares, he'd said. It was the snacking you could cut out. And the cream sauces.

"Is this for another interview?" Charla called to him from her window.

"What?" Nelson said. At least when Charla had to come around with coffee, he could hear her better.

"Are you doing another article?" she said. "Is it about what happened at the Fivemile?"

"No." Nelson shook his head. "This is just for breakfast."

"Oh," she said.

"What?" He sat up straighter in his chair. "What's wrong with that?"

"Nothing," she said. "Why are you nervous, then?"

"I'm not," he said.

"Nelson." Charla had her hands on her hips.

He didn't want to talk about why he was fidgeting in his seat, why his hands felt clammy this early in the morning. His head actually felt fairly clear. "They'd have to interview Shoe if they were going to write what happened at the Fivemile," Nelson said. "But judging from yesterday's *Chronicle*, it sounds like he's not talking."

"I don't blame him." Charla planted her hands on her service counter.

"That's right," said Nelson. "Actions talk louder."

"That's right," Charla repeated.

"Which means everything's already been said."

Which was what Bethany had said, anyway. She'd read the Sunday paper with him yesterday, and dropped him at Liberty this morning, and Nelson was glad Charla hadn't had any reason to go out in the parking lot and wonder why his car wasn't there. He was going to take the bus home when he was done—the number two, corner of Memorial and Stout, every eleven minutes. As if saying it to Bethany ten times wasn't enough, she wrote it on a piece of paper and put it in his pocket. Like he was a child. Like anyone wouldn't be nervous with their every breath put under a microscope. Nelson wanted to see Hailey—he was happy she'd pulled him aside at the party and asked him to have breakfast—but he was also glad, for now, to be relatively alone. He was thankful Charla had been in the kitchen when he'd arrived and hadn't seen him go on back behind the bowling counter to his cubby.

If Hailey hadn't asked him to have breakfast, Nelson wasn't sure when he would have given her the painting.

"I think Shoe was strong to do what he did," said Charla.

Nelson nodded, but he was thinking that if he'd never been in the newspaper—if he'd never met Hailey—he'd never have done the painting in the first place.

"It took guts," Charla said.

"Yes," Nelson said, but what also got to him was how no one was calling Shoe Sanders crazy for setting fire to his own place. Strong, crazy, nervous, criminal. Whatever he actually was, Shoe was being cracked up closer to a hero.

"I think he knew it was the only thing to do," Charla said.

Nelson tried to get his mind off the painting. Instead he thought about the newspapers. Maybe this was what they did, cracked people up to be heroes.

"It was coming down either way," he said about the Fivemile.

Charla was shaking her head.

Nelson was thinking maybe that was the only way to get people to read the news, to turn it into something that they wanted. At least it was a way to make people remember what went on. He himself had to admit he wouldn't forget the look of Shoe Sanders finally emerging from the Fivemile at sunset. Shoe standing there, with cops on either side, saying his thank yous, saying how it was everyone else who'd made things possible all these years, and then you started to see what you thought was more of the sunset in the window. A little bit of glow. And then the smoke. And then the pop of glass. And then that hulking, useless wrecking ball, sitting there, no longer necessary. According to the *Chronicle*, Shoe had used some old rags that he soaked in his own drink, the one he called Shoe's Sandman. But that was all he'd say. "I think he was proud of himself," Nelson said. He figured now Shoe could open a new bar, sell only Shoe's Sandmans, and make a living.

Charla was back to planting her hands on the counter. "So why are you and her having breakfast?" she said.

Nelson looked into his coffee. He feared his hand might shake if he picked up the mug, because he was that nervous, and he didn't want Charla to see. He started to tell her this was where he always had breakfast, but he knew that wasn't what she meant, and so he didn't say anything at all. He flattened his hands on the table.

"Nelson?" she said. "Are you okay?"

"Yes," he said, and he wished even one person would skip asking him that. It felt like a lot of the time he was. Okay. But all of the time, now, there was someone worrying about him, someone breathing down his collar, and that was enough to make him stop worrying altogether and just say that he was fine. There'd be someone else asking him again in five more minutes. "We're friends," he said about Hailey. "She doesn't have family here."

"Do you have family here?" Charla asked. "In town?"

"What's that supposed to mean?" he said. He had family all over the state.

"Nelson," Hailey called as she entered the dining area. She was wearing her red coat, with a white scarf. She dumped her bag on an empty chair and leaned down and gave Nelson a hug. The scarf's white tassels tickled his face. Her scent of cold air and fresh shampoo brightened him up. "I didn't see your car," she said.

"It's in the shop," he said. He'd thought this through ahead of time.

Hailey studied his face like she had a hunch this wasn't true.

"I took the bus," he said.

"I could have picked you up," she said. She sat down and blew into her hands. "Anyway," she said. "Here we are. How are you?"

"That's what everyone wants to know."

Hailey looked at him. "Well, I'm fine, thank you," she said. "But I'm tired. I skipped dinner last night, and then I lay in bed with my stomach growling—"

"Honey, I told you—"

"I'm kidding." She touched Nelson's hands on the table. "I ate Chinese. We had beef with broccoli and sesame noodles."

"As long as you don't skip a meal," said Nelson.

"My future is going to be happy and productive," Hailey said. "According to my fortune."

Then Charla was there, pouring Hailey's coffee. It turned out Nelson and Hailey would share the one small pot.

"I'm in the mood for French toast." Hailey was talking fast. "I haven't had that since I was a kid."

"I don't make French toast," said Charla. "I make hotcakes and eggs."

"You can do French toast." Nelson tugged on Charla's apron, and she shot him a look.

"Hotcakes sound perfect." Hailey didn't bother to reach for a menu. "Is that what you're having?"

"Yes," said Nelson. "I start with one."

"I'll start with two," said Hailey.

Nelson raised his eyebrows. "Last I heard you weren't one for breakfast."

"I'm trying," Hailey said. She looked at Charla. "There's no law against that, is there?"

"Not unless you burn down the place," Charla said, and headed back to the kitchen.

"We were just talking about that," Nelson said to Hailey. "Are you going to get ahold of Shoe?"

Hailey shook her head. "No."

"Because he's not talking?"

"Because I'm not on the Fivemile anymore."

"What do you mean?" Nelson made two fists on the table.

Hailey waved a hand. "It's nothing," she said. "My editor doesn't like what I've been writing. He read what I wrote after Friday, and he thought I didn't write about the people I should have written about, and that I wrote too much about other people I shouldn't have bothered with." She unrolled her paper napkin. "It doesn't matter," she said. "I wrote what I wanted."

"Well, can't you fix it?" said Nelson.

Hailey shrugged. "Maybe." She looked at her lap.

"You wrote about us, didn't you?" Nelson studied Hailey, those pink cheeks and broad cheekbones, and, he noticed this time, long eyelashes. He wondered if he'd ever be able to get her face just right. He would need a photograph first.

To work from. And another canvas. He might get a little better each time. "You should get ahold of Shoe," he said, wanting to be helpful.

"Today's *Chronicle* says he got a lawyer."

"I didn't look at today's," Nelson said, though the truth was he would have if Bethany hadn't taken it. "I just did the crossword."

"They quoted Fran."

"They did?"

Hailey nodded. "The police wanted to find out whether she'd known what Shoe was planning to do, since she was the last one with him, but she said she didn't know anything. In the paper, she says she was as surprised as anybody when she saw the fire. She figured Shoe was sad but not a loon."

"That's the word she used?" Nelson leaned over the table.

"About him setting the fire," Hailey said.

Then Nelson unrolled his napkin, too, and lined up his utensils evenly. "It was like fireworks," he said.

"Like a bonfire," Hailey said, and Nelson was thinking how this was so different from an interview. How this was just a shooting-the-breeze, a back-and-forth, and how it was impossible to remember not knowing a person once you got to the point where you did.

"That's what my dad said." Hailey was stirring vanilla creamers into her coffee.

"In Pennsylvania?" That confused Nelson.

"On the Internet," Hailey said. "The *Chronicle* has pictures of it on their Web site. The *Free Press* doesn't. I was telling my dad about my story." She smoothed her hair, which wasn't as wet as the last time they'd had breakfast, but it wasn't all the way dry either. "I called him," she said.

"Oh," Nelson said. Hailey's father.

"I called my brother, too," she said.

Nelson had a hard time picturing that. Hailey's family.

"He said my mother's on some retreat in Mexico," Hailey was saying. "He's living in a converted warehouse in Brooklyn with a new girlfriend who paints 'industrial impressions,' whatever that means. I'm not sure the place is zoned for living, but he sounds happy." Hailey licked her spoon.

She sounded happy to Nelson—in fact, she'd seemed happy all-around since she'd walked in—and he wondered why this fact should unsettle him. She was so much more familiar to him now than when they'd first met, and yet she seemed different. Closer and farther away at the same time. Could that be true? Would he be wrong to give her the painting? And how could she not know her mother was all the way in Mexico?

"Well, they have impressionists in painting," he said. "That might be where she's coming from. The girlfriend."

"Maybe," said Hailey.

"I do mostly scenery," he said. "I've never been any good at painting faces." He was tempted to say more—he wasn't very good at keeping surprises—but he felt his hands go clammy again.

"Maybe I could see some of your paintings," Hailey said. "When you get to your new place."

And suddenly he felt that if he didn't go get his painting right then, it would be like lying. But he didn't want to give it to her until the end of breakfast, when they could go back to the cubbies together, like they'd done before. The more he thought about it, the more worked up he got about showing her. He didn't know if he was good at painting anymore. At the same time, the one thing he did know was that on this last go-round, amid all this fuzziness and all this talk about whether he was okay, he had been pleasantly surprised by the cool, clear space that opened up, like a secret room in his jam-packed brain, on each dark morning and each quiet afternoon that he'd worked on this painting. Of course he couldn't say for sure—no one could in this life— but he hoped it wouldn't be the last one he did. He looked now at how Hailey's upper lip was redder than her lower lip, like it was chapped.

"Unless they're already packed," she said.

"What?" Nelson had lost track.

"Your paintings," Hailey said. "I don't know how much you've packed." She was fidgeting just like him, which made him feel better. "And I hope I'm not inviting myself," she said. "But at the party, Bethany told me that maybe I could stop by next weekend. I could help with the move."

"Oh," Nelson said. He didn't really want to think anymore about moving, or about the party. Nice as the evening had been, he hadn't liked the idea of everyone showing up to make a big deal about him. He thought the whole thing was embarrassing, but Bethany kept calling it a celebration. Forty years in one house? Who did that anymore? she said. The way Nelson saw it, who wanted to celebrate being so turned around you had to go live in a one-bed-room where there was a lever attached outside the front door so people could monitor if you'd gone out each day, or if you'd died in your sleep, and there wasn't even a separate room to paint. Where you had to set up the easel right there in the living room for everyone to see. It didn't sound like anything to cheer about to him.

"You keep finding the good," he said, which was what Bethany kept on telling him. "It's going to be there somewhere."

"What?" Hailey said.

"It wouldn't have been a party if you weren't there."

Charla set their breakfasts down in front of them.

"You had a good time," he said to Charla. "Right?"

"I had enough beef Stroganoff and brandy to last me to Easter," she said. "Did we leave you a big mess?"

"No," Nelson said. "Clarette stayed and did dishes. Bethany and I finished up the rest yesterday. And packed."

Charla rubbed his shoulder. "It was a celebration," she said.

Which Nelson wished everyone would quit saying.

Charla gave him and Hailey a couple of extra napkins, because Nelson liked to have them when there was syrup, and then she went back to her window to get started on the napkin rolls.

Hailey was putting margarine all over her hotcakes. She was pouring syrup both on top of them and in between.

"You are hungry," he said to her.

"Would it be all right if I brought Nate?" she asked him. "To your new place?"

"Who's that?" he said. Was he supposed to know?

"My boyfriend," she said, and she was looking at him with a grin like this should mean something, only he didn't know what.

"You have a boyfriend?" he said.

"Yes," she said, without elaborating. She took an enormous bite of soaked hotcake.

"I didn't realize that." He sorted through the jellies for a strawberry one.

Hailey drank her coffee and wiped her fingers on one of the extra napkins. She seemed so much less like a reporter to him than she had before and so much more like just a person. She took the strawberry jelly packet from him, since he was having trouble opening it, and opened it with her fingernails. Her fingernails had no polish. "You'd like him," she said.

But again, he wasn't sure if this was something he was supposed to know. *This* was the worst part, he thought, the not knowing when you were stumbling.

"Why did you want to have breakfast with me?" he said.

Hailey stopped. She'd been reaching for her fork, but then she didn't. "Nelson?" she said.

"Well, usually when a person asks another person to have breakfast it's for a reason."

"Oh," Hailey said. She clasped her hands together and lowered them to the table's edge. Her elbows rested on nothing. It didn't look natural. It looked like she was trying hard to find the way to say something. Not that everyone hadn't already said—buried in a dozen different pep talks—how they felt sorry for him.

"I don't know," she said. "Because I wanted to."

Nelson wanted to know the difference between people spending time with him and people keeping an eye on him. He wanted to erase that consideration altogether. "Well, I wanted to, too," he said.

"I don't think we have to have a reason," Hailey said.

He wanted to believe her. "Say that again," he said.

She leaned over the table, and he could see that, yes, her lips were chapped. "I don't think we have to have a reason," she repeated.

Nelson nodded, though he was getting fuzzy on what they were talking about. He was thinking about Hailey's chapped lips and her unpolished nails, and how if he painted her nails he would give them a color anyway. Probably red, because that was the color of her coat, and now her lips. "Thank you," he said about opening the jelly. He could feel tension in his shoulders, like he'd been on edge about something, but he let it go. He relaxed into his seat. "I would like to take pictures," he said. "If you come to visit."

"Okay," Hailey said.

"I'm not sure I got any of you at the party."

"Clarette was taking a lot of pictures," she said.

"Bethany might have," he said. "I'll have to check."

There had been a lot of cameras at the party. Fran had taken the most pictures, but he didn't want to bring up Fran right then. He felt a little foolish for the way things had gone. From saying she was the big lover of his life to ending up right back under Bethany's thumb. In fact, he wasn't so much embarrassed about being back under Bethany's thumb as he was about not thinking much about Fran. After all the buildup and the hoopla. About not reading his own mind—or heart, or gut, or whatever you wanted to call it—not even doing that much, at the end of the day, the right way.

"Are you done packing?" Hailey was asking him.

Then again, he wouldn't have changed anything about the past two months. This part about the move, yes, but not the rest of it. The part where Hailey showed up and opened this space inside his life.

"I could help you," she said.

Was it the same space as where he'd done his painting, or was it a coincidence that they'd both eased open around the same time, give or take?

"Or maybe you're all finished," she said.

"I think they might be," he said.

"I'm sorry?"

"I have something for you," he said. Only then he looked at her plate. She wasn't nearly done eating. "After you're finished," he said.

Hailey looked at her hotcakes like she was trying to decide if this was fair. She took another bite. "You don't have to give me anything," she said.

"I want to," he said.

She poured herself more coffee from the small pot between them and topped off Nelson's, too. Making use of this new pot pleased him. It was a good idea. "Do you have much to get rid of?" she asked. "Before you move?"

He hadn't thought of it that way, that she might think he was giving her something he was trying to throw out. He had plenty of junk to get rid of, yes—no one needed a drawer full of broken calculators or years' worth of cleaned-out margarine containers and yogurt cups—but that wasn't what he was talking about here. "No," he said. "I'm giving you something new."

Hailey put down her fork. Her brow creased, and Nelson worried that he'd missed something.

"It's nothing to lose your appetite over," he said.

"I don't have anything for you," she said.

Nelson didn't know what to say to that. He didn't know how to say to a person like Hailey that being who she was was plenty. Hailey, who wasn't any of their grandchildren, or their girlfriends, or anything like that. She was just a person, and she had a lot more time on her horizon than him. "You should eat," he said.

She did. She picked her fork back up and ate more of the hotcakes and added more syrup when she wanted. Nelson watched her mix in sips of coffee and water, and he watched how she ate around the outside edges of the hotcakes first, which he understood, because the centers always soaked up the most margarine. They were the best last bites, a fact Hailey knew too, a fact they'd both probably learned when they were children. He himself ate slowly this morning. He was more interested in watching Hailey, her white fingers and her pink cheekbones and her eyes lit up with coffee and sugar. He didn't care if it didn't make exact sense, but he was satisfied, watching her eat all of her breakfast, like it meant that he had done something right. Nothing to write about, certainly, but something he would remember nonetheless. "There wasn't even a kitchen here until 1980," he said.

Hailey topped off their coffees.

"This was where the shoes went." He pointed to where they sat. "And over where the counter is there wasn't anything. When we'd have the spring banquet at the end of the league season, we'd bring the food ourselves. Now they serve us a whole dinner right here."

"There's still a banquet?" Hailey asked.

"Oh, yes," Nelson said. "Right here. And they do a raffle." He ate another bite of hotcake himself, but it took effort. He was feeling too jumpy to be hungry. He wasn't interested in his food. He was interested in what Hailey was going to think about his painting. "The first year, Jim brought the tables," he said. "And a woman named Lucy brought the roast, but she's gone now." He put his napkin under his plate. "Fran painted napkin holders out of those shower rings, and Bethany made sheet cakes." He could still see the sheet cakes, one for each of the four long tables, two vanilla frosted and two chocolates, with red flowers in the four corners of all of them. "There wasn't a bar then, either, so I packed up coolers of beer and soda. And Clarette brought these tablecloths she'd made herself out of the curtains that the people in her house had left behind when her and Dean bought it. They had orange and brown diamonds on them."

"When was that?" Hailey asked.

"1978," said Nelson.

"It's funny, the things you remember," she said.

He wasn't sure if she meant *him* or everyone in general. "You mean the year?"

"The diamonds."

"Oh," he said. He thought about that. He supposed that he agreed. Why would anyone remember those curtains? "You're all done," he said.

"You're not."

Nelson looked at his plate. He'd only made it through half a hotcake, and his heart was scrambling. "Charla," he called toward her window. "She's done with hers, but you can leave this here."

Charla was still doing her napkin rolls. "Okay, Nelson," she said.

"We'll be right back." He stood up. Clammy hands, wobbly legs. What if she didn't like it? He almost wanted to can the whole thing. What if he was no good?

"Where are we going?" Hailey stood up, too, and put her napkin on her plate.

"Over this way," he said, and started walking toward the shoes.

"I'm not taking your shoes," Hailey said. "If that's what you think you're giving me."

Nelson was ahead of Hailey, so he couldn't see whether her face was serious or joking. He'd never heard anyone make demands about something they were being given. "My shoes aren't new," he said.

"They're beautiful," she said. "I'd never let you give them away."

Nelson liked the way that sounded. He lifted up the counter and let her through and then slipped ahead of her like last time. He led her around the front cubbies and behind the office, into the leftover space with the second set of cubbies. Earlier that morning, when he'd propped up the painting facing against his cubby, he'd pushed a couple of stray bowling balls out of the way. He'd also been sure to turn the lamp on so he wouldn't have to fumble for the light at the same time he was trying to give Hailey the painting. He wanted her to see it just right from the beginning. His hands were so clammy now he wouldn't have been able to work that lamp's switch. In fact, he wondered if he'd be able to hold the painting steady for her to see.

"Okay," he said. He could see she'd noticed the back of the painting, but she was being polite not making more guesses. "Close your eyes," he said.

She closed her eyes. Nelson looked at her calm face and her long eyelashes that appeared even longer in the shadowy light of the one lamp, and as scared as he felt right then, he figured he didn't have much to fear. He figured she would tell him she loved it no matter what she thought.

"Okay," he said again. He was gripping the frame to his chest, the painting facing her. "You can look."

Hailey opened her eyes. She didn't say anything. She just put her hand over her mouth.

He thought his heart might explode, waiting for her.

"Nelson," she said through her hand. "Nelson, you did this?"

He nodded. "I was never any good at painting faces," he said.

"That's not true," she said, opening her arms toward him. "Nelson." Then she cupped both hands over her mouth and released them, like she was shoveling in air. "Nelson, this is—this is spectacular," she said.

He couldn't feel his feet beneath him. It was like from the knees down, it was clouds. "I've been practicing," he said.

"Yes," she said.

"Here and there," he said. "I felt like I should."

She took the painting from him. She stepped closer to the lamp and held the painting out in front of her so that the bottom of the frame rested across her hips. It wasn't a huge painting, but it was good-sized. Nelson watched her take a closer look—it was a moment he could have watched forever—and then he saw her face open one thought wider. "This is from the *Free Press* cover," she said. "Isn't it?" With one hand, she pointed to where the bowling pins would have been if he hadn't skipped them. Then she ran her fingers through the air above his eyes. "It looks just like you," she said.

"I don't know," he said. "I'm just trying it."

"Just *trying* it," Hailey said like she didn't believe him. Nelson loved the sound of it.

"I wasn't sure what you'd think," he said.

"I'm so glad you didn't paint the bowling pins," she said. "I never liked them."

"I would of done you," he said, "but I didn't have a photo." He stood beside her so they were both studying the painting. His first face ever. His first self-portrait. It wasn't exactly what he'd hoped, but it was a beginning. "I needed to do it from a photo," he said.

"You're in a tie," Hailey said then.

It was true. He'd put himself in a tie. On the *Free Press* cover he was in one of his plaid shirts, but that didn't feel right for a portrait. For a portrait, he'd given himself a plain blue tie, and a white shirt, because they were easy to paint and they seemed like the right thing to have on. "I wear ties on occasion," he said.

"It looks just like you," she said again. Then she looked at him. He looked at his painting. He thought about all those hours. How it had been odd, to stare and stare at himself for so long, the same sensation as when you said the word *hamburger* a hundred times. By the end, you weren't even sure if the thing that had once been so familiar had any definition at all.

"I kept the bar in the background," he said.

"Yes," she said. "Nelson, this is so good. I don't know if I can take this."

Which was what every woman said when you gave them something nice. The best women, anyway, in his experience.

"I want you to have it," he said.

Lou Ann had fought before putting on that ruby pendant. Bethany had returned the loveseat he'd had delivered last year. She'd given it the sixty-day tryout but then said it was plain too much.

"Don't you want to keep it?" she said.

"That wouldn't make much sense," he said.

He'd tried not to take Fran's heart-shaped piece of flint.

"Or your children?" Hailey said.

Nelson shrugged. "They've seen my other paintings. They're far away."

"Or Bethany?" She wasn't going to quit.

What was it, he wondered, about not taking what a person wanted to give you?

"You don't have to have it if you don't want," he said.

Hailey didn't say anything to that. She ran one hand slowly up and down the frame, and she got a hurt expression on her face. Her eyes squinted, and her lips pushed together so tight they disappeared. If she cried, Nelson thought, he might die.

"Did I make you mad?" he said.

"No," she said right away. She looked at him, and in the one light the whites of her eyes glowed. "No." She took a deep breath. "This is so good, Nelson," she repeated. "No one's given me something like this before."

"Like a picture of themselves?" he said.

"This is more than a picture," she said.

Yes and no, he thought. "It's what I wanted to do."

"It's a lot of work," she said.

"So you'll remember me."

And there it was, a glistening in her eye. She blinked it away, and maybe it hadn't been the start of tears at all; maybe it had only been the kind of shine you got from a yawn or from being tired—it was early in the morning, after all, it was barely sunrise and still single digits. But in any case the shimmer was gone. She whisked it away and got on with it.

"Nelson, you're only going across town," she said.

He, though, didn't want to move beyond that moment.

"A few miles," she said.

He wanted to say something, but at the same time he didn't. Nor did he want to reach for the lamp, or lead her back through the office, or ask Charla for their bill. Which he was going to pay. Really the only thing he had any interest in right that second was staying exactly where they were. Not finishing his breakfast, not showing anyone else his painting, not budging from this quiet space with the one lamp and those couple of bowling balls pushed off to the side. Except for Charla, no one in the world knew where he and Hailey were right then, and even Charla might not have known exactly. She might have thought they'd gone outside to get something out of his car. Which wasn't there. Anyone driving by Liberty Lanes wouldn't even know that he was there. What a time, he thought. He watched Hailey put the painting down gently. Then he felt her arms around him, hugging him. He felt himself hugging her back. He felt her shoulder blades. He smelled the fresh shampoo in her hair. He breathed the last traces of cold air she'd carried in off the morning and thought how lucky he'd be to skip the sunrise, leave his last boxes unpacked, and call it a day right there.

······ ★ ······

Acknowledgments

Liberty Lanes is a work of fiction inspired by a group of bowlers who first invited me to join them for a drink in 2003. Through their friendships, they save and shape and brighten each other's lives. For doing the same for me, I am grateful to:

Drs. Juliet and Tony Aizer, Nicolette Barber, Shana Halsey Beladino, Dr. Clarissa Bonanno, Dr. Nancy Brown, Nancy and Sam Celone, Lois Lake Church, Dr. Dennis Cooper, Lacy Crawford, Martha Elizabeth and the everlasting spirit of Jim Crumley, Dr. Eric David, Paul Dietrich, Debbie Doucette, Joy Kealey Drakonakis, Jack and Jeri Fisher, Devon Chivvis Fowler, Kate Gadbow, Matt Gibson, John and Dana Gale, Jen Chapin Giering, Brock Gnose, Laura Gronewald, Grace Halsey, Chad Harder, Will Hochman, Sara Holland, Sandy Johnson, Catherine Kiernan, Sara and Sean Kiffe, Chris Knight, Rayon Lennon, Bruce and Christy Lindsay, Dr. David Lima, Jessica Davis McNamara, Dr. Ryan Martin, Melissa McClain, Clay McKee, Megan McMorris, Elisa Lufler Milano, Mimi Munson, Richard and Debbie Nason, Chris Nichols, John O'Loghlen, Dr. Michael Paidas, Chona Panes, Dr. Tripler Pell, Peter Picard, Dr. Carol Portlock, Elaine Portnov, Clara Everts Quinlan, Dana Remley, Margaret Roberts, Lorie Rustvold, Daniel and Allie Sargent, Patsy and Nick Schanz, Anne Heavey Scheinfeldt, Laura Koerckel Selvig, Jocelyn Siler, Anne Battle Slater, Len Slater, Andy Smetanka, Jeremy Smith, Jan Ellen Spiegel, George and Nancy Stromberg, Keila Szpaller, Denise Taliaferro, Dr. Hugh Taylor, Brad Tyer, Patrick van den Broek, Liza Ward, Audrey, Bev, Bill, Dee, Dick, Ed, Evaun, Herb, Irene, Jean, Larry, Larry, Lou, Mary Lou, Mick, Raynita, and, forever in our hearts, Norm.

Special thanks to Dee McNamer and Debra Earling at the University of

Montana; my colleagues at Southern Connecticut State University, especially Tim Parrish, Jeff Mock, Margot Schilpp, Vivian Shipley, Nicole Henderson, Mike Shea, DonnaJean Fredeen, and Selase Williams; Tom Jenks at *Narrative* magazine; copy editor John Mulvihill; and the University of Nevada Press, particularly Barbara Berlin and, most of all, Margaret Dalrymple:

Margaret, thank you for believing in this story. Thank you for your wisdom and your spirit. Let's climb a mountain one day soon. Let's be each other's hero for many, many years to come.

And, to my family—Mom, Dad, Mike, Quinn, and Reed: I love the way we live our lives. Thank you for making everything possible.